"How

~~going to know me?"~~

"I'm against it." Luke met the challenge in Meredith's eyes head-on.

Oh, God, was she going to lose her child a second time? She forced a calm she wasn't feeling into her voice. "Then why did you come here today?"

"Because I'll do anything for Michael. And he wants to meet his birth mother. I need to know you can handle this. It's not going to be easy."

You don't understand the half of it, Mr. Rayburn. "What exactly do you mean?"

"Michael's a complicated kid, and he's stubborn. He wants to get to know you now that his mother...my wife...Sara...is gone. But I know my son. He's going to have some trouble with...with the fact that you gave him up."

Meredith's hands went clammy and her insides contracted. She struggled to gain control over her emotions. No one must ever know the circumstances surrounding Michael's birth.

Not Luke—and *especially* not Michael.

ABOUT THE AUTHOR

Michael's Family is Kathryn Shay's third Superromance novel, and the second in which teenagers play a role. She draws on her experience of twenty-six years as a high school teacher to portray the kids realistically. "Michael is typical of many of my kids," says Kathryn. "He's bright, lovable, fun and yet also under some of the same stresses—peer pressure, athletic competition, death of a parent and adoption.

"This book also came from the mother in me. I have a fifteen-year-old daughter and a twelve-year-old son, and as I wrote *Michael's Family*, I thought a lot about how I would feel if I had been separated from them and was only now getting a chance to know them. This helped me understand what Meredith Hunter went through."

Kathryn really enjoys hearing from her readers. You can reach her at P.O. Box 24288, Rochester, NY 14624-0288

Books by Kathryn Shay

HARLEQUIN SUPERROMANCE
659—THE FATHER FACTOR
709—A SUITABLE BODYGUARD

Don't miss any of our special offers. Write to us at the following address for information on our newest releases.

Harlequin Reader Service
U.S.: 3010 Walden Ave., P.O. Box 1325, Buffalo, NY 14269
Canadian: P.O. Box 609, Fort Erie, Ont. L2A 5X3

MICHAEL'S FAMILY
Kathryn Shay

Harlequin Books

TORONTO • NEW YORK • LONDON
AMSTERDAM • PARIS • SYDNEY • HAMBURG
STOCKHOLM • ATHENS • TOKYO • MILAN
MADRID • WARSAW • BUDAPEST • AUCKLAND

ISBN 0-373-70727-4

MICHAEL'S FAMILY

To *my* family—Patty, Dee Dee and Bill, Joanie and Herb, Joe and Lynne and Stacey, who have supported me not only in my writing career, but in all areas of my life.
I love you.

CHAPTER ONE

"HEY, DAD, do you believe that sixty-three percent of the men in this survey say they don't have sex as often as they'd like?"

Michael's sixteen-year-old voice preceded him into the den, where Lucas Rayburn sat, having just made one of the most difficult decisions of his life. He stared at the boy who was almost a man, and felt his heart constrict. God, he loved the kid.

"Daaad. He-llo?"

"Yes, Michael. I believe that."

Green eyes focused on Luke as Michael plopped his nearly six-foot body into the wing chair, rolled the magazine he held and tapped it on his knee. "What's wrong, Dad?"

"Nothing. Why?"

"You usually rib me about my project."

"With good reason. I'm still wary of a year-long term paper on the sexual practices of the average American."

"Hey, the new English teacher said we should choose a topic we're interested in. It'll make learning the research skills easier. Julie Anne's doing hers on the rights of adopted children."

Luke's smile disappeared abruptly at the mention of the topic Michael's best friend had chosen for her paper.

"Dad?"

"I've decided, Michael."

He watched his son grip the chair arm hard. "And?"

"I've thought about your request. A lot." The words stuck in his throat, but Luke got them out somehow. "We'll contact your biological mother."

Michael swallowed, his youthful Adam's apple bobbing. "That's great."

Great? It was obscene, that's what it was. The fact that Michael had asked, weeks ago, to find the woman who'd given birth to him stunned Luke at first. Now it just hurt. He tried hard to keep his face neutral and concentrate on what was best for Michael.

"Listen, Dad, I promise it won't change anything between us. You know, how it's been for the last three years. Since Mom died. We'll be buddies, like we've always been."

Luke's throat clogged. "I know you mean that, son. But you've got to realize that when we find her our lives will never be the same."

Michael shrugged his shoulders. "Maybe our lives will be better."

"Maybe."

But Luke doubted it.

LUKE PULLED his Bronco into the parking lot next to a sleek silver Corvette, and took the time to admire its clean lines and subtle construction. It was not out of place here at the swank condominium complex in an upscale suburb of Romulus, New York. Michael's birth mother must have done pretty well for herself.

He shut off the engine and leaned his head against the seat. He tried to quell his resentment but his effort was futile, as it had been on the interminable one-hour drive from Sommerfield to Romulus. The only thing his internal debating had achieved was to enhance the dull ache at his temples.

What did it matter how well she'd fared in the intervening years? When Michael was born, she'd turned him over to a family who could raise him better than she could, and Luke had thanked God for it then. It wasn't fair to judge her now for what he had considered the greatest gift a mother could give her child.

"But she's *not* Michael's mother," he said aloud, pounding his fist on the steering wheel. "Sara is."

No, Sara *was* his mother.

Yanking open the door, and determined to leave the bitter feelings and morbid thoughts behind, Luke made his way to number thirty-four. Before he could change his mind, he reached up and rang the bell. Impatient now, he tapped his foot on the brick steps as he looked around at the lush greenery. Large maple and birch trees swayed in the early-afternoon breeze, infusing the air with the scents of fall. The grass and shrubbery were meticulously clipped, like the grounds of the golf course at the country club Sara had convinced him to join. He was about to ring again, when the door opened.

Luke froze. Staring up at him were Michael's eyes. His son had the most unusual eyes Luke had ever seen—oval, with large black pupils, surrounded by light green or dark green—depending on his mood or what he wore—and rimmed in black. They'd always reminded Luke of the marbles he used to play with as a kid.

"Hello." Her voice was strained, and she coughed to clear it. "Mr. Rayburn?"

"Yes. You must be Meredith Hunter."

She nodded, then inched back to allow him in.

Luke couldn't shake the feeling that once he entered this house, his life would change forever. But he'd promised Michael. He stepped through the doorway.

Softly she closed the door, and circled him in the large foyer. "Come on in here," she said, her voice a little stronger. She preceded him into a huge living room.

He tried not to notice that her hair was light brown, and streaked the same as Michael's with end-of-summer highlights. He tried not to observe that she was about five-eight, tall for a woman. It must be where Michael got his height. Oh, Lord, he told himself, he had to stop these comparisons, or he'd go crazy. He had to remember that this woman gave birth to his son, but he and Sara had given Michael everything else.

"Why don't you sit down, Mr. Rayburn," she said, standing beside an overstuffed white leather couch.

He sat. She perched on the matching chair across from him, and was framed by high, arched floor-to-ceiling windows. Vertical blinds allowed in afternoon sunlight which softened her somewhat formal outfit—a navy blue suit with a white blouse.

Stop staring and say something. "Nice place you have here." *Oh, now that was clever.*

She scanned the room absently. "Thanks, I like it."

"Lived here long?"

"Um, yes, about seven years. I was one of the original tenants. That's how I could afford it."

He nodded.

"Can I get you something to drink?"

He glanced down at her hands, clasped so tightly in her lap that her knuckles were white. It was the first time he noticed she was trembling. The small show of vulnerability thawed some of his resentment of her. "Not unless you have a magic potion that will make this any less awkward."

She smiled then, a half smile that Michael often gave Luke when he'd done something right. "This is hard," she said.

Luke sat back against the comfortable cushions and sighed heavily. "I don't even know where to begin. I was hoping our mothers could be here to break the ice." When she didn't say anything, he added, "You know, because they arranged the adoption."

Again, the wisp of a smile. "I wish they were here, too."

"Bad timing that they're both traveling."

"Yes, it would have helped if they could have filled us in on the details of each other's lives before we met." Her eyes turned bleak. "And of...Michael's."

She said his son's name reverently. Instead of impressing Luke, it irked him. He didn't want to know how she felt about Michael, or what it had been like to give up her child. "What *did* my mother tell your mother?" he asked.

"Just that Michael wanted to meet me. And...that his...that your wife had died three years ago."

"Yes, his mother died of cancer."

Luke watched her carefully. She'd flinched when he called Sara Michael's mother, but she'd repressed it immediately.

"I'm sorry," she said softly. "For you and Michael."

"You knew nothing about us?"

"No. I assume you knew nothing about me, either."

He shook his head.

"I agreed with my mother that was the best way to

handle the…adoption.'' She paused again, and her hands clenched tighter in her lap. "Didn't you want it that way?"

"Of course. I never thought this day would come."

"I'm sorry," she repeated.

"My mother said that she and your mother cut off all contact sixteen years ago—when they arranged the adoption—so she didn't know how your life turned out."

"My mother said the same thing. About you, and your life."

Luke smiled in spite of the gravity of the situation. "We're parroting each other. This is the stiffest conversation I've ever had."

"It *is* awkward."

"I always felt bad my mother gave up her best friend from law school for me."

Meredith stared over his shoulder. "Me, too. They both made a big sacrifice for Michael's welfare. I…appreciated it." She smiled again. "Did you know that they were the only two women in their graduating class at Stanford?"

Relaxing, Luke nodded. "They got each other through, from what I heard. My mother talked about Lydia a lot before the adoption. She never mentioned her afterward."

"Same here."

Luke sighed again, watching her. "Well, where do we start?"

"Tell me about him." Luke thought he saw moisture glaze her eyes, but she blinked and it was gone.

He hesitated. It was hard for him to begin, but he knew he had to start the ball rolling somehow. "He's a great kid," he said finally. "He's a junior in high school—gets good grades but doesn't have to study much for them. Like most kids, he plays his music too loud, he's addicted to MTV. He wears my clothes without asking. English is his favorite subject, and he writes a lot since his ninth-grade teacher got the kids to keep a journal.''

The intensity on her face reminded Luke of a POW starved for information about the outside world. He felt a pang of sympathy.

''Let's see, his best friend is Julie Anne Sherman, who lives next door. They're together most of the time, though he has a lot of buddies from the soccer team who hang around the house.''

Meredith Hunter bit her lip hard.

''Are you all right?'' he asked.

She took in a deep breath. ''Yes, I, um…it's all a little overwhelming. Finally…knowing about him.''

She'd either just lied to him, he decided, or hedged. He knew the signs well. She'd reacted when he'd mentioned soccer.

Nervously, she reached up and fingered the braid that fell over one shoulder. She wore no polish on her short fingernails; her hands were unsteady. ''What else?''

Probing, to see if she would react again, Luke said, ''He's an excellent soccer player.''

Her shoulders tensed. ''What position?''

''Forward. Do you know the game?''

''Yes. Does he drive yet?''

Luke nodded, but let go of the cross-examination. ''We kept Sara's car for him after she died. He uses that.''

''A nice legacy for a teenage boy.''

For some reason the comment angered Luke. ''Sara gave him a lot more than that.''

"I'm sure she did." Meredith swallowed hard. "Look, I'd like some coffee. I'll be right back." She fled from the room faster than a beaten dog.

Damn it. Luke hadn't meant to hurt her. He hadn't known what to expect—how she'd felt about giving up her son—so he hadn't thought out his reactions to her. Hell, she seemed pretty controlled to him in general. Almost cold. But one thing was clear. It hurt her to talk about Michael, and about the woman she'd given him to. Luke didn't want to deal with that. He had his own conflicting emotions to sort out.

So he got up and wandered around the room. Its tidy sparseness added to his impression that this was a woman in control. Everything was in its place, neatly stored or displayed. There were none of the springy plants Sara had populated their house with. Only two pictures graced the bookshelf: one of an older couple, the woman resembling both Meredith and Michael. The other photo was of two guys, arms linked, in football jerseys and shorts. Was one a lover? Michael's natural father? All Luke knew about the man was that he had died before Michael was born, and that they had no health records from him like the ones he'd gotten from Meredith. Even recently, when Luke's mother had told him the whereabouts of Meredith Hunter, she'd said that there would be no discussion of the man involved. Which was fine with Luke. Even mention of the guy made his stomach churn. *He didn't want to know any of this! He was Michael's father.*

In the kitchen, Meredith gripped the countertop and took several deep breaths. She reached over and cranked open the window, then splashed some cold water on her face.

Oh, God, this was hard. She'd known it was going

to hurt, she just hadn't planned on the details sucker punching her in the gut.

He was a soccer player. She had a brief flash of herself in the last game she'd ever played, booting in the winning goal from almost midfield.

Shake it off, Meredith. This is too important, to fall apart now.

Taking out the canister and filter, she assembled the coffee machine, and watched it brew. Mr. Lucas Rayburn would have to wait until she got herself together. Judging from the looks he'd shot her, she was certain he wouldn't miss her presence at all. Which was fine with her. Arrogant, intimidating men were her least favorite people.

Eight minutes later, she returned to the living room more composed, a tray containing their coffee in her hands. She found Luke standing in front of her music collection. "You have a lot of jazz." He held up a Rippington's CD. "Michael likes this group, too."

Quelling a surge of joy at yet another shared interest, she set the tray down on the low, glass-topped table. "How do you take your coffee?"

"Black." He came toward her then, and took a mug. A lock of hair fell across his forehead. It was the color of fall chestnuts. His eyes were slightly darker, she noted, allowing herself to look into them.

She wished she hadn't. They were a deep, dark masculine brown—and they were filled with wariness.

Nothing you didn't expect, Meredith.

When they were seated again, she tried to warm her ice-cold hands by circling them around one of the steaming mugs. He watched her.

"Mr. Rayburn, I know this is difficult for you. It's hard for me, too. Would you answer a question?"

"Maybe."

"How do you feel about Michael getting to know me?"

He set his mug down on the table, then linked his hands between his knees. For the first time she noticed he was dressed casually, in blue jeans and a gray T-shirt under a blue plaid flannel shirt. Her work suit, tailored yet stylish, seemed formal and fussy for this occasion. "I'm against it," he said simply.

Oh, God, was she going to lose the boy a second time? She forced a calm into her voice, as she did in the courtroom when she was unsure of her facts. "Then why are you here?" she asked. Susan, her therapist, had told her to focus on what she needed from the situation.

"Because I'll do anything for Michael. And he wants to meet you."

Meredith let out a revealing breath. "So you'll let us...him...see me?"

"Of course. Look, I don't want to know anything about why you gave him up. All I really need to know is where your head is today." He paused, then said, "Answer a question for me. Can you do this for him now? Do you want to?"

"Yes, I do. More than you could possibly know."

"It won't be easy," he warned.

You don't understand the half of it, Mr. Rayburn. "What exactly do you mean?"

"Michael's a complicated kid. And he's stubborn. He wants to get to know you now that Sara's gone, and no one can convince him differently."

"You've tried?"

"I've explored all the angles with him. Ultimately, it was his decision."

"But had it been yours, we wouldn't be here talking."

"Absolutely not. I know my son. He'll have some trouble with…with the fact that you gave him up."

Meredith felt sick, but she forced herself not to react to his articulation of her worst fear.

"Are you prepared for that?" he asked.

"I honestly don't know."

"Why did *you* agree to this?"

Anger flickered inside her. Could he possibly think she didn't want to know her own child? His eyes narrowed on her, so she must have reacted outwardly, something she took great pains to avoid doing. "I want this, too."

"All right." He sat back and picked up his coffee. "I'd like to know more about you, then."

Meredith studied him. *Know thy enemy.* "I feel the same way."

He smiled and she had the odd feeling it was a rare occurrence in his life these days. "You go first," he said. "Give me the basics, then I'll do the same."

Wanting to relax, she eased back into the chair. "Let's see. I'm thirty-five. I have an older brother, Nathan, and as you know, my mother is a retired attorney, living in New York City. My dad's dead. I read and spend time with my best friend, Belle. I like jazz and have an interest in cars. I watch sports on television, but not much else. I work out at a health club four times a week. And I'm an assistant district attorney for the city of Romulus."

His thick eyebrows raised when she finished. "I didn't expect the last thing."

"What do you mean?"

"We have something in common."

"What?"

"The law. I'm a federal public defender for the counties that include Romulus and Sommerfield."

Meredith's hands went clammy and her insides contracted. But she struggled to rein in her conflicting emotions. Luke Rayburn could never know about her bias against public defenders. Of everything in this whole emotional mess, that was the one thing that he could never, ever find out.

She'd go to the grave with that secret.

LUKE SUCKED IN AIR as he ran up the hill; he glanced over at his son, who wasn't even breathing heavily. Ah, the advantages of youth. But he wouldn't trade places with Michael today for anything in the world. When they hit the top of the incline, and Luke was able to talk again, he asked, "Nervous about meeting her?"

Michael's pace slowed almost imperceptibly, and his face flushed. But he kept running. "Yeah. Stupid, huh?"

Not breaking stride, Luke reached over and squeezed Michael's arm. "I'd be the same if I were in your shoes."

"Dad?"

"Hmm?"

"What if I don't like her?"

I'd fall down on my knees and thank God. Not fair, Rayburn. Maybe the kid needs this. "Well, none of this is irrevocable, you know. You don't have to continue any relationship with her if you don't want to."

"Would that be fair to her?"

Sometimes, good parenting came back to haunt you. You taught your kid to care about others, not to use or abuse them, and then at the worst possible times, they did exactly what you said. "Mike, we haven't made any promises. We just decided to meet her and see how it goes. It will probably be hard for her if it doesn't work out." The memory of sad green eyes appeared before him. "But we're going to do what's best for you."

The boy smiled weakly and picked up the pace of their jog. They ran about a quarter of a mile before he spoke again. "I know you want me to form my own opinions about her. But, ah...is she nice? What's her personality like?"

Cold. Meredith Hunter definitely struck him as cold. Except when she spoke about Michael. "She seems very reserved to me. Very cautious."

Another few yards. "She's smart, though, right?"

Luke smiled, surprised at his son's question. "I'd guess she's very bright. Those articles I dug up from the *Romulus Herald* cited a pretty successful career."

Once he'd discovered she was an assistant district attorney, he'd done some investigating and found Ms. Hunter had caused quite a stir in the Romulus law community during her seven years in the D.A.'s office. She'd taken the track most county D.A.'s did—putting in a stint of several months in city court, and about a year in town court. Then, she'd prosecuted nonviolent felons, and finally settled in the Major Felonies Bureau. "Champion of Women's Issues," one headline had called her, and another newspaper dubbed her as part of the "Sensitive Bureau."

"And she went to Princeton, right?"

"Yep."

"Did you ever meet her when you were kids, Dad?"

"Once or twice. But we lived on opposite coasts so it was tough getting the families together." Luke glanced at his son. "I don't remember much about those visits."

"What about as an adult? Your jurisdiction is Romulus, too."

"Yeah, it is. But I never met her. That's not unusual. When I was a county public defender, there would be little chance of meeting her since Sommerfield and Romulus each have about forty or fifty A.D.A.'s. No reason for me to come in contact with her. And I've only been with the federal department for a year, so it's not unusual."

"It's strange, all the law connections, though."

"No, son, it isn't. You know that your grandmothers arranged the adoption. And they were both lawyers. Their children chose law."

"At least Grandma will get to see her good friend now."

Luke stopped running; Michael went a few paces before he realized his father wasn't beside him, then stopped, too. "What is it, Dad?"

"Michael, it's important that you don't take responsibility for anything that's happened here. Your grandmother made her own choices. She got you in the exchange, and never regretted it for a minute. As far as Meredith Hunter is concerned, she also made her own decisions. If this doesn't work out—letting her into our lives—she'll learn to live with it."

Michael grinned at his father. "Okay, Dad, I get it. But can I at least have a minute to feel bad for them?"

Relaxing, Luke returned the grin and walked to Michael, encircling his son's neck with his arm. "Sorry, kid. But I'm not going to let you get hurt by this." *Please, God, let me be able to do that.*

Michael leaned into him for a minute.

"I love you, Mike."

"Me, too, Dad." Then he pulled away. "Race ya? Last one home gets to wear your new Broncos' sweatshirt."

"You're on."

An hour later, Michael, wearing Luke's Broncos' sweatshirt, lay sprawled in front of the VCR playing his favorite video game. Luke had just reached the bottom of the stairs when the doorbell rang. Michael dropped the controls and looked up at his father. For all his height and muscle, he seemed a child today. "Want me to get it?" Luke asked.

His son shook his head and uncurled his long frame. His body was rigid when he stood.

"Mike?"

White-faced, he turned to Luke.

"Remember, this isn't irrevocable," Luke lied. "We don't have to take it any further."

Nodding, Michael crossed to the foyer.

OH, DEAR GOD, he looks like me. The thought came uncensored when Meredith saw her son for the very first time. She ground her heels into the concrete and gripped her purse strap. Mostly it was his eyes, but his other features resembled hers, too. And his hair was the same color.

"Hi." His voice was raspy. Nervous.

"Hello."

Meredith watched as he scanned her. She'd changed clothes four times, and hoped the casual knit skirt and hip-length top were the right choice. *This was really her son, standing here, looking her over.*

And his eyes betrayed him. Used to reading people, she saw a myriad of emotions flood him: curiosity, wariness, pleasure and finally, some distrust, which reminded her of Lucas Rayburn—who materialized behind Michael.

"Ask her to come in," he said gently.

The boy's face turned red. "Oh, sure, sorry. Come in."

Michael stood to the side, next to Luke, as Meredith entered the house. Trying to calm her churning stomach, she scanned the interior. Their home was lovely, if not her taste. A large, well-appointed living room sprawled to the right, dining room to the left. Ahead, a hallway led to the rear of the house.

"Come on back," Luke said, heading down the hall. Michael waited politely for Meredith to go first, and his proximity made her dizzy. She could feel his presence looming behind her.

The family room was huge and airy, decorated, like the rest of the house, in expensive Colonial motif. Luke preceded her into the room, and as Meredith followed, she stumbled and lost her balance. She grabbed for the post that separated the dinette from the family room, as Michael grasped her to steady her.

"You missed the step down," he said.

The breath went out of Meredith as she looked at the large masculine hand enfolding her arm. *Her son's hand.* She struggled against the swell of emotion building within her. She'd promised herself she'd stay in control. Damn it, she wouldn't cry. She'd handle this well. But, God, her *son* really touched her. If nothing else ever happened between them, she'd gotten more from him now than she'd ever imagined having.

"Sorry," she said hoarsely, pulling her gaze away. "I'm not usually this clumsy." Glancing over, she saw Luke staring at her, examining her. She knew that somehow he sensed what had just happened to her. The distaste in his eyes told her he didn't like it—and that he felt not a whit of sympathy for her. So be it. She wasn't going to let him stand in her way. Not if Michael wanted her in his life. *You have some say in this now, Meredith,* her therapist had said. *Go for it.*

"Have a seat, Ms. Hunter." The ice in Luke's voice confirmed her impressions.

Knees shaking, Meredith crossed to the blue plaid sofa and gratefully sank onto it. Luke leaned against a six-foot-long mahogany wall unit, hands stuck in his jeans, a long-sleeved gray T-shirt hugging his muscles. His whole stance was hostile. She turned from him to Michael.

He, too, was watching her from a distance. He stood by the step she'd stumbled over, head cocked, posture only slightly less tense than Luke's. The sweatshirt he wore stretched across his wide shoulders.

"Can we get you something?" Luke asked, breaking the silence. When she stared at him, wide-eyed, a ghost of a smile played on his face. "A glass of water, or something? You look like you could use one."

He'd broken the tension. Even though he hated her presence here, he'd done it for his son. Reluctant admiration swept through her.

"I *am* a little overwhelmed. Water would help."

Michael's shoulders relaxed as Luke walked by and squeezed his arm. Meredith bit her lip, moved by the supportive gesture. She was a bundle of nerves and needed to get control before she started to bawl in front of the Rayburn men.

Taking a deep breath, she focused on Michael. "This must be hard on you," she said softly.

His eyes—the exact color of hers—watched her. Then he shrugged. "Yeah, it is. For you, too?"

She nodded. "But I'm glad that you wanted to meet me."

"Yeah?" The grin that split on his youthful face gave her the encouragement to go on.

"Yes, I am. You'll never know how much."

Michael moved into the room, and sat down on a chair adjacent to her. "Okay, good." He held eye contact. "So, how do we do this?" Meredith smiled inwardly at the similarities between his gestures and words and those of the man who had raised him.

Luke returned with the water, and Meredith hoped neither of them noticed the slight trembling of her hand as she took it. She gulped it down, then set the glass on a coaster on the fancy end table and turned back to Michael. "We'll do this however you want."

He glanced at his father, who'd retreated to the wall; Luke gave his son an encouraging smile and nodded.

"Dad thinks we might want to spend some time alone together."

An unexpected gift. Pure joy shot through her. "I'd love that."

Michael shifted in the chair and looked longingly out the window. "Want to go for a walk? We're only a half mile from the high school. I could show it to you."

"I'd like that."

He scanned her outfit. "You gonna be okay in those shoes?"

Peering down at her one-inch pumps, she shook her head. "Probably not, but I've got my Nikes in the car."

"Cool." He stood. "Let's go then."

Meredith risked a glimpse at Luke. His face was inscrutable as he pushed away from the wall and followed them to the foyer. "You need a jacket, Michael?"

The boy tugged at his sweatshirt as he opened the front door. "Nah, I got to wear this, remember?"

A smile full of love and pride suffused Luke Rayburn's face. It made him look young—and handsome, even if Meredith didn't understand the exchange.

"Don't rub it in, buddy," he said gruffly. He turned to Meredith. The warmth drained from his eyes and he scowled. "How about you?" he asked. The strain in his voice told her he was trying hard to inject some concern into his question. "You got a jacket?"

"Ah, no. I don't. I didn't think…I was a little rattled this morning when I left Romulus."

Luke's features softened. "That's understandable." He reached over, opened a closet and yanked out a white nylon jacket. Meredith caught the Sommerfield blue lettering on the back. "Here, you can wear this," he told her.

She felt the room sway as he placed the jacket over her shoulders. Her son's jacket. She was actually wearing her son's jacket. Michael stepped outside; Meredith was forced to follow, though she did so in a daze. A quick glance down to see *Mike* on the upper left almost destroyed her equilibrium completely. The subtle smell of after-shave surrounded her as the smooth material caressed her arms. She halted on the porch, closed her eyes briefly, savoring the scent of her child. Thank God both men were distracted by Michael's comment, "Wow, Dad, look."

Meredith watched Luke and Michael take the steps two at a time and stride to the Corvette parked in their driveway. Michael reached out his hand and smoothed it over the silver-metallic paint and chrome. Luke held himself back, but couldn't take his eyes off the car.

"What year is it?" Michael asked.

Meredith was about to answer, when Luke said, "A silver-anniversary edition, I'll bet. 1977."

This from the man who drove a Bronco—a late-model, pricey one, but still a family car. Interesting.

As the two men examined the car and traded comments, Meredith stuck her hands into the pockets of Michael's jacket. She pulled out two movie-ticket stubs, a pack of gum and a dollar. She swallowed hard. Clues to her son's life. Traces of his daily activities.

"Ready to go?" she heard him ask.

"Sure, as soon as I get my sneakers."

She took the stairs carefully, not wanting to repeat her earlier clumsiness. Opening the passenger side of the car, she grabbed the shoes and socks, sat down and slipped off her pumps. When she was ready, she looked up to find Luke's gaze focused on her legs. He tore his eyes away, like a kid caught doing something he shouldn't, then cleared his throat. "Well, enjoy your walk." Peering over the hood of the car, he stared hard at Michael. "I'll be right here when you get back, son," he said meaningfully.

Involuntarily Meredith winced at the term. On the other side of the car, Michael didn't notice. But when she caught Luke's eyes, she knew he had.

Damn, she'd have to be more careful around this guy. He saw too much. And it would be a cold day in hell before she'd let any man in on her vulnerabilities. Especially Luke Rayburn.

MIKE STRUGGLED to maintain a slow pace so that the woman beside him could keep up. He jammed his hands into his corduroy jeans and wracked his brain for something to say to her. How did you talk to a mother you'd never met? Man, he didn't even know what to call her. Meredith, he guessed. His Interpersonal Skills Course never covered this one.

"My dad says you're a lawyer."

"Yes, I'm an assistant district attorney in Romulus."

"You like it?"

"I love it."

They walked a little farther. "It's funny, you being a lawyer... Dad's a lawyer and Grandma Rayburn and your mother are all lawyers."

"It *is* a coincidence."

"But I guess that's how I got to...to Dad, right?"

She moved away from him, like Julie Anne often did when he pushed her about something she didn't want to discuss. Must be a girl-thing.

"Yes, Mike, it is. My mother and your father's mother arranged the adoption."

His stomach went queasy at the topic. *You can ask her anything you want,* Dad had said, *but don't feel you have to get into things you're not ready to discuss.*

"Tell me about your job."

He tried to listen as she told him about the case she was working on now. An eighty-year-old woman had been attacked and Meredith was prosecuting the alleged attacker. She had a strong voice, a lot like the news reporter on channel ten. His mother—Sara, his *real* mother—had had a soft, feminine voice. He could still hear it sometimes, calling up the stairs for him to come to supper, laughing softly with his father in the den, and in the end, telling him he had to be strong. God, he missed her.

The woman next to him was nothing like her. She

was tall. His mother had been barely five feet. Meredith was healthy and athletic-looking. His mother had been sick for all of his life. And fragile. He remembered trying not to do anything to upset her because she was so vulnerable. When he did, he felt guilty about it for days. Just as he felt guilty now. For wanting to know this woman.

The school loomed ahead. Meredith had fallen silent as they walked toward the bleachers. Taking a seat on the first row, he stared out at the field.

"You're a soccer player, right?" she asked, joining him.

"Yeah."

"It's a great game."

He turned to her. "You know it?"

She smiled, the first real, unselfconscious one she'd given him. "Yep."

"How?"

"I used to play."

"Really? What position?"

"Center forward."

"No kidding, that's what I play."

"I know. Your father told me."

"He didn't tell me you played."

She frowned. "I didn't say much about it. It was a long time ago."

"Wow, maybe you can come and watch a game sometime."

He heard her suck in her breath. When he turned to look at her, her eyes were watery. Damn, he hoped she didn't cry. The few times when Julie Anne had cried, it killed him.

"Are you all right?" he asked.

She coughed again. She'd done that a lot. And

cleared her throat. He figured she was pretty choked up about all this. Well, so was he.

"Yes, Mike, I'm okay. And I'd be honored to come and see you play." She took another deep breath. "Am I going to get to do that?"

Was she? Good question. He wanted her to. He thought he did, anyway. Sometimes. Most of the time. Then there were times he never wanted to lay eyes on her.

"You know, *I* asked to see you."

"Yes, I know."

"Dad thinks it's a mistake."

"Did he say that?"

"No, but I can tell. He throws his shoulders back and shoves his eyebrows together whenever he doesn't agree with something I want to do."

"Well, that's understandable. This is a difficult situation."

"Is this really hard for you, Meredith?" Saying her name for the first time felt strange. When he looked at her, he could tell she sensed it, too.

"Very hard." Her reply was breathless.

Something pushed at him from inside. He knew he should ignore it. He always knew when he should stop himself from doing things. Like when he was on the soccer field and had the urge to take the ball down alone. He always *knew* when he should pass. But he often went solo, anyway, believing he could score alone. So, knowing he was making an error in judgment once again, he asked, "Yeah, well, if this is so hard for you, why did you give me up in the first place?"

CHAPTER TWO

"READ THAT AGAIN."

"Forty-eight percent of women have had sex as a result of having had too much to drink, fifty-eight percent of men have."

Julie Anne shook her head. "Well, now you know why I don't drink." She paused. "And why I worry about you hanging out with the boozers on the soccer team."

Mike stared at the ceiling of her room, tracking the stippled paint's path with his eyes. He didn't rise to the bait of their ongoing argument. More important things worried him.

"Michael? What's wrong?"

When he didn't respond, she said, "Mike?"

"Do you think that's when she did it? How it happened?"

In an even voice—Julie Anne Sherman was the coolest girl he knew—she said, "I don't know. Why don't you ask her?"

"I did."

Julie Anne got up from the twin bed she was lying on and crossed the room to perch on the edge of the matching one where Mike lay sprawled. "You haven't said much since you saw her yesterday."

"I know."

"Why?"

Mike thought hard. "Because it hurts, I guess."

When Julie Anne sighed, he knew what was coming. "Remember when your mom died? You wouldn't discuss it for a long time. Once you did, you started to feel better."

Mike drew his arm up to his forehead and nodded.

"Maybe it'll help to talk about this."

He glanced over at the girl beside him. They'd grown up together, and though he felt like a brother to her, he could appreciate how beautiful she was with big blue eyes and blond hair to her waist. "Okay." He sat up, stuffed a pillow behind him and leaned against the white wicker headboard. "Like I said, I did ask her. Not too nicely."

"So? You don't owe her anything."

"You wouldn't say that if you'd seen the look on her face. I thought she was going to puke."

Again, Julie Anne sighed and scooted back to the end of the bed, curled her legs under her and rested her chin on her knees. "What was her answer?"

"She gave me some crap about being eighteen, pregnant and unwed. She'd made a foolish mistake. Knew she couldn't take care of me. Gave me to people who could." He recited the bare facts aloud, as if he was reading them from a textbook. Hell, he *had* read them, from one of the magazines Julie Anne had gotten for her project.

"You don't believe her?"

"It's not that. I just don't think that's all of it."

Julie Anne rolled her eyes. "Michael, you didn't expect the gory details, did you? In the back seat of a car...after a football game...whatever."

This was one thing he valued about his next-door neighbor. She cut right to the quick, as his father would say. His father...now *there* was a major-league problem.

"No, I didn't expect the details. It's just such a cliché."

"Well, adoptions *are* pretty clichéd. Girl gets pregnant, not married, gives up kid. End of story. She could have gotten rid of you."

Mike jerked back on the bed. "Oh, nice thought, Sherman."

"Well, it's true. Give her some credit."

"Since when did you start taking her side?"

"Don't be such a dweeb, Rayburn. I'm trying to help here. I've been researching this topic for a couple of weeks. It's all pretty cut-and-dried."

Mike tried to relax, settling back into the pillow. After a few minutes, he asked, "What do the adoptive parents usually do, Jule? When the kid wants to find his birth parent?"

Knowing blue eyes fastened on him. "Various things. Scream and threaten. Cry. Send out big-time guilt trips. Not many handle it as well as Lucas Rayburn."

Michael saw again his father's eyes, full of the hurt Mike's request had caused. The fact that he'd disappointed his dad had almost made Mike take back his words. "He may handle this okay on the outside, but it's tearing him up inside. He looks so worried all the time. Like he did about Mom."

"Your father's a saint."

"You wouldn't say that if you could hear him swearing when he can't find something."

Julie Anne frowned. "At least he's not ragging on you like *somebody* we know."

Automatically, Mike looked toward the door. "Your mom still upset about the topic for your term paper?"

"A mild word for a major temper tantrum."

"I told you she'd flip out. Your mother has always been closemouthed about the fact that you're adopted. My parents were a lot more open about my adoption, but your mom has never wanted to talk about it."

Julie Anne moved away from him to lean her back against the wall.

"And, Jule, you're sixteen. She's your mother. You got built-in conflict going for you. This research project is bound to cause waves."

"More like typhoons. She won't believe I don't want to find my biological parents. I just think kids should have the right to if they want. Like abortion. I'm pro-choice, not because I'd have one, but because I think every woman should have the right to decide."

Against his will, an image of Meredith Hunter popped into Mike's mind. Had she considered an abortion? It was weird to think he might never have been born.

"What's on your mind now, Rayburn?"

"I'm thinking about Meredith. You'd get along well with her, Jule."

"Why?"

"My dad says she's done some neat stuff in the D.A.'s office. Champion of women's issues, I think he called her."

"I'm sure she and my mother will get along great," Julie Anne put in dryly.

"Oh, God, your mom will give her grief, won't she?"

"Don't worry. Good old Teddy may be flippin' out now, but it'll blow over eventually."

"At least she's honest about her feelings. I wish my dad would come clean about his. Like he always does, he's holding it in. For my sake. I *hate* that. Saint Lucas is going to end up with an ulcer before this is all over."

"Well, just so his devil of a son gets what he needs." Julie Anne smiled. "What do you need from this, Michael?"

"I'm not sure. I want to get to know her, see what she's like. Sometimes. Other times I want to forget she exists."

"Typical male response."

Mike threw a small flowered pillow at her.

"Are you worried about how the jock squad will react?"

"What do you mean?"

"Michael, they're jerks. They'll get on your case when they find out who she is." Julie Anne frowned. "Or they'll cut you down behind your back."

"Hell. I hadn't thought about that."

"It's not written in stone that you have to follow through on this, you know."

"That's what Dad said. I'm so mixed up."

"Want some advice?"

"When didn't I?"

"When you asked Barbara-with-the-big-boobs to the prom."

Michael grinned and moved his eyebrows up and down, then sobered. "Yeah. I want some advice."

"Only one way to sort those feelings out."

"What?"

"Keep seeing the lady. Otherwise, it'll eat you alive."

IT WAS EATING him alive.

So Luke slammed the ball low into the right-hand

corner of the wall, sending it spiraling onto the floor before bouncing back to his opponent.

Seth Sherman dived for it, missed and crashed into the wall.

You two play like you're teenagers, Lucas. You're going to get hurt. Luke could still hear Sara's gentle chiding over their aggressive racquetball games. God, he missed having her worrying about him and fussing over silly things.

"Lucas, it's your serve."

He'd stopped playing and had been staring into space. Something he'd done a lot of the last two weeks. Smiling weakly, he went to the service box and tossed up the ball. He hit it hard, slicing it back into his opponent's left-hand corner. Seth missed the shot.

"Game point next," Luke said. He repeated his earlier serve. Again, it was impossible to return. He pivoted and looked at his friend of fourteen years. "Want to go again?"

Wiping the sweat off his forehead with the hem of his white polo shirt, Seth shook his head. "Are you kidding? Not the way you're playing. I need to be able to walk this week. Those line drives are bound to hit this poor, old body eventually."

"Yeah, right. That forty-year-old body is in better shape than some teenagers I know."

"Let's get a drink, anyway," Seth said. There was something about his tone—its gentleness—that set Luke on edge. But he said nothing, collected his gear and followed his friend to the lounge of Bridgeview Country Club.

Seated at a table overlooking the lush greenery of Sommerfield's finest golf course, Luke was reminded of Meredith Hunter's condo complex.

Not that he needed reminding of the woman. He'd been unable to banish her from his mind. For the most part, he was angry and distrustful of the woman who could steal his son from him. But every once in a while, he'd remember the vulnerability in those jade eyes, the tense set of those slender shoulders, and he'd actually feel sympathetic...for the mother who'd given her baby away.

Sipping his springwater, he caught Seth staring at him.

"You wanna tell me about it?" his friend asked.

Luke wanted to confide in Seth. But he was afraid to articulate his worst fears. "I...ah, can't stop thinking about this situation with Meredith Hunter."

"That's pretty normal."

"It's hell."

"How?"

"I'm scared, Seth."

"Of?"

"Losing Michael. I already lost Sara. I couldn't bear to—" Luke broke off, shaking his head in disgust.

Seth leaned over on his elbows and faced Luke squarely. "The boy loves you, Lucas. You two have the most...special relationship I've ever seen between a parent and a kid."

"It's because Sara died."

"No, it's always been that way. Although, I believe it is because of Sara."

"How so?"

"You two had a bond because of her. Over taking care of her."

"Yeah, I suppose."

Seth cleared his throat, and it alerted Luke.

"What?"

His friend stared hard at him. "Nothing. What's she like? This Meredith Hunter?"

An image of her two days ago in the dressy green outfit, pulling on Nikes, flitted through his mind. "Hard to tell. My guess is she's full of contradictions. Appears one way, has a lot buried inside her that peeks out when she's not looking."

"Like?"

"Her feelings for Michael, for one thing. God, they were written all over her face, but she tried to hide them."

"This can't be easy for her."

Luke ignored the comment. The last thing he needed was encouragement to feel sorry for this woman. "And she's nothing like Sara. Sara was small and fragile, all soft and feminine curves. Meredith is tall, angular, looks tough." But then he remembered the glimpse of tears glazing her eyes that day at her condo, and wasn't so sure of the assessment.

"We watched out the front window to catch a look at her," Seth said. "Great car."

In spite of his reservations, Luke smiled. "Yeah, wasn't it?"

"Speaking of which, did you ever go back to check out the Mustang?"

"Nah. I'm going to save the money for Michael's college fund. It was a stupid idea, anyway."

This time, Seth's scowl was too obvious to let go.

"Something on your mind, Sherman?"

Seth gulped his drink and set it down hard. "Yeah, there is. You already have enough money saved for Michael's education. I'd like to see you do something for yourself, for a change. I'm sick of watching you always putting yourself last."

Luke sat back, stunned. "Where did all this come from?"

Shaking his head, Seth said, "Truthfully, I've felt it for years. I've watched you give in on everything your family ever wanted, and never, ever take for yourself. Not even something as relatively insignificant as a car. I thought once Sara was gone, you'd allow yourself a little pleasure. But now you're putting Michael's every wish ahead of your own."

Luke was shocked at the vehemence of Seth's feelings. "Seth, you're exaggerating. So I let them both have their way a lot. Now that Sara's dead, I'm glad I did."

"It's more than that."

"No, it's not. Besides, I didn't give in on the public defender thing," Luke argued.

"No, you didn't. It's the only thing you did for yourself."

And Sara hated it. He still remembered her objections. *Lucas, you went to Stanford. No one goes to that kind of school then works as a public defender. You could get a job in a prestigious law firm. Or join Daddy's company...*

"I was right to give in to her on everything else. Sara was sick. She didn't need conflict in her life."

"So you've spent yours making sure she didn't have it. Incidentally, so has Michael."

That got him. "What do you mean?"

"He tiptoed around her just like you did."

Luke felt the blood drain from his face.

"Look, Lucas, the only reason I'm bringing this up is because I'm worried that you're doing it again with this adoption thing. Suppressing all your needs in order to meet Michael's."

"What do you think I should do? Forbid him to see her? Act like Teddy about Julie Anne's research paper?"

His friend's eyes widened.

"Oh, hell, Seth, I'm sorry. That was out of line."

"No, it wasn't. Teddy's being impossible about this issue because she's scared. It's tearing me apart to watch her suffer. But at least she's being honest about her feelings."

Luke took the comment stoically. "I'm being honest. Inside, at least," he admitted.

"Talking it out might help."

"Maybe." He looked around the pine-paneled room; Sara had loved to have lunch here. "I'm afraid Meredith is going to replace Sara in Michael's life." He hesitated. "And replace me."

"Well, that's a normal fear. If unwarranted."

"Meaning?"

"Michael loved Sara unconditionally. She'll always have a mother's place in his heart."

Feeling engulfed by the familiar frustration over Sara's death, Luke's hand fisted on his knee. "I guess. I just couldn't handle... What if he wants to go live with Meredith Hunter?"

"Why would he?"

"To get to know her better."

"He'd never leave you to do that. The kid hates even to disappoint you. He worships the ground you walk on."

"That's a little extreme, isn't it?"

"Not in my view. But even if it is, you've got to have faith in your parenting, in how much a part of Michael you are."

"Oh, God, I hope so. I don't...if she took him away..."

"She can't, Lucas. She can't."

But his best friend's assurance didn't ease the terror that gripped his heart when Luke voiced his worst fear. He knew he could survive his wife's death—somehow adults managed when a spouse died. But there was no way in hell he could live through the loss of his son.

"THERE'S SOMETHING about the way he looks at me. Wary. Almost afraid." Meredith sat at Belle's table, shredding lettuce for the tacos her friend was preparing for dinner. The spicy aroma of Mexican food surrounded them like a comfortable blanket. "I got the definite impression Lucas Rayburn thinks I'm trying to take Michael away from him."

Five-foot-tall Belle stood on tiptoe to reach a pan from the cupboard. "Understandable, given the circumstances. What's he like?"

"Serious. Perceptive." Meredith popped a chunk of tomato into her mouth. "One thing's for sure, he loves Michael. And they're close. Really close," she repeated softly.

Belle slid the pan in which she was heating oil to the back burner, then crossed to Meredith and sat down. Taking her friend's hand, Belle said, "I'm sorry about this."

Meredith shook her head. "No, Belle, never be sorry about it. I'm so grateful I've been given a chance with Michael. And I'm praying he wants me in his life. I never expected this. It's a blessing."

"It could be a curse."

"Why?"

"Look at you. Your face betrays how much this is hurting you."

"No, no, Belle, I loved seeing him. He looks like me. Did I tell you that?"

"Yes, you told me that."

"And he plays soccer."

"The game, and scholarship, you had to give up when you were...when you got pregnant."

"You don't pull any punches, do you?"

"Not when your happiness is at stake. Not when you were living a contented, productive life before last week, when this kid came barging into it. Don't expect me to be happy about all the pain this resurrects for you. I was there sixteen years ago, honey, right after you gave him up. I saw how it tore you apart."

"I know you did." Meredith squeezed Belle's hand. "I couldn't have gotten through it without you. But Michael *has* contacted me. Surely, you don't expect me not to see him."

"No, I don't. I'm just worried."

Meredith closed her eyes. "I know, so am I."

Her friend rose, and went back to the stove. "So, tell me more about Lucas Rayburn."

Might as well get it over with. "He's a public defender, Belle. For the federal government."

The spatula Belle held clattered to the floor and she pivoted to face Meredith. "No, tell me he isn't."

"Yes, I'm afraid so. Life plays dirty tricks, doesn't it?"

Belle let out a few obscenities she usually reserved for the more negligent parents of the children in her subsidized nursery school. After a few minutes, she asked, "What's the difference between a federal public defender and a regular one?"

"County P.D.'s work for the state. They defend ninety percent of the local cases who can't afford representation. The federal public defender deals with crimes involving drugs, weapons, bank robberies and of course, assaults on federal employees."

"So they help really dangerous criminals get off."

Meredith smiled sadly. They'd had this discussion before. "No, Belle. They defend people who have no money to hire other lawyers. The law says everyone's entitled to a defense. Just because I've had a bad experience doesn't mean all defense lawyers are unethical."

"An ethical defense lawyer is an oxymoron."

"That's not true. In all branches of law, you find a lack of ethics in *some* attorneys."

"Like Mark Rath."

The name from the past, the horrible, haunting name, clawed at Meredith's insides. "It was a long time ago."

"Seventeen years."

"Listen, Belle, I know it's a terrible coincidence. But I can't change the fact that my son's father is part of a system that hurt me. I spent a lot of time in therapy dealing with the fact that I have to get beyond my biases about P.D.'s. I've done it pretty well by dealing with each defense lawyer on an individual basis. It's worked so far."

"But it isn't easy for you, is it?"

"No, it's very hard. Sometimes the cases they win are painful to me."

"Well, this only stacks the deck, as far as I'm concerned. This whole thing is spelling out nothing but trouble for you."

Wistfully, Meredith remembered the feel of her son's

jacket, his essence surrounding her. "It has potential for great joy, too." Luke Rayburn's face materialized before her. Grim. Suspicious. Wary. "I'll stay away from Rayburn as much as I can. But I'm not giving up Michael a second time. At least not without a fight."

"What about the other? The…real reason you gave Michael up for adoption?"

Stark terror engulfed Meredith. She fought it. "No one else will ever know about that, Belle. Ever."

LUKE LET the papers drop onto his desk, unable to summon enough energy to slam them down. He hadn't had a good night's sleep since Meredith had come into his and Michael's lives. Exhaustion was beginning to catch up with him.

The door opened and his colleague, Pete Johnson, poked his head in. "Your lucky day, Counselor. There's a looker out here to see you. Our next case?"

Lucas frowned at Pete. "No, this is personal stuff. I was supposed to meet her out of the office, but since you scheduled the Washington case at two, I had to change my plans."

"Sorry, buddy. New lady in your life?"

"No way."

Pete sobered. "It's been a long time since Sara died, Lucas."

As if he needed reminding. "Send her in, will you?"

In seconds, Ms. Meredith Hunter, Romulus assistant district attorney—and the woman who had the power to wrench his life apart—appeared at his doorway. Against his will, he scanned her tall, athletic form.

Pete was right—she was attractive. Elegant, slender, with an aura of strength about her. All right, he *had* noticed her great legs when she'd donned her Nikes the other day. And he'd wondered what her hair would look like down. Today she wore it in some kind of knot at her neck. Every time he'd seen her, it was tied up or back.

"Hello, Mr. Rayburn."

"Ms. Hunter. Come in."

She walked gracefully into the room. "Sit down." She sat, crossing one knee over the other, and for the first time in what, years?—the sight of a woman's legs affected his pulse rate. "Thanks for meeting me here," he said, trying to stifle the awareness. "I would have kept our original arrangement, but I've got an appointment in an hour."

"That's all right. I didn't want to wait until you could fit me in again." Her voice was strong but strained.

Luke remembered how she'd watched Michael, devouring his every word. Luke steeled himself against allowing any sympathy to soften his feelings toward her. He sat back on the edge of his desk, towering over her, and fleetingly wondered at his need for this power tactic. "I can imagine you want this settled. Sometimes uncertainty is the worst thing."

"Not the worst," she said absently, her eyes straying to a shelf behind him. Her lips tightened before she tore her gaze away. He angled his body to see what she'd been looking at and caught a glimpse of a collage of pictures displayed in a brass frame. They were all soccer photos of Michael.

Meredith looked at him again. "You said you wanted to iron out some things with me. Does that mean you've...you and Michael have come to some sort of decision about all this?" she asked bravely.

Had to give the lady credit. She went right to the

point. But he noticed, once again, her hands clenched tightly in her lap. "I want to clarify some issues, and set some ground rules. But, yes, Michael's decided he wants some time to get to know you."

Lids lowered over her green eyes before he could read them. But her soft expulsion of breath, and the way her shoulders relaxed told him of her relief. Damn, he didn't want to notice that any more than he wanted to admit she had great legs.

"It's not going to be easy," he said to diffuse his emotions. "And it may not work. You should keep that possibility in mind."

It was as if he'd doused her with cold water. All the tension crept back into her body.

"But it may work out," she retorted quickly. "Depending on how it's handled."

"What does that mean?"

"If you don't try to sabotage it."

He laughed, a sound holding no mirth. "Look, lady, if I planned to do that, I would have done it before we even contacted you."

As she watched him, he resisted the urge to squirm under her scrutiny. She'd hold her own in the courtroom with that piercing, analytical gaze. "Your point, Mr. Rayburn."

"You probably should call me by my first name."

Her features softened, and the half smile she gave him did funny things to his insides. "All right, Luke."

He cocked his head.

"What is it?"

"No one has called me that since I was a kid. I go by Lucas."

"Really? You...look like a Luke."

"I'll call you Meredith, if that's all right." When

she nodded, he continued, "We need to talk about some things."

"What things?"

"First, I think it's best if you get to know Michael on his own turf. I realize it's almost an hour's drive from Romulus to Sommerfield, but I think it's better if you come here."

"I don't have a problem with that."

"And I think you should limit your visits initially. Give us all time to adjust."

"That's probably a wise idea. Was it Michael's?"

"No. He thought this whole meeting was needless."

"But you insisted."

"Yeah. For a change."

"For a change?"

"I've tried to give Michael as much control over his life as I could, since he was a child. But I've insisted a few important things be done my way."

"Fair enough."

Her acquiescence irritated him. He felt an unnatural—and unkind—urge to rattle her. "You're pretty agreeable. Don't you have anything to say? Any feelings about the situation?"

Her grip tightened on the arms of her chair, and her face flushed. "I have a lot feelings about it. It's just that I'm well aware that I don't have any rights."

That zinged his lawyer's heart. He was a man who had spent his whole life protecting people's rights. He ran his hand through his hair, eased off the desk and paced. "I'm sorry. That was unfair. This is...not easy for me, but attacking you isn't going to help."

He heard her sigh behind him. "I know. I'm pretty raw about it myself, Luke. Ah, Lucas."

Pivoting, he dug his hands into his suit pockets.

"Let's start again. My parents are in town. They want to see you. Why don't you come by the house Saturday morning. You can meet them, have an early lunch then spend the afternoon with Michael."

Luke had seen women weep with joy, men burst with happiness and children cry with glee. He had never, ever seen a look that mirrored the one on Meredith Hunter's face. Suddenly he felt shamed by his fears and his pettiness. As much as he didn't like it, the fact remained that this woman gave birth to Michael. And right now, it was crystal clear that the hardest thing she ever did was to give him up.

She swallowed hard. "Thanks." Then she frowned. "How are we going to—"

The door burst open, cutting off Meredith's question. A woman with a black eye, dressed in a torn blouse and a too-tight skirt, was followed by the receptionist Meredith had met earlier. "I'm sorry, Lucas," she said. "I couldn't stop her."

"That's all right, Dee. Mrs. Washington, is something wrong?"

"I need to see ya. Now."

"I'm busy right now. But I can—"

"Now. Before you meet with me and my old man at two. I ain't gonna say what I have to say in front of Terrence. You wanna hear it, you hear it now."

Meredith stood. "I can wait outside. I'd like to have just a few more minutes with you when you're done, though."

He gave her an apologetic look. "You can wait here. We'll go into the conference room. Thanks, Meredith."

His smile, combined with the gentle way he said her name, unnerved her. She watched as he led the overwrought woman into the adjoining room and softly closed the door. Shaking off her awareness of him, she scanned the office.

It was large and airy, unlike her own cramped quarters in the county building. The interior had obviously been modernized, but still had the original tall, thin windows that overlooked Broad Street. A credenza, covered with a computer, files and a phone, lined one whole wall, and his desk grew out from it in an oval shape. The office was big and powerful—a lot like the man himself. She could picture his wide shoulders hunched over the desk, a lock of unruly chestnut hair falling onto his forehead. Bemused by her uncharacteristically whimsical thoughts, she finished her study of the room. Several large modern prints hung on one wall, which also had several file cabinets. On the other side, floor-to-ceiling shelves were crammed with books and personal effects. Like the pictures of Michael.

Reluctantly, but unable to stop herself, she wandered over to them. Like a man picking up a newborn baby, she lifted the frame. "Oh, God," she said, cupping her hand over her mouth. In front of her was the history of Michael's soccer career from about the age of four. A quick perusal told her there was a snap shot of him for every year he'd played. Slowly, she ran her finger around the little face in the first photo.

But it was too much, seeing him like this. Too much too fast. She set the picture down, facing it away from her, and moved to the window overlooking downtown Sommerfield. Hugging her waist with shaking hands, she forced herself to calm down. It took minutes before she was breathing normally.

To distract herself, she crossed to Luke's bookcase. Familiar law books, tomes and treatises of their trade, occupied most of his shelves. But tucked in between were some others. A bestseller about the law profession, popular about a year ago. A slim volume of poetry. And a book of jokes about lawyers. Two books about cars. She plucked one called *Classic Cars* off the shelf and opened it. On the first page she read, "To Dad—will you please get one? Love, Mike." It was dated Christmas of last year.

She leafed through the book, wondering about this piece of the puzzle that was Lucas Rayburn. Why did he have a Bronco when he obviously loved fast cars? It wouldn't be the money. Even on her salary, she could afford the payments for a Corvette. Federal P.D.'s earned a lot more than she did.

Sighing, she turned the pages. The more she learned about him, the more complicated he appeared to be. She'd seen the gentle side of him with Michael, but toward her, he'd been the tough public defender. God, she'd hate to face him in court. Usually she relished professional competition. Maybe he was so intimidating because Lucas Rayburn could easily reopen so many personal wounds for her. She needed all her wits about her to hold her own around him.

Ten minutes later, he emerged from the conference room. He was scowling. "Don't worry, Mrs. Washington, I'll certainly deal with these facts."

The woman muttered something to him, and when Meredith looked closely, it was obvious she'd been crying.

After she left, Luke went to the phone and picked it up. "Dee, get me Pete right away." He put his hand over the receiver. "I'm sorry, this will only take a minute."

Meredith smiled. "It's okay. I know the routine."

He stared at her until he was pulled away by a voice on the phone. "Yeah, Pete. Mrs. Washington just came to see me. There's more to this than we knew. We've got to confer before the two o'clock meeting.'' A pause. "No, it's not going to help us defend her husband. But...Pete, she has relevant, significant information about him..." Luke glanced at his watch, then looked to Meredith with raised eyebrows. His face, which she previously thought was handsome enough, glowed with anticipation. His rich brown eyes sparkled. Meredith was momentarily struck by how attractive Luke Rayburn could be. "Ten minutes?" he asked Meredith. She nodded.

When he hung up, he took in a deep breath. "Sorry to cut this short. It's something new we have to deal with...something I didn't know about."

She admired his honesty, and thought back to her discussion yesterday with Belle.

"What is it?"

"Nothing."

"You look...surprised."

"No. Not exactly."

He crossed his arms over his chest. "I guess I might as well know this from the outset. Are you one of the prosecuting attorneys who feels we're in the trenches together, and fighting for the same kind of justice? Or are you on the fringes, and believe we public defenders will sell our own mothers to get a client off?"

She chuckled at his phrasing. "Neither, I guess. I don't believe P.D.'s are worse than any other type of lawyer. There are some good ones, some bad ones. I do have some philosophical differences with what you do. And...I've also had some personal experiences that haven't been too positive."

"Care to elaborate?"

Never in a million years. "No." When he continued

to stare at her, she added, "Let's just say I agree with the Supreme Court ruling in 1963 in the *Gideon versus Wainwright* case that instituted public defenders."

"I feel like there's more going on here than you're saying."

Meredith did not want to get into this. She checked her watch. "Don't you have to go?"

He looked disappointed as he replied, "Yeah, I do. But you were about to ask a question when we were interrupted. So, shoot."

Uncomfortable, Meredith shifted from one foot to the other. "I was wondering how you were going to explain my presence in Michael's life. I don't want to embarrass him or make him deal with anything too soon with his peers. I know kids can be cruel."

Luke sighed. "I hadn't considered that. I'll talk to Michael about it tonight. We'll think of some way to explain you," he said, watching her with dangerous questions in his eyes.

Had she revealed too much to this man?

As Meredith said goodbye and left his office, she was thankful for the reminder that she had to watch her step around Lucas Rayburn. She had to keep up her guard because he held too much power over her.

Usually she didn't need to be reminded. She didn't trust easily—for good reason.

CHAPTER THREE

LUKE'S FATHER glanced over and winked at his son as he addressed his wife, "Truthfully, Peg, do *you* have sexual fantasies about famous people like twenty-six percent of the women in this survey?"

Luke had been watching his parents pore over one of Michael's infamous sex surveys. Every once in a while his mother would lean into his father, her white-haired head touching his salt-and-pepper one. She'd point something out to her husband, who would grab her hand and kiss it. Their intimacy emphasized Luke's loneliness. He envied their closeness, their friendship, their ability to share everything, including this outrageous project Michael had chosen. Sara wouldn't have wanted to discuss the topic with Luke. And she wouldn't have been able to tease in public, like his parents. But she'd been his best friend, and now he was on his own.

"Quiet, Grandpa. Michael will hear you." Peg's face flushed a becoming shade of red as she adjusted the jewel-necked collar of her blouse.

"Michael's upstairs, with Julie Anne. And besides, it's *his* project." Paul Rayburn's brown eyes twinkled at his wife.

Luke's mother laughed softly. "I guess it is. But you don't expect me to disclose this information in front of witnesses, especially our son." Then, in a fake whisper, she said, "I'll tell you later."

Valiantly, Luke smiled and tried to hide the heaviness in his heart by crossing to the row of windows and pretending interest in the leaves swirling around in the front yard. Late September had just begun to color the trees red and orange and their vibrancy mocked his somber mood.

He should be more at ease today, having laid some ground rules, moving on to the next step of integrating Meredith Hunter into their lives. He had everything under control. At least he thought he had until he woke up sweating in the middle of the night wondering what surprises hid around the corner. God knew, he couldn't handle any more ambushes in his life.

"Lucas? Are you all right?" Peg asked.

"Just restless, I guess." He dug his hands into his tan corduroys. *And scared.*

He felt her come up behind him and touch his arm. "This is so hard for you, dear. You don't have to be brave in front of us."

Pivoting, he gave her a grateful smile. For the thousandth time, he thanked God for giving him a mother like her. "I know. I'm glad you're here. Among other things, it will diffuse the tension when Meredith arrives."

Peg Rayburn cocked her head. "It's been bad?"

Luke had a fleeting image of Meredith Hunter watching Michael with anguished eyes that devoured his every move. "Emotions are running high for everyone."

He sensed his mother was about to probe further, when the doorbell chimed.

"That's her." He smiled. "You ready for this?"

"Of course. It will be a joy to meet Lydia's daughter."

At least Grandma will get to see her good friend now, Michael had said. Luke had intentionally not allowed himself to ponder what his mother had given up for him. Just thinking about it was tough, so he forcefully brushed aside the pangs of guilt, strode to the door and pulled it open.

Lord, Meredith looked even more vulnerable today. Clearly taking her cue from him and Michael, she'd dressed casually in tailored beige pants and a long-sleeved blue-green cotton sweater. She had her hair tied back in a loose ponytail. When she looked at him, her eyes were the color of the lake on a summer morning, a mixture of dark greens reflecting the blue of the sky. They were also wary. Very wary. His body tensed.

"Hi," she said, then stepped aside. "I hope it's okay. I brought my mother. She flew in unexpectedly this morning."

Meredith's face pleaded her case eloquently. She was afraid she'd made a mistake, that the appearance of Lydia would rock the boat even more. His heart went out to her, despite the churning in his gut. He smiled at Lydia Hunter and held out his hand. "Of course it's okay. Mrs. Hunter, I'm Lucas Rayburn."

Once again, Michael's eyes stared back at him. "Lucas. You...look like your mother." The older woman's voice was husky with emotion as she shook his hand. "I invited myself here because Meredith said she was planning to meet your parents." Lydia raised her chin, and Luke could see this woman facing down a jury from hell. "It's been so long, I couldn't resist the temptation to see Peg right away."

"I wouldn't want you to pass up the opportunity," Luke lied smoothly. Another variable in the equation to muddle things up, just as he'd feared.

"Thank you." Her knowing gaze silently added, "Even if you don't mean it."

Disconcerted by her astuteness, Luke motioned the women into the foyer and then led them into the living room. He moved to the side as Meredith and her mother came full face with the Rayburns.

For a moment, it was like a freeze-frame on the video screen. No one moved; the air was hushed; all eyes focused on Lydia Hunter and Peg Rayburn, two sixty-five-year-old women who had given up the friendship of a lifetime for the sake of their children. And their grandchild.

"Oh, God, Lyddie." Peg was the first to break the tableau, covering her mouth with both hands, her eyes filling.

"Hello, Peggy." Meredith's mother, though prepared for the meeting, was only a little more controlled. Luke saw her bite her lip in a gesture reminiscent of her daughter, and blink back the tears.

Then they both flew across the room. Neither made any pretense of poise. Or sophistication. They wrapped each other in a bear hug, more intense, more heartfelt and warmer than Luke had ever seen between two people. And they didn't let go. Weeping openly, they held each other as tightly as possible after sixteen years of separation.

It hurt to watch them, so Luke averted his eyes. Unfortunately, his gaze fell on Meredith, whose jaw was clenched hard enough to be painful. Her eyes were wide and sad; her face was pale.

He checked the impulse to go to her and ask if she

was all right. What would she say? Of course she wasn't all right. Both of them were responsible for having deprived these two women of each other. It didn't matter that neither Luke nor Meredith had understood exactly what they'd done all those years ago. It didn't matter that they'd do it all over again, given the same circumstances. It still hurt to be confronted with a loss that they had caused.

After a few gut-wrenching minutes, the women pulled apart. Still grasping Lydia's hand, Peg turned to Paul. "You remember Lydia, of course."

Paul Rayburn had stood back to give the women some time. Luke knew his father understood only too well the significance of this reunion. "Yes, Lydia. Good to see you again." He went to his wife's friend and hugged her warmly. "You look wonderful."

"So do you."

Paul glanced quickly behind Lydia, then back to her face. "Nick?"

Lydia's features softened. "Nick died ten years ago."

Peg grasped her friend's upper arms. "Oh, no, Lyddie. I'm sorry. I wish I could have been there for you."

"So do I." Lydia's words were simple, but rife with emotion.

Out of the corner of his eye, Luke saw Meredith turn her back to them, and walk over to the glass étagère in the corner. Ostensibly, she was examining the knick-knacks displayed there; Luke would bet Michael's college fund that she was crying. Or that she was close to it.

Reining in his own conflicting feelings, he took a step toward her, just as he heard thundering footsteps on the staircase. Michael barreled into the living room, unaware of the emotionally charged scene.

"Was that the doorbell? When no one called us, we decided to come and check."

Behind him, Julie Ann studied the adults. "Mike," she said in warning, touching his arm.

He looked around. "Oh, we...have more..." His eyes sought Luke's. They said, "Dad, help me."

Veering away from Meredith, Luke stepped around the older people and went to his son. Purposefully, he stood in front of Michael, blocking the boy from view. Grasping his son's shoulder, Luke said, "Meredith's mother came with her. Can you handle it?"

Michael grinned, though it was a little wobbly. "Sure. I'd like to meet her."

Pivoting, Luke looked to Lydia. "Lydia Hunter, this is Michael."

The older woman smiled. Though her eyes were watery, and her chin quivered a bit, she crossed to her grandson and stood tall before him. Luke knew where Meredith got her grit. "I'm honored to meet you, Michael."

Michael studied Lydia with eyes shrewd beyond his years. Then, though a blush crept up his neck, he said, "You could hug me if you want."

Luke watched, fascinated. Never in his life had he been more proud of his son. Lydia's face beamed at the precious gift she'd been given. She reached up— she was tall, like Meredith, but Michael topped them both—and took her grandchild in her arms for the first time. From behind them, Luke watched Lydia swallow and close her eyes. He saw his own mother wipe hers, and his father squeeze her shoulder. Even farther behind them, Meredith stood back, her face ashen, one hand at her waist, another fisted at her mouth.

"Well," Lydia said, drawing back but holding on to one of Michael's hands. "This is wonderful. Really wonderful." She glanced over to the right of Michael. "And who is this?"

"Oh, sorry. This is my friend Julie Anne Sherman." He glanced from Julie Anne to Lydia. "Jule—this is...my...um...I..."

Lydia said smoothly, "I'm Lydia Hunter. And I hope to be Michael's friend, too."

Luke let out a breath. Another disaster avoided. What *was* the protocol in a situation like this? Damn, it was hard.

Michael looked past Lydia to Meredith, then glanced around the room assessing the dynamics of the situation. Slowly, he left Julie Anne and Lydia and walked over to Meredith. She'd straightened, and was a little more composed by the time Michael faced her. Reaching out, he took her hand. Meredith squeezed his fingers and let him tug her to the center of the room. "Grandma, Grandpa, this is Meredith. Meredith, Peg and Paul Rayburn."

"Hello, dear," Peg said, leaning over and giving Meredith a kiss on the cheek. "You're as beautiful as your mother. You look just like she did when she was your age."

Meredith nodded, and Luke prayed she wouldn't start crying. "Thanks," she said huskily. "I hope this wasn't too much of a surprise."

"Never," Peg said.

"Meredith, it's wonderful to meet you," Paul said, taking her hand.

Coughing self-consciously, Michael pivoted. "And

this is Julie Anne Sherman. My next-door neighbor, good friend and sometimes pain in the butt."

Like an old married couple used to signaling each other, Julie Anne took Michael's cue to lighten up the situation. "Watch it, Rayburn. I could tell tales on you," she said in a singsongy voice, making her way to the group. She reached out her hand to Meredith. "Hi, nice to meet you." She angled her head to Michael. "He's an okay kid, once you get to know him."

Meredith smiled gratefully at the girl. Luke decided it was his turn to do his part.

"Why don't we all sit down."

Immediately, Lydia and Peg took side-by-side seats on the sofa, with Paul flanking his wife. Luke noticed the two women joined hands once again. Meredith edged onto the love seat, where, after a moment's hesitation, Michael plopped down. Julie Anne sank to the floor by the fireplace, and Luke leaned against the doorjamb.

Though a little stilted, conversation flowed remarkably well in the following half hour. By degrees, the three old friends on the couch relaxed. Eventually, Michael and Julie Anne participated enthusiastically in the small talk.

Only Meredith did not let down her guard. Instead, as the minutes ticked by, she became more and more tense. Every time Peg and Lydia reminisced, Meredith sat up a little more rigidly. Each comment about Michael made her hands clench tighter in her lap. Her color was terrible, and he thought he saw her shiver when the topic turned to soccer. She looked as if she was about to pass out when Peg asked Michael to get out his photo album. Then the boy went to sit between the two older women and opened the book.

Luke watched Meredith as long as he could. Before they could ask her to join in this stroll down memory lane, he said, "I'm going to get lunch on the table. Meredith, do you think you could help me?"

"I'll help," Julie Anne said.

"No, thanks, Jule, I wanted to talk to Meredith about a few things, anyway."

Zombie-like, Meredith rose from the love seat, grabbed her purse and followed Luke down the hallway to the back of the house, out into the kitchen. He went directly to the sink, got a glass of water and handed it to her. Mechanically, she dropped her purse, took the drink and gulped it. Her face was still white and her bottom lip quivered. Her struggle for control caused something to shift inside him.

"Do you want to sit down?" he asked softly.

She stared at him for a moment, then shook her head. Instead, she walked to the sliding doors that led out to the deck and leaned her forehead against the glass.

Please, God, don't let me cry. Please, give me the strength to get through this.

Meredith felt Luke's presence behind her before she opened her eyes and saw him in her peripheral vision. She ordered herself to be strong in front of this man. Instinctively, she knew she couldn't afford to show any weakness.

"Are you all right?" he asked, his tone gentle.

Oh, God, she could have handled his scolding, which was why she thought he'd brought her out here, to tell her to get a grip on herself. But his gentleness...

She nodded, unable to speak.

"It's acceptable to feel bad. This has to be hell for you."

That did it. The tears started, and fell silently down her cheeks. She turned farther away from him.

He grasped her shoulders, his touch so tender it made her raw emotions push to the surface. She swallowed hard to keep from sobbing.

"Hey, it's all right to cry," he said. "I feel like bawling, myself."

Raising her hands, she covered her face with them. Slowly, with exquisite gentleness, he moved his palms over her shoulders, down her arms. "It's okay, Meredith," he said for the third time.

As if the repetition had convinced her body, the sobs finally racked her entire frame. The bullet-burst of emotion refused to be suppressed any longer.

He circled her to face him. Only she couldn't, and kept her head down, her hands up. As if he sensed she needed closer contact, he tugged her to him. Her hands automatically flattened on his shirt, then fisted in it. She buried her face in his chest. He felt so solid; warmth radiated through his flannel shirt. And she craved that warmth. She'd been floating in a cold sea of regret and recrimination in the living room, watching the old friends get reacquainted. She'd observed the reunion of grandmother and grandson, whose separation she'd been responsible for. The knowledge had chilled her like arctic wind.

At first she was only aware of the pain erupting inside her. But gradually it cleared out and other stimuli invaded her senses. Luke's strong arms were now around her. They held her in comfort, in soothing solace, which was exactly what she needed. Large hands rubbed her back in lazy circles, then one went to her hair, causing the band that held it to fall to the floor. His fingers smoothed her hair, over and over. She sensed soft crooning, then heard words, and finally ze-roed in on what he was telling her, "It's all right. Cry it out. No one will see you."

Embarrassed, she tried halfheartedly to pull back. He held her where she was. "Come on, Meredith. We're in this together. Without you, I wouldn't have Michael. Let me comfort you."

So she stayed where she was—incredibly—locked in Luke Rayburn's arms. And he didn't feel like the enemy. He was just one kind human being helping an-other.

After a few minutes, he said, "Your hair is the same texture as Mike's, do you know that?"

She shook her head, feeling his fingers studying the strands. "And it's lovely. Why do you wear it back all the time?"

"I... don't," she mumbled into his chest.

"We've never seen it any other way."

She raised her face to look at him. "I wear it like this in court."

"I see." He examined her features. "Michael has your eyes. You must have noticed the resemblance."

She nodded. "And my mother's." Sniffling, she bur-rowed into him again. "They gave up so much."

Luke's arm tightened around her back. His voice gruff, he said, "I know. But now I see that it was worse for your family. At least my mother had Michael. At least we all had him." After a pause, he said, "I'm sorry, Meredith."

She savored his comfort for a few more seconds, then drew back. "No, don't be sorry. You've given him a wonderful home, a wonderful family." She glanced toward the living room, then back at him.

"And our mothers would *not* want us stewing about them."

Luke smiled at her, which made her stomach spin. "Yeah, they're two of a kind, aren't they?"

Meredith was mesmerized by the combination of humor and compassion in his eyes. Suddenly, she wanted to inch close to this man, touch him from head to toe. The rhythmic motion of his hands on her back and in her hair caused a pull deep inside her.

And it scared the hell out of her.

So she tried to draw back even farther. His eyes bored into her before he eased his grip, and she moved away fractionally. Wiping the tears from her face, she became aware of her hair tumbling around it. "I'm a mess," she said, pushing the stray locks away.

Luke Rayburn's smile was all male. "No, not a mess." Then he sobered. "Pretty fragile, though, compared to the tough cookie you present to the world."

She shook her head. "I *am* tough. This was an aberration."

"I believe that."

She took a deep breath. "Listen, thanks for all this. Getting me out of there. Letting me get this off my chest."

"Tell me something, Meredith. Have you cried at all since this whole thing started?"

"No, that's why this was Niagara Falls. I guess I needed to."

Suddenly, there was an awkwardness between them. She was acutely conscious of standing between his legs, even though she'd pulled back. "I…ah…should get cleaned up. Good thing I brought my purse out… I'll need to…" She stopped when she realized she was rambling.

He angled his head to the right. "There's a bathroom over there, off the laundry room."

"Thank you." She sidled away from him.

At the door to the bathroom, she turned. "Luke, why did you do this? Up until today, I felt as if we were on opposite sides...like I was the enemy."

He stared at her for a long time. "No, Meredith. You aren't the enemy." He drew in a deep breath. "You're my son's mother, who had the strength to do what was best for him sixteen years ago."

Meredith was unable to speak for several moments. "Thank you. I didn't expect you to be kind."

He watched her intently. "Maybe you should expect more from life."

When Meredith came out of the bathroom, face scrubbed, light makeup covering the ravages of the afternoon, she was in control once more. Crossing to the dinette, she saw that Luke had the table set and had spread out plates of salads and cold meat.

"You okay?" he asked huskily.

"Yeah. Do I look all right?"

His eyes darkened again. "You look fine."

"Want me to call everyone?"

"Sure."

Minutes later, the kitchen was filled. Lunch was hectic and noisy. As Lydia and Peg talked about their college adventures, Meredith found herself listening comfortably, even enjoying their reminiscences.

Michael listened, too, as did Paul. Meredith hadn't dared look directly at Luke since the group joined them, but had the distinct impression that he was avoiding her gaze, too. Julie Anne was quiet, glancing from Luke to Meredith frequently. Fleetingly, Meredith wondered what signals the teenager was picking up.

Eventually, the talk turned to Michael's upcoming soccer match. "Want to come see my next game, Meredith?" he asked hopefully. "And you, too, Lydia."

Meredith digested her son's invitation as if it were the richest caviar. "I'd love to, Mike. When is it?"

"Next Wednesday, under the lights."

"A night game! We never had those in high school."

"Meredith was quite a soccer player," Lydia told her grandson. "Have her show you her trophies sometime."

"I'd love to see them," Michael said.

"I'd like to see yours, too," Meredith told Michael.

"Sure, they're upstairs. Want to come now?"

Both Meredith and Michael started to rise.

Luke stopped them. "Michael, before you take off, there's something we need to discuss." He looked at his parents, then at Lydia. "And since we're all a part of this, we could use your input."

Meredith's stomach knotted. He was going to make an issue of something; despite what he'd said about her rights as Michael's mother, he was going to limit something, to take something away. She could just feel it. She regretted her loss of control earlier. *Never let them see you weak, Meredith. They take advantage of it later.*

"What is it?" she asked as she sat back down, her tone sharper than she'd intended.

He turned to her. She saw disappointment flicker in his eyes. But he doused the reaction, folded his arms over his chest and said in a neutral tone, "As a matter of fact, it's an issue you've raised. What are we going to tell people about your presence in Michael's life? If you suddenly start appearing at his games, showing up around here, other kids are going to wonder about it. This suburb is a small community.''

Michael sighed, his big body deflating.

"I mentioned this last night," Luke said. "Have you thought about it, son?"

"Yeah. Julie Anne and I talked about it, too. I don't know if it's even going to be a problem. Or how I feel about it. Let alone what I should do."

Meredith said, "Mike, there's no need for you to jump into anything. You don't have to make any declarations as to who I am yet."

Lydia and Peg both frowned.

"Kids can be cruel," Peg said. "No use complicating the situation further."

"So how do we explain Meredith's presence? And Lydia's, since it looks like she kind of likes Michael." Paul Rayburn's teasing brought a few weak smiles around the table. But no one spoke.

Then Julie Anne sat forward. "I've got a great idea. Meredith can pretend to be dating Mr. Rayburn."

Meredith gasped, and Luke's fork clattered onto his dish.

"Not a bad idea," Paul said easily. "You wouldn't have to actually state that she's your girlfriend, just act like she is and let people assume it. You aren't seeing anyone, son, so it wouldn't look odd. And it would keep the kids from asking Michael embarrassing questions until you all feel comfortable with the situation."

For the first time since their closeness in the kitchen, Meredith met Luke's eyes over the table. His were inscrutable, so she shielded hers, too. But she noticed he swallowed hard, and his hand gripped his glass.

"What about you, dear?" Peg asked Meredith. "Do

you have a male friend this could cause problems with?''

Meredith said, ''Well, I do date one of my colleagues, Ken Dobson.'' She hesitated when she saw Luke throw his shoulders back and shove his eyebrows together. For some reason, the reaction made her uncomfortable. ''But it shouldn't interfere if we decide to…to do this.'' When she averted her gaze, she caught Julie Anne's.

The girl looked from Meredith to Luke, then smiled innocently. ''Geez, it's a great idea. Even if I do say so myself.''

CHAPTER FOUR

AS MEREDITH WATCHED Michael warm up on the field, she chuckled to herself, thinking of the survey he'd shown her before she'd left last Saturday. *Twenty-three percent of all men asked said they get more enthused over a sports match than they do making love with their spouses.* Though she wouldn't go that far, she understood the sentiment.

She hadn't been on a soccer field in seventeen years but she remembered well the thrill of athletic competition. Especially if you were good. And she'd been among the best. *A possible contender for the women's Olympic soccer team,* her high-school coach had told her dad.

"Meredith, did you see that?" her mother asked. Lydia Hunter sat on her left, bundled up in a plaid stadium blanket she shared with her good friend Peg. "He waved to us when he came from the field to the bench."

From behind her, Meredith heard the stringent reply, "Michael always waves to us before a game." Teddy Sherman's voice gave the unseasonably cold September night competition. Meredith glanced behind her to see Julie Anne's mother staring straight ahead, not even looking at them. She would have been pretty if her features weren't so pinched.

Lydia said smoothly, "How sweet."

On her right, in the packed bleachers, Meredith felt Luke's arm tense. Luke Rayburn, her *date*. From the corner of her eye, she could see him dressed in a battered bomber jacket and denims so worn they were white at the knees. "Is everyone warm enough?" he asked.

"You guys are getting old," Julie Anne said from where she sat between her parents. "It isn't even forty degrees."

"Quiet, brat," her father said mildly. "The wind is picking up."

Luke hunched over his knees in the cramped space, locked his hands together and turned to Meredith. "You forgot your gloves?"

She nodded, her eyes involuntarily traveling to the lock of hair that fell over his forehead. She wondered what the texture of it would be if she touched it. Though the wind had made his cheeks ruddy, he looked tired tonight. The lines bracketing his mouth were more pronounced.

"I thought we were having Indian summer," she said. "I'm not prepared for this."

"Aren't you?" His words, uttered softly so only she could hear, took on another meaning.

She shook her head. "Truthfully, I'm not sure."

He reached over and squeezed her hand. "It'll be fine."

The shriek of the whistle ended their conversation. More than two hundred spectators stood to sing "The Star Spangled Banner," then cheered as first the Morrisville players then the Sommerfield team were introduced.

And for the very first time, Meredith watched her son run out onto the field to play soccer. Her stomach clenched tight and for a minute her breath was cut off. She heard her mother exclaim in a hushed whisper, "He runs just like you, dear."

Meredith nodded, her eyes glued to Michael. His white jersey was tucked into baggy blue shorts. Large blue numbers labeled him 15. The wind had tousled his hair; she could see it from where she sat. He cocked his head the way Luke often did, and listened attentively to the official; then he turned and nodded to two of his teammates, and the game began.

Mesmerized, she watched his footwork. He was quick and agile. Meredith's own feet began to move on the concrete flooring. She heard Luke chuckle beside her. When he leaned over, the scent of his woodsy after-shave surrounded her. "It's a common reaction from athletic parents. They try to maneuver a phantom ball from the stands."

She smiled at him. The look on his face was one of tender empathy, and for a few brief seconds she allowed herself the luxury of trusting this man.

"Lucas, wouldn't Sara have loved seeing him as co-captain this year?" At Teddy Sherman's intrusion, Luke arched away from Meredith. His whole body stiffened and he nodded but said nothing. He also sidled a few inches down the bleachers.

Disappointed, Meredith turned her attention back to her son in time to catch him heading a ball right for the goal. She gripped her hands together as she watched the opposition's goalie float into the air to capture it. Morrisville's crowd went wild.

The goalie booted the ball back down the field. Michael glided after it. Just as she used to, quick as the wind and as fleet-footed as a deer. Again, a cold knot formed inside her at the bittersweet similarity.

Another cheer went up, this time from Sommerfield supporters. A halfback had elbowed his way into a row of the opposition right in front of the goal and kicked the ball out of play.

Michael trotted over to the boy who'd stopped the score and slapped his shoulder.

"He's a good team player," Meredith said.

"Not always." Luke's voice was tinged with that ruefulness parents get when acknowledging their children's faults.

"Lucas, he *is* a team player," Teddy said from behind her. "His mother wouldn't have had it any other way."

Meredith stood up abruptly and drew her coat closer around her. "I can't sit still. I'm going down to the fence."

"I wondered how long it would take you," Lydia said, laughing.

"I'll go with you," Luke said, also standing.

Quickly they left the bleachers and made their way to the fence surrounding the edge of the field.

Meredith leaned against the metal barrier and fingered the chain links as she watched the play. "This is a lot better," she said evenly.

Luke rested his arms on the top of the fence and looked over at her, nodding. "It's a lot farther away from Teddy Sherman."

She met his purposeful stare. There was a sadness in those brown velvety depths that caused Meredith to catch her breath. "Teddy misses Sara," he confessed. "They were best friends."

Meredith nodded and they both returned their attention to the game. Within seconds, Michael took possession of the ball and sped toward the goal on a fast break, the right wing for his team shadowing him.

Meredith's nails dug into her palms and she stood on tiptoe so as not to miss anything. "Go, Mike. Go for it."

An opponent closed in. She heard Luke say, "Pass, son, pass."

About ten feet from the net, Michael kicked the ball to the other side of the field. His teammate stopped it on a dime, then angled it into the goal.

The crowd roared, and so did Meredith and Luke. She clapped her hands together and allowed herself a swell of pride at Mike's unselfish assist. When the noise died down, Luke moved closer and bent his head to say something to her.

From behind them, they heard, "Great play. That kid's got talent, Lucas."

They sprang apart like illicit lovers caught in an indiscretion. Luke turned, stuck out his hand and said, "Dave, nice to see you. Yeah, Mike's in good form tonight."

The tall, thin man shook Luke's hand and looked at Meredith. "Hello."

"Hi."

"Meredith, this is Dave Lockhart. Michael's social studies teacher. Dave, this is...a friend of mine." Luke deliberately raised his hand to Meredith's back. His palm rested heavily on her neck and tiny pinpricks of sensation radiated through her. She had the absurd urge to lean into him. "Meredith Hunter."

"Nice to meet you," the teacher said.

After a few brief comments, Lockhart left, and the rest of the first half flew by as Meredith watched her son dribble and pass, leaping and twisting like a pro.

He was really good. The opposition tallied a goal on a penalty—a direct kick, and at halftime, the score was tied.

The Rayburns, the Shermans and Lydia joined them at the fence during the break. Paul and Luke dissected Michael's play and Peg and Lydia chatted.

Teddy Sherman glared at Meredith before turning her back on her to talk to some of the players' mothers. Meredith felt the brittle pain of being excluded and it served as a stark reminder of her place in Mike's life.

Well, she'd just have to forge her own way into his life—and his heart.

"Meredith, want to get some hot chocolate?" Julie Anne asked. Despite her disregard of the cold, her pert nose had turned red.

"Sure."

"Bring us old folks some coffee, would you, kid?" Seth asked, handing her a ten-dollar bill.

Meredith and Julie Anne walked to the refreshment stand at the far corner of the field. The girl was almost as tall as she, with long coltish legs that matched Meredith's stride. Halfway there, Julie Anne said, "My mother's being a bitch."

Startled at the teenager's candor, Meredith hedged. "She doesn't seem pleased that I'm here."

"She hates that you're here."

"Because she was friends with...Sara?"

"Nope, because she's scared."

Meredith stopped walking. "Scared? Why?"

A frown marred the perfection of Julie Anne's skin as she looked at Meredith. "Somebody should've told you this. I'm surprised Mr. Rayburn didn't."

Meredith felt a sinking sensation in her stomach. "Told me what?"

"I'm adopted, too."

The puzzle fell into place. Teddy Sherman's hostility made more sense in light of that piece of evidence.

"And I've made it worse," Julie Anne added.

Meredith schooled her face to show no emotion. "You don't want me here, either?" How could she have been so wrong? She'd pegged Julie Anne as an ally. Suddenly, Meredith felt terribly alone.

"No, that's not what I mean. I encouraged Mike to meet you. To get to know you. I made all this worse because I'm doing my paper on the rights of adopted children. My mother's taking it personally. She won't believe I've got no interest in finding my biological parents."

"You don't want to?"

They began walking again, and neared the refreshment stand. The crowd around it was thinning. "No," Julie Anne said simply. "Why should I?"

Five minutes later, they returned to the others and distributed the coffee. The grandparents and the Shermans went to the bleachers as the game resumed. Luke and Meredith stood by the fence watching their son. The score remained tied as the ball volleyed back and forth between the two teams.

With four minutes left, Michael got a clean breakaway. Again the right wing flanked him and they were set up for a perfect pass. But halfway between midfield and the goal, Michael ignored his teammate.

Meredith froze, her fingers digging into her palms. "Pass it, Mike," she said under her breath.

From the corner of her eye, she saw Luke shake his head.

Michael did not pass. Instead, he kicked the ball toward the goal. Bulletlike, it shot through the grass. The goalie dived for it. And missed.

The crowd erupted. Sommerfield fans danced in the stands.

Meredith saw Luke raise his fist, then cup his mouth and yell something at the players. He pivoted, reached out and hugged her to him. In the excitement, she went willingly. His jacket was cold against her cheek and he smelled of fine, rich leather scented with his after-shave. For a moment, Meredith let her face rest there. His hand caressed her hair and smoothed it, loitering a little too long in its strands, which she'd left loose. She chided herself for the sexual pull inside her that his touch generated. Everyone was hugging. There was no significance to his gesture.

When the tumult died down, she drew away. Luke leaned over and said, "It was great, but I wish it hadn't been another of his solo flights."

She understood—and empathized—right away. "He should have passed."

A rueful smile turned up the corners of his mouth as Luke nodded. "His tragic flaw."

It was mine, too. "Sometimes it's hard. When you're so good. And you know you can do it."

Luke frowned; the warmth left his deep brown eyes. He stuck his hands in the pockets of his jacket. "He works at it. He just can't seem to beat it every time." Straightening his shoulders, Luke eyed her cautiously. "He needs encouragement *not* to grandstand like that, Meredith."

She stiffened and took a step back, sliding her own hands into her stadium coat. Opponents again, they faced each other as they would if they ever met in the courtroom. "Give me some credit, Luke. I don't have much experience with kids, but I'd never tell him it was all right to hog the ball. I just understand because—'' She broke off. No more confidences with this man.

"Because?"

"Never mind. Let's just watch the game."

He opened his mouth to say something, but she forestalled any further comment with a subtle shift of her body away from him. Training her eyes on the field, she blocked out the man and focused on the boy.

Soon there was another jolt from the crowd. The ball had come back to the opposing team. They had it at their end...and scored on a beautiful head shot by their center forward.

With two minutes remaining, Michael's team took the kickoff. The ball went back and forth...back and forth... Eventually, the clock showed only forty-three seconds remaining in the game.

Then there was déjà vu. Michael had another breakaway. He bolted down the field, his long legs eating up the distance to the goal. He had the ball in total control, easing it between his feet, never losing contact. The right wing caught up to him, as did the defender, who shouldered closer and closer to him.

Clearly Michael should pass.

He didn't look. He didn't hesitate. Instead, he took the shot himself, fifteen feet from the goal.

This time, the goalie was there to catch it.

MICHAEL SWORE as he exited the locker room alone, using words his father would kill him for. He walked fast, his light jacket flying open in the wind, ignoring comments from his teammates.

Why hadn't he passed? Damn. Damn. *Damn.* He'd

done it again! Sometimes he just couldn't seem to get it together. It was like something took over inside him and he couldn't control it. *Sure, Rayburn. Blame it on Dr. Jekyll and Mr. Hyde. It's your own freakin' fault and you know it.*

Grasping the battered gym bag his mother had given him for Christmas years ago, Mike jammed his free hand into his pocket and stomped all the way home. His foul mood increased when he reached his driveway and saw Meredith's sports car parked behind his Dad's Bronco. "Shoot," he said, and sagged against it. He'd been so happy to have her see him score; then he'd blown it. And she'd know just how much. As an athlete, she'd read his mistake loud and clear.

At the house, he yanked open the side door, stepped inside and tossed his bag into the laundry room. Laughing and talking, everyone was gathered in the dinette, far across the kitchen. He thought briefly about fleeing up the back stairs, but he decided not to. He might be a jerk, but he wasn't a coward.

"Hi, buddy." His father was the first to spot him when he entered the room. The understanding look on his dad's face made Mike feel worse; he hated disappointing him.

"Hi." Mike sniffed. "Something smells good."

Peg Rayburn stepped forward. "Your dad made chili. Your favorite."

"Great."

"It's your mom's recipe," Mrs. Sherman said from the table.

He saw his father's head turn toward Meredith. She was sitting on a stool with a glass halfway to her mouth. She paused briefly, then took a slow sip.

Nonchalantly, Julie Anne crossed to Mike and playfully punched him on the shoulder. "Take off your coat and stay a while, handsome," she said. Her flippant comment broke the tension in the room, though Mike didn't quite understand what had caused it in the first place.

Easing farther into the kitchen, he went to the refrigerator in the far corner to get a drink. Luke followed him, then stood before the open door blocking out everyone else. He squeezed Mike's shoulder, and Mike let himself lean into it a bit. "Tough time after the game?" his dad asked.

Sighing, Mike grabbed a can of pop, slammed the door shut and turned to his father. He noticed everyone but Meredith talking on the other side of the room. She sat silently watching him. "The coach chewed me out bad," he told Luke.

"Think you deserved it?"

Disgusted, Mike rolled his eyes. "You know I did." He glanced across the kitchen. "Meredith say anything?"

"Not much." His father gave him another brief squeeze on the shoulder and said, "You'll get it together, son. If you work at it." He smiled and Mike had the stupid urge to throw himself at his dad and let him hug him. He hadn't felt like doing that since his mother's funeral when he'd sobbed openly in his father's arms. "Hungry?" Luke asked.

Mike shook off the feelings. "Yeah." He went to say hello to his grandparents and neighbors, grabbed a bowl of chili, then made a beeline for Meredith. "Hi," he said, pulling out the stool next to her and plopping down. "Thanks for coming."

Her smile washed over him, taking away some of

the sting of his self-disgust. "I wouldn't have missed it."

He ducked his head. "I should've made that goal," he said, wondering why he didn't just tell her he shouldn't have gone for it alone. For some reason, it was harder to admit his faults to her than his dad. Why did he care what she thought of him, anyway? Hell, she was the one who'd given him away. The knowledge settled sourly in his stomach and he pushed away his chili.

Meredith glanced at his father, who was within hearing distance. "Your assist was great in the first half."

Michael didn't say anything.

"But you should have passed. Both times."

The anger came out of nowhere. He turned it on her. "I made the first one."

"Yes, you did."

"It's not my fault we tied."

"It's never one player's fault."

She didn't have to finish the accusation. It glowed from her green eyes. Michael scraped his stool back and stood. "I'm not hungry, after all. I'm going to take a shower."

When he saw the expression on her face, he could have kicked himself. She bit her bottom lip, then looked away. He thought her eyes were glassy.

Upstairs, the shower improved his mood. Someone knocked on the door to his room just as he pulled on his jeans.

"Come on in."

"You decent, Rayburn?" Ever since the time she'd caught him in his skivvies two years ago, Julie Anne always checked before she burst in on him.

"Yeah."

She opened the door, sauntered in and sank onto his bed, bending her elbow and propping her head on her hand. The thermal top she had on was tucked into tight black jeans. "Bad night?"

He gave her an annoyed glare.

"All right, so you blew it."

"Twice."

"Yeah, but you came through with the first goal."

"I'm a jerk."

Julie Anne was silent for a minute, then scowled. "What did you say to Meredith?"

He pulled on a sweatshirt, and as he poked his head through the top, asked, "Why?"

"She looked like she was going to cry."

"I don't want to talk about her, Jule."

"What's going on?"

"*Julie Anne,*" he warned.

His best friend just waited. Mike crossed to the window and stood looking out. The stars twinkled overhead, bursts of brightness against a blue-black sky. He'd wished on those stars too often. That his mother wouldn't die. That he could fill his father's life so full that he wouldn't ever see that hollow look there again. And—guiltily—that he could meet and know the woman who had given him life.

Mike faced Julie Anne. "All this stuff with her—it's hard. It gets mixed up with everything else."

Quiet, Julie Anne watched him with clear blue eyes. "You want to talk about it?"

"Nah. We've already hashed it out. Besides, I'm in a rotten mood."

"Okay," she said. "Let's go play a video game. It'll take your mind off things."

"Sure. But I gotta do something first."

He found Meredith in the living room, staring out the window, her arms wrapped around her waist. Her shoulders were hunched, and she didn't look so tall, so strong in the muted light. "Meredith."

She spun around. "Feel better?"

"Yeah. I'm sorry I snapped at you."

"That's okay." She gave him a weak half smile then walked toward him. A few feet away, she reached out and settled her hand on his arm. It felt good when she touched him. He wished she'd do it more. Then she said, "You're a great player, Mike. Agile. Quick. Lithe. You've got natural talent."

"Thanks."

She sighed. "I used to—"

"Oh, there you are." Meredith sprang back from him as his father's voice came from the doorway. Mike turned to see his dad watching them. Then Luke said, "Brad called while you were in the shower. The guys are all going to Chunkie's for pizza. He said they'd stop by here on their way to see if you want to go."

"I don't think so," Mike said. "We've got that makeup game tomorrow and they'll be...I just don't think I'll go."

His dad eyed him suspiciously. To avoid questions, Mike turned to Meredith. "Last week's game was called because of lightning. We're making it up tomorrow. Want to come?"

"What time?"

"Seven."

Meredith shook her head. "I'm sorry, Mike, I can't."

Again the anger flared, fast and unexpected. Why the hell couldn't she go to his game? Hadn't she missed enough of his life? Knowing he was being unreasonable, he shrugged. "Sure, you've got a life. It's cool."

Meredith reached out to him again. "You're a very big part of my life now, Mike. It's just that I made a commitment weeks ago and I have to keep it."

"Michael," his father started. "Meredith can't change every—"

"You got a date?" Mike asked, his tone surly as he stepped back.

"Well, yes. It was arranged—"

The doorbell rang. "I'll get it," he heard Julie Anne say as she appeared in the doorway.

Julie Anne flew gracefully by them into the foyer. Mike strode to the front of the room and heard her say, "Well, if it isn't the in-crowd."

"Hi, Sherman. You look sexy in that long underwear. Got anything under it?"

Michael stiffened and walked toward the foyer. Julie Anne always baited these guys, but he'd be damned if he'd let them insult her, no matter how much of a pain in the butt she was being.

"Get your mind out of the gutter, Sloan," she said before Mike could get to her. Then she came through the doorway. "The *boys* are here, Mike."

Brad Sloan stepped into the room, a cocky grin on his face, the sleeves of his Raiders' jacket pushed up to his elbows. "Ready to go, Rayburn?"

Mike looked at his father, whom he'd let down on the field tonight.

He looked at Meredith, who was too busy to come to his game tomorrow.

He *didn't* look at Julie Anne, knowing the disgust he'd see in her eyes.

"Yeah, I'm ready. Let's go." He scanned the room.

"'Bye everybody," he said sharply, and walked out the door.

"CAN I HELP?"

Luke glanced over from the sink into the drawn face of Meredith Hunter. Silhouetted in the archway of the kitchen, she looked vulnerable as she spoke to him. "Sure, grab a towel," he said.

Crossing into the room, she picked up a pan from the rack and began to dry it. "The chili was great. You're a good cook." She smiled self-effacingly. "Unlike me."

"Thanks." Her controlled voice tugged at him. "Meredith, Michael won't care if you can't cook."

"It's just never been my forte."

He watched her precise movements as she dried the chili pans. "I'm sure you have other talents." God, he hadn't meant the words to come out husky. To cover his embarrassment, he plunged his hands back into the hot soapy water.

They worked together, making companionable chatter. Since Sara died, Luke had missed the closeness of doing little things like this with someone—doing the dishes together, raking leaves, figuring out which room to paint first.

"Where are our parents?" Luke asked to stifle the feeling.

"Playing Mortal Kombat." They both chuckled. "Sometimes they act just like kids."

Luke unplugged the drain, wiped his hands on a towel, turned and leaned against the counter. Meredith had moved to one of the stools, and perched on it, ever cautious. He was reminded of a doe poised to bolt. "Speaking of kids..."

Meredith's face paled. He had the urge to draw her to him for comfort, like the last time they'd been alone in this kitchen. Her soft curves had fitted against his body, and he was shocked to realize how clearly he remembered the sensation of having her tight against him.

"Meredith, not everything is going to go smoothly with Mike. He's a teenager—moody, self-absorbed at times, rebellious." Luke scowled. "Though I have to admit I don't like him hanging out with Brad and those other guys."

"Why?"

"I'm not sure what they're into. Mike doesn't spend a lot of time with them. When he does, Julie Anne doesn't like it. Something's going on there."

"He's complicated, isn't he?"

"Yes."

"And I've made his life even harder by my presence."

"It was his choice." Crossing his arms over his chest, Luke studied her. The fuzzy pink sweater she wore made her look all soft and fragile. And he'd noticed the way her jeans hugged her hips earlier. She looked very feminine. The thought led him to ask, "Who's your date with tomorrow?"

Her delicate eyebrows arched, but she answered, "Ken Dobson."

"The guy from the D.A.'s office?"

Meredith nodded.

"You said this situation with Michael—with us pretending to be involved—wouldn't be a problem."

"It isn't."

Something inside Luke prodded him to push. "If there's a man you're serious about, it could definitely affect Mike. I'd like to know about it, so I could help him deal with it.''

She cocked her head, as if assessing his honesty. "Ken and I have worked together for a long time. We've dated off and on for two years."

Luke felt a spurt of displeasure at this information. "That's a long time."

"It isn't serious. I'd cancel tomorrow night, but Ken has political aspirations and this dinner is a black-tie fund-raiser. I promised months ago I'd be his date." She sighed. "I can't back out on such short notice."

At the mention of the formal event, a fanciful image of Meredith caught him off guard. A short, sophisticated dress...her long legs encased in misty black stockings...they might be attached to a garter belt and...he halted the fantasy before it could go further. Already, his jeans felt uncomfortable. He straightened and turned his back to her, afraid she might see his involuntary reaction to the vision he'd spun.

Reaching up, he opened the cupboard, grabbed a glass, drew some water and gulped it down. It didn't help.

He was still hard, thinking of his son's mother in ways that were clearly not maternal.

The recognition rocked him.

CHAPTER FIVE

ONLY ABOUT FIVE PERCENT *of all men and women say they have never had a sexual fantasy.* Luke sighed as he read the magazine over his Sunday-morning coffee in the dinette. Well, he'd admit to a sexual fantasy or two. He'd drawn some pretty detailed, erotic images in his mind when he couldn't fall asleep Friday night after the soccer game.

Of Meredith Hunter.

The people who have the fewest sexual fantasies have the most sexual problems. Did he have sexual problems? Was abstinence a sexual problem? Today, it felt as if it was. How long had it been since he'd felt that intense, driving need for sex that he experienced Friday night? Sara had been dead three years. She'd been sick for a long time before that. A year after she died, he'd let himself try a casual relationship with a woman he knew at the office—a woman he liked and respected. After a few months, the lack of true intimacy made him feel worse. He'd tried with another woman a year later...with the same result. So he'd given up.

Luke threw down Michael's latest survey, stood and walked to the sliding glass doors. It seemed his body was responding to the deprivation at an inopportune time. He could *not* allow himself this attraction for a very good reason. What if Luke pursued his feelings for Meredith and it didn't work out? How would that affect Michael's already tenuous relationship with her?

He heard Seth's words: *I've watched you give in on everything your family ever wanted, and never take for yourself...I thought once Sara was gone, you'd allow yourself a little pleasure...I'm worried that you're doing it again with this adoption thing. Suppressing all your needs in order to meet Michael's.*

Luke had given Seth's accusation a lot of thought and begrudgingly admitted that he *had* put aside many of his own needs. Except for his career as public defender. Sara had been against his decision. Meredith seemed to feel the same way. He wondered why.

Irritated that he'd spent the last forty-eight hours thinking about Meredith Hunter, he swore softly and concentrated on how the early-October winds swirled the leaves around the backyard. Maybe he'd go out and rake them. He remembered how six-year-old Michael used to sneak up behind him and jump into the piles.

"Hi."

Luke turned and saw his son standing in the archway, his green eyes sleepy, his hair disheveled. Clad in sweatpants, he leaned against the wall, almost a man now.

"Hi. Sleep well?"

"Sort of."

"I heard you come in. It was a little late, wasn't it?"

"I guess."

"I thought we agreed on two."

"Yeah. We did." Michael brushed his hair out of his eyes and came farther into the room. "I should have driven. The guys wouldn't leave the party when I wanted to."

"You could have called me. I thought we'd agreed to that."

Michael crossed to the refrigerator and pulled out a carton of orange juice. He opened the top, raised it to his mouth and guzzled.

Which did Luke deal with this morning? The issue of his son breaking curfew or his own fastidiousness— or was it Sara's?—about not drinking from the container. Luke let the latter go.

"Mike? We decided a long time ago—"

"Dad, we decided I could call anytime, no questions asked, no lectures, if I was in a spot with other kids who were doing something dangerous. If I couldn't get home without risking my safety. I wasn't in any danger last night. Marty was driving. He hadn't done any drugs or liquor. They just didn't want to leave. I'm the only one who has a curfew, you know."

"Yes, I know. Okay, let's drop it. Julie Anne called about ten last night. She said to call her back today."

Michael sank onto a chair. "Anybody else call?"

Luke shook his head. "Anyone in particular?"

"I thought maybe Meredith would call to see about the game."

Ah, his son kept handing him opportunities to drive a wedge between him and his biological mother. All he'd have to say was, "No, she was too busy with her date last night for you." Instead, he said, "She said she was going to a black-tie fund-raiser. It was probably pretty tough to get to a phone." Why the hell was he defending her? When had this shift taken place? Luke glanced around the kitchen. That day she'd cried her heart out in this room. In his arms.

Shredding a paper napkin that had been left on the

table, Michael didn't meet Luke's eyes. "Think she's mad at me?"

"Should she be?"

"Maybe." Mike looked up and in his eyes was a blend of regret and confusion. "I...ah, shoot, I shouldn't have left Friday night. I don't get to see her much, and she was here and I left."

"Why did you leave?"

"'Cause I was pissed off at her for pointing out what a jerk I was on the soccer field. And then she said she wouldn't come to my next game."

Again the ever-present parental choice. Chide the kid for his inappropriate language or stay with the point? "It doesn't help to run away from your feelings, Mike."

Yeah, Rayburn, you're one to talk.

Yet Luke didn't really have feelings for Meredith Hunter. He was just attracted to her. That was all. Hell, she was a beautiful woman.

Michael shrugged, grabbed the local section of the Sunday paper that was stacked at the end of the table and leafed through it—his signal that he didn't want to talk anymore.

Luke crossed to the counter and poured himself another cup of coffee. It tasted bitter—like a lot of things in life these days. Shaking off his thoughts, he returned to the table, plucked up the business section and began to read.

After a stretch of silence, Mike said, "Hey, Dad, there's a car show near Romulus today. Says here they've got some restored Mach I Mustangs. Wanna go?"

"I'd love to. It would be nice to spend the day with

you for a change." He reached out and ruffled Michael's hair. God, he loved this kid.

Michael watched him for a minute.

"What?" Luke asked.

"Nothing."

"Mike, something's on your mind."

"No, it's okay."

Luke hated this teenage evasion. Michael was growing out of it, but not fast enough. *"Michael?"*

"All right. I was wondering if we could ask Meredith to go with us. But then you said that about spending the day with me. I don't want to disappoint you."

Luke winced inwardly. For two reasons. First, he didn't ever want to smother Michael with his need for him since Sara died.

And second, he was going to have to spend the day with Meredith Hunter. Damn, it had taken all his willpower to erase her from his mind. Now he'd have to look at her all day. And maybe even worse, he'd have to share with her his love of old cars, and Michael's interest in them—something bound to bring them all closer.

"Dad. It's okay. She doesn't have to come with us."

"Think she'd like it?"

Mike's grin was like dawn breaking through the sky. "Yeah. We were looking at some books one time she was here. It's one of her hobbies. She even gets a subscription to *Car Magazine*."

In spite of his conflicting feelings, Luke chuckled. "A dedicated woman. Okay, go ahead and call her."

Michael glanced at the clock. "It isn't too early?"

"Eleven o'clock?"

"Well, she was out last night."

Against his will, Luke's body tensed. Without his

conscious consent, the fantasy possessed his mind again, like a demon waiting to strike. Meredith in a short dress and high heels…out with another man. "I think it's an okay time to call."

The first thing Luke noticed was that Mike didn't have to look up her number. He went right to the phone and began dialing. But he hung up before it would have had a chance to ring. "Dad, could we…could we pick her up?"

"Why?"

"I don't know," Michael said, gripping the phone. "I guess I don't like her driving everyplace alone. She comes here a lot all by herself. Sometimes I worry."

"Sure, we can pick her up."

Mike gave him another million-dollar grin and redialed. Luke leaned against the counter and watched him. Soon the smile disappeared. "Ah…is this Meredith Hunter's?"

A pause, then Michael said, "Okay," and covered the mouthpiece. "Dad, a man answered."

Oh, hell. How did he handle this one? And what was wrong with Ms. Assistant District Attorney that she didn't have enough sense not to let her overnight guests answer her damn phone? "Mike—"

"Hi, Meredith. It's Mike.… You did?… You were?… Um, well, I was just wondering if you wanna go to the car show at Ricky T's just outside of Romulus today with me and Dad. If you're not busy."

After her response, Mike raised questioning eyes to him. "What time, Dad?"

"About two?" Luke said stiffly.

"Two. Oh, great. Well then…we'll pick you up, okay?"

Another pause. "No, we want to.... I don't know....
Okay, see you then." And he hung up.

Luke could feel the tension in his neck. He did *not*
want to deal with this. For more reasons than he cared
to admit. Purposely keeping his voice even, he said,
"She's coming?"

Mike's sixteen-year-old shoulders shrugged.
"Yeah."

"A man answered?"

Mike nodded. "Think that was this Dobson guy?"

Yeah, that's what I think. "Well, we shouldn't jump
to any conclusions."

"She said they weren't serious. Why would she..."

When his son didn't finish the question, Luke said,
"First, we don't know that she *did* anything. But Mike,
Meredith's an adult and she's entitled to a private life.
This really isn't any of our business." The idea stuck
in his craw. It sure as hell felt like his business, but he
was trying to be objective. "However, if any of this
bothers you, you should talk to *her* about it."

"Are you kidding? Ask Meredith?"

"No, son, I'm not kidding. If she's going to be an
important part of your life, you're entitled to have some
idea what her values are."

"Yeah. It's not like we're prudes or anything."

"No, we're not." Again Luke was ticked off at Meredith for making this talk necessary. "I happen to believe sex is a beautiful thing between two people who
care about each other. Otherwise, it's pretty empty—
and dangerous." Though he felt mildly hypocritical,
given his experimentation after Sara died, what he said
was nonetheless true, and his own value system. "I
hope you believe that, too."

"Yeah, I do." Mike looked around the kitchen, then

met his father's eyes again. "What if she doesn't? I mean, what if she sleeps around or something?"

Luke struggled hard to be fair. "Would that really affect your relationship with her?"

"Well, yeah. I think it would, anyway."

"Then you'd have to deal with that, I guess, if it turns out to be the case." He walked over and put an arm around his son's neck, playfully pulling him close. "We've gone through a lot together, kid. We'll get through this, too," he said, carefully lacing his voice with humor.

But Luke saw nothing funny in the situation.

In fact, he was angry. Angry at the thought of Meredith sleeping around and possibly causing his son more pain? Or at the thought of her being with another man?

MEREDITH COULD TELL something was wrong with both Rayburn men as soon as they pulled into the condo parking lot and got out of the Bronco. It dampened some of the enthusiasm she'd let herself feel for the upcoming afternoon. Enthusiasm about spending the day with Michael. And with Luke—a man she'd spent far too much time thinking about in the last two days.

She and Nathan were waiting outside; her brother had to get back to his home, but he'd wanted to meet Michael. Both Luke and Mike walked stiffly toward the bench where Meredith sat with Nathan. Michael's face looked...pained. Luke's was full of thunderclouds.

She stood up, briskly rubbing her arms with her hands. "Hi," she said cheerfully.

When they reached her, Mike stuck his hands in his back pockets and Luke stuck his in his jacket. "Hi," they said simultaneously. Then both their gazes fell on Nathan with unabashed hostility.

"Hi," Nathan said evenly. Her brother was over six feet and could meet their eyes directly. He held out his hand. "I'm Nathan Hunter, Meredith's brother."

"Meredith's *brother?*" Michael's jaw fell open and his eyebrows rose.

Meredith glanced at Luke. He was better at concealing his emotions, but the red tinge on his cheekbones told her that he, too, had tried and convicted her. But of *what,* exactly? Surely she was allowed a man in her life.

"Yes, I'm Meredith's brother. And your uncle, Mike."

"Wow! I got an uncle. Both Mom and Dad were only children so I never thought...hey, you got any kids? Do I have *cousins,* too?"

Nathan laughed and filled Michael in on his twin girls.

Meredith focused on Luke. He was watching the exchange between the man and boy. Today, he'd dressed in beige corduroy jeans, which he wore beltless. He had on a navy blue T-shirt under his bomber jacket. For a brief moment—and to her chagrin—her palms itched to touch his sinewy chest.

"Is that okay?"

"What?" Meredith asked.

"Nathan has some pictures in his car of my...cousins. I'm going to look at them before he leaves. Okay?"

"Sure." Luke held out his hand. "Nice to have met you."

Nathan smiled. "Same here." He turned to his sister. "'Bye, sweetie." He reached out and encompassed her in a bear hug, then said quietly, "Remember what we talked about."

She could feel Luke watching her; he wasn't supposed to hear what Nathan said. As before, she didn't want him to know too much about her.

Uncle and nephew trotted down the walkway to the parking lot. Meredith watched until they were out of sight, and out of hearing distance, then faced Luke.

She glared at him, her hands fisting on her hips. "Let me get my facts straight, Counselor. When Mike called this morning, you assumed the man who answered was my date from last night. Right?"

Something flickered across Luke's face but he only nodded.

"And I'm not entitled to have a man in my life?"

Luke lifted his chin. "You'd said you weren't serious about the guy from your office. So, if you'd let him spend the night, well…"

"Oh, I see. Then the implication is that I sleep around."

Luke scowled but didn't retort.

"I hope you're more fair with your clients, Mr. Rayburn. I'd assume an attorney would wait until he heard the whole story before passing judgment."

In what she guessed was a deceptively casual stance, one he probably affected in the courtroom, he relaxed his shoulders, crossed his arms over his chest and stared her down. "Listen, I told Michael this was only circumstantial evidence."

"But your tone and body language tell me you've found me guilty—of promiscuity, I gather." She shook her head. "You know, sometimes I think my bias against public defenders is not all that unwarranted."

"What do you mean?"

"Nothing."

"Meredith—"

"I will tell you one thing. I'll be damned if I let you poison Michael's mind against me."

"Look, lady, I've got Michael's best interests at heart. I've done my damnedest to instill some solid values in him and I'm not about to let someone who's flouting them compromise him."

"In case you haven't figured it out, I wasn't *flouting* anything."

"We didn't know that at the time."

"Would you have cared?"

"What do you mean by that?"

"Does it really matter to you who's guilty or innocent?"

A spark of anger flared in Luke's eyes. "Of course it matters, though I hardly know you enough to judge. You're still a stranger to us in many ways. We don't know your moral values…except for what we can intuit from the…circumstances of Michael's birth."

She felt the color drain from her face. It was a low blow. One she hadn't expected. The pain that it caused bounced around inside her for a minute then settled with a thud somewhere in the vicinity of her heart. *Foolish, Meredith. You let down your guard with him.*

With a Herculean effort at keeping her voice even, she said, "This conversation is over, Mr. Rayburn. Excuse me, I'd like to say goodbye to my brother."

LUKE WISHED he could take back his words. As he watched her wander from car to car with Michael, he admitted there was no excuse for his cruelty. Of course, she'd made some prejudicial comments about public defenders, but he was pretty sure her remarks were part of a knee-jerk reaction to his behavior. The problem, he admitted to himself, was that he was afraid of Meredith Hunter—afraid she'd hurt Michael, afraid she wasn't the type of person they could count on—afraid of his attraction to her and how it could complicate their lives. So he'd struck out at her. Right where it would hurt the most.

If only she didn't look so good today. She was dressed in those tight leg things Julie Anne always wore, black ones over which she'd donned a black turtleneck and a pale green sweater that made her eyes glow like a cat's. She'd left her jacket in the car and he hoped she was warm enough. His own temperature soared at the sight of her.

She'd been keeping her distance from him emotionally and physically all day. And he didn't blame her. By the time her brother had left, she was composed, though her color wasn't quite normal. She and Michael climbed into the truck and Meredith pointedly took the back seat. She'd addressed all her comments to Michael for the entire trip to Ricky T's. Luke felt left out. Damn, when had he developed the desire to share simple Sunday-afternoon conversation with her?

"Hey, Dad, come over here," Michael yelled from behind him.

Slowly, Luke left the 1969 Mustang he'd been pretending to inspect and joined them at the vehicle they were fawning over. Meredith had her head stuck through the driver's-side window, and her nicely rounded backside was all that showed of her.

"Isn't she a beauty?" Michael asked.

"Huh?" Luke tore his eyes away guiltily.

"The car. It's exactly what you're looking for."

Forcing himself to look at the Mustang, he inspected it from a distance. It *was* a beauty.

"It's even yellow, Dad."

Meredith pulled herself out of the front seat. "It's got some great options, Mike. Did you feel the leather inside? It's like butter."

"Think it's restored?" Michael reached in and fondled the upholstery.

"Yeah."

"Come closer and look, Dad."

Since *closer* was the driver's side, he crossed the short distance to the door. Before he got there, Meredith rounded the car, ostensibly to peruse the trunk. He caught her eye, but she looked away quickly.

"Dad? Is something wrong?"

Luke shook his head.

"I'm going to check out the '71, Mike," Meredith called over her shoulder as she walked away.

Michael stared after her, then looked at Luke. "Dad, what's going on? The vibes between you two are really wacky."

"I...ah..."

"Hi, Rayburn. Whatcha doin' here?"

Michael turned to face a boy Luke had never seen before. He was a little guy, reaching only to Michael's shoulder. Slender, the kid wore glasses and looked small and pale next to his son's large frame and vibrant presence.

"Hi, Joey. I came to see the cars with my Dad." Mike introduced him to the boy.

Joey pushed his glasses up his nose. "You like these things?" he asked Michael.

"Sure. Do you?"

"Why do you think I'm always drawin' them in art class?"

Michael smiled. "Who you with?"

"My mom and dad. Your mother here?"

"She's over—" Michael stopped abruptly, then continued, "Ah, no. My mom's dead. She died before you started at Sommerfield High."

Luke felt as though he'd been hit by lightning. Michael's eyes locked with his and Luke smiled weakly at his son.

"Want to come and see the '70 Mustang my dad might buy?"

"All right." Michael said to Luke, "I'll meet you inside in ten minutes, Dad. Okay? We can eat then."

Luke nodded, still reeling from Mike's slip. The punches to his emotional equilibrium were coming left and right, and he wasn't sure how many more blows he could withstand. Digging his hands into his pockets, he took a couple of deep breaths as he watched his son maneuver through the throng.

"Where's Michael?" Meredith kept her tone neutral as she approached Luke. She'd been cautious all day around him, but the naked emotion on his face right now tugged at her heart.

Luke looked surprised to see her. Clearly, his mind had been somewhere else. "Um, he met a friend and went to check out a car. He said he'd meet us inside in ten minutes." Luke checked his watch, the muscles of his arm bunching with the movement. It had gotten warmer and he'd traded his jacket for a cranberry sweatshirt. It emphasized the broadness of his shoulders. For a minute, Meredith let herself remember what it was like to lean on those shoulders.

"You hungry?" Luke asked.

"No. But I wouldn't mind a soda."

"Can I buy you one?"

She crossed her arms over her chest.

"As a peace offering?" he said lightly.

In spite of her reservations, she softened at his boyish grin and the innocent way he raised his eyebrows, like a kid trying to wheedle his way out of trouble. Only this was no kid; he was all adult male. Dangerous adult male. "I'm not sure, Luke."

He stepped closer to her. Her senses were filled with the sight and smell of him: a woodsy after-shave, the small nick from his razor on the underside of his chin, how his front teeth were just a little uneven. "I'm sorry, Meredith. I was an ass earlier." He sighed and looked off over her shoulders. "This is tough for me. I jumped the gun this morning and I shouldn't have." He looked back to her. "Sometimes it…scares me to see Michael getting close to you." He scanned her features, his gaze resting briefly on her mouth. It made her insides quiver. "There's a little more to it than that, but suffice it to say, I know I was out of line. I apologize."

What was she supposed to do with that? How was she supposed to resist that kind of honesty? She smiled up at him and rolled her eyes. "You're entitled, I guess. You've been really good about this whole thing. I shouldn't have reacted so badly to what you said." She stuck out her hand.

He took it. He didn't shake it. He held it. He caressed it. Meredith's breath caught as the sensations from that light touch worked their way up her arms and then spread warmth through her entire body.

His eyes went liquid as he stared at her. Meredith

read in them something that she never expected to see, was sure she didn't want to see. Especially from him.

JOEY LUBMAN WAS a dork. All the jocks at school teased him, and Brad had stuck him in a locker once and closed the door.

Mike had let him out.

"Hey, here's your dad," Joey said.

Mike glanced over to the door to see his father and Meredith enter the large diner. They spotted him and wove through the aisles to get to him. His father's hand rested lightly on Meredith's elbow, guiding her around the tables. Strange. These two were acting really strange today. He wished Julie Anne was with him—she'd be able to figure it out.

"Hi guys," his dad said.

"Hi." Mike introduced Meredith to Joey. "I asked Joey to eat with us. His parents are still working on the owner of that great black Mustang."

"They're buying it?" Luke asked.

Joey nodded and stuffed his mouth with a French fry.

"Yeah, Dad. They are. Now it's your turn." At Meredith's questioning look, Mike said, "Dad's wanted a yellow Mustang all his life. When Mom was alive, he didn't get it because—" Mike stopped short. "Why didn't you, Dad?"

"Your mother said I should have outgrown the need for a fast car. I had to set an example for you." His dad smiled with the memory. "She was right."

Mike glanced at Meredith, then said to Joey, "Meredith's got a '77 silver-anniversary 'Vette. It's awesome."

Joey's small brown eyes widened. "Holy cow! You rich or something?"

Meredith shook her head and the scarf that held her hair back fell onto the table. His father picked it up but didn't give it to her. Instead, he stuffed it in her purse. She looked at him for a moment, then shook out her hair and turned back to Joey. "No, I'm not rich."

"What do you do?"

"I'm an assistant district attorney in Romulus."

"Yeah, and my dad's a public defender," Mike said. "Funny, huh?"

Joey giggled and said, "You guys must have some terrific arguments."

"Why would you say that?" Luke asked.

"Aren't you on opposite sides of the law all the time?"

"Well, we do come at things from different angles. But basically, we're all trying to get justice done," Luke replied.

"Not all of us," Meredith said. Mike looked at her and then decided the comment had just slipped out. She confirmed his feeling when she smiled and added, "But most of us."

"Then you two have a lot in common," Joey said. "Not like my mom and dad. He's a computer analyst and my mother's a computer-phobic."

Well, it had worked, Mike thought. Julie Anne's idea to have his dad and his biological mother pretend they were dating had worked on Joey, who, although he was a dork, was probably the smartest kid in the school. Mike looked at his father and Meredith. They made a nice-looking couple.

"Got any hot cases going on now?" Joey wanted to know.

His father's eyebrows scrunched together. He'd just finished defending a man accused of promoting child pornography on the Internet. The soccer players at school had ragged on Mike about it. Must be Joey didn't read the papers.

"Tell him about your eighty-year-old woman, Meredith," Mike said, switching the direction of the question to her.

"My client was assaulted on the sidewalk in front of her apartment building by someone trying to steal her purse," she told Joey. "In the process, the victim fell and broke her hip. When a neighbor tried to help, the guy pulled a gun and shot him. That's how the case got to me. I work in the Major Felonies Bureau."

"Why'd you want to be a D.A.? There's not much money in it, is there?" Joey asked. "Couldn't you make a lot more in private practice?"

"I suppose," Meredith said. "But I firmly believe in law and order. Besides, I love to go to court, and only D.A.'s get as many trials as I like."

"You could've been a P.D. like Mr. Rayburn."

Meredith gripped the straw she'd been toying with. "Ah, no, I couldn't."

"Why?"

She glanced nervously at Luke. Mike didn't like the way she looked at his father.

"Yeah, Meredith, why couldn't you?" Mike asked her, his tone sharper than he intended.

The brief flash of hurt that flickered in her eyes made him feel bad. Then she angled her chin. "Because just like I could never prosecute someone I think is innocent, I could never defend someone I think is guilty."

"But it isn't a defense attorney's place to decide those things." His father jumped in, though Mike could tell he was trying to restrain himself. "We simply present the best possible defense. It's not our job to decide guilt—the jury and judge do that."

"You mean, you defend people when you know they're guilty?" Joey asked. His freckled face was flush with interest.

"Truthfully, Joey, most of the time, I don't know if they're guilty or not."

"I think that's the big difference," Meredith said. "I couldn't defend anyone I really thought was guilty."

"Do you judge others who do it?" Luke asked.

"I try not to, although sometimes I find myself thinking lawyers are really wrong to go ahead with a case when they obviously know the defendant is guilty."

"Well, my feeling is that public defense is the purest form of the law. It adheres to our profoundest judicial tenet. Everything is in the hands of the judge and jury. Now, if you want to argue whether or not the American judicial system is right, that's another thing."

Ignoring his father's last point—boy, Mike bet she'd be good in court—Meredith said, "But have you ever made a witness for the other side look like she's lying even though you suspect she's telling the truth, to get your guy off?"

"I'm morally responsible to give my client the best defense. I grill all witnesses without judging if they're telling the truth or not."

"That sounds pretty convenient."

Mike watched, fascinated, as they flung comments at each other faster than Ping-Pong balls. He'd seen his father's face light up with this kind of argument before. Long ago, Mike himself had talked to his dad about his job, and now he felt comfortable with his father's choices. But, watching Meredith argue with the same…passion…was interesting. Her eyes glowed just like his father's did when he talked about law. Her fist clenched and unclenched as she made a point. His dad's hand slapped the table once for emphasis. Interesting.

Very interesting.

CHAPTER SIX

"WHAT TIME will he be home?" Meredith asked.

"I imagine he'll drag his feet tonight, even though it's a school day tomorrow." Luke's voice was indulgent, but tinged with concern.

Meredith sighed and turned to look out the living-room window, waiting for her son. The full moon peeked out from behind the clouds, smirking.

She'd been so proud of him after the last two games, where he hadn't had one "solo flight." Tonight, he'd gone for two and missed both. Sommerfield had lost the game.

"I'm going to get a sandwich. Want something?"

"No, thank you."

Luke left the room, and Meredith sighed again. He was cool and distant. There had been a chill between them since the car show. She didn't want to examine why.

Deliberately, Meredith forced her attention away from Luke and onto Mike. Now, *they* were making progress. Last weekend, they'd sat on the floor of his room, listening to the new Rippingtons' CD she had bought him, browsing through some magazines for his project. She'd suspected there was a hidden agenda in his suggestion that she help him with his research, and she was right.

"Look at this," he'd said, not so innocently. "This

survey shows how many sex partners people have had in their lifetime.''

Meredith had taken the magazine and read the numbers for American men and women. They were high, given today's awareness of the dangers of promiscuity. Fifty-six percent of all men and thirty percent of women had had *five* or more partners.

She'd read it, then uncurled herself from the floor, walked over and turned down the music. When she came back, she'd plopped close to Michael. ''Mike, is there something you want to ask me about last weekend? Or anything else about me you want to know?''

He'd blushed, and Meredith had bit her lip trying not to smile. He was a kid in a man's body. ''Yeah, I guess.''

''Okay, shoot.''

''I thought that guy from the D.A.'s office had spent the night at your house. I know it's none of my business…''

Reaching out, she took his hand. It was bigger than hers, muscled and sprinkled with dark hair. ''You can ask me anything you want. If I think it's too personal, or don't feel comfortable answering it, I'll tell you.''

His direct gaze and the set of his jaw reminded her of Luke. ''Okay. I guess I want to know what you think about…sleeping around.''

''I think it's foolish. And dangerous.'' She watched him for a minute. ''I don't sleep around, Mike.''

''But, um, you, um…got pregnant with me.''

''Yes, I did. But I wasn't sleeping around. I'd gone with a boy all through high school. I was very much in love with him. I *did* make love with him.'' When Michael didn't respond, she said, ''You should know, Mike, that your biological father is dead.''

Mike had looked at her as if he was going to pursue the matter. She hadn't lied, exactly...but what she'd told him had been deliberately misleading. And if he pushed, she *would* lie. Until the day she died.

He hadn't pushed. "I don't want to know about him. I've got Dad. He's all I need." Then he'd blushed again. "And now you."

Meredith's heart had soared with happiness at his including her, and with relief that he didn't pursue the other topic.

"But I talk to Dad a lot...about morals and stuff, you know. It's confusing sometimes. I guess I...just want to know what you think about things."

Meredith had smiled and talked for an hour to her almost-seventeen-year-old son about her firm belief in loving someone you slept with, monogamy and the profound joy that came from joining your body with someone you cared about.

The back door slammed, drawing her away from the bittersweet memory. As she made her way out to the kitchen, she heard low masculine voices deep in conversation. Then, Michael raised his. "Don't you think I know that? Damn it, Dad, I don't need this."

When she reached the doorway, she saw Luke cross his arms over his chest and lean back against the counter. Scowling, he calmly studied Michael. She loved the way he thought things through before he reacted. Even when his son was out of line.

"Hi, Mike," Meredith said.

One glance at his face when he turned to her told her he was hurting...but trying to cover it with teenage bravado. When had she come to know him so well? That slight tilt of his head and the angle of his chin meant he was insecure. "Hi." His tone was surly. "Are you gonna rag on me, too?"

Taking her cue from Luke, she said nothing at first. Crossing into the room, she leaned against the dinette table. Finally, she answered, "I hadn't planned to."

"Why not? Everyone else is. Two of the guys said I was a grandstander. Coach might bench me for the next game. And Dad..." He glanced at his father. "Dad's disappointed."

"Mike, I—"

"No, don't say you're not. You should be. You are. I can see it in your face." He looked at Meredith. "And what do you think, former star athlete? Are you gonna tell me what I did wrong? What I could've done better?"

Maybe it was the unfair way he'd treated his father. Maybe she was feeling secure enough with him after their closeness last weekend. Maybe she thought it was time to stop feeling so guilty about having given him up seventeen years ago. So she said, "I think you're out of line, Mike. Actually, I think you're striking out at us because you're disappointed in yourself."

He looked at her with mutinous eyes.

"I *will* tell you, as a *former star athlete,* that there are invariably times when you're going to feel bad about your performance. But as you mature, you learn to put things into perspective better...you can..."

His eyes frosted over. Stunned by the depth of contempt in them, Meredith didn't finish her point. He said, "Yeah, and you'd know all about maturity, wouldn't you?"

Something constricted inside Meredith. She always knew, intuitively, when she about to be attacked. Her quick self-protectiveness and shrewdness was one of the things that made her such a good A.D.A. She stepped back to ward off the psychological blow she knew was coming. "What do you mean?"

"How old were you when you got pregnant?"

She swallowed. "Eighteen."

"Only about a year older than me."

"That's right."

"Yeah, well, don't lecture me about maturity. You weren't so mature at my age. You got knocked up and then ditched me as soon as you could. I don't call that very mature."

The room began to spin. Meredith's knees started to buckle so she grasped the doorway. Her other hand went around her waist, poor armor against the assault of his words. This was the one thing she'd dreaded in getting to know Mike. That he'd bring this up.

Because he could never, ever know the truth.

LUKE LISTENED to the door click closed as Meredith left. He took two steps away from the counter to go after her, halting when he heard something slam on the floor above. "Don't defend her, Dad," Michael had said, before he'd stamped upstairs. Luke had tried to intervene, but now he had to think about Michael. Not Meredith, although the look of anguish on her face was something he'd never forget.

So instead of following her, he crossed to the breakfast bar and sank onto a stool. He noticed Meredith's jacket tossed over the back of a chair. Reaching out, he fingered the fur around the hood and rubbed his hand over the soft, beige suede. She'd be cold out there tonight. And alone. And very upset.

He ran his hands over his face. It didn't take a genius to know why Mike had lashed out at her. And at him, though not as vehemently. Meredith was right—the kid was disappointed in himself, and took it out on those he cared about. Luke could withstand the blow of his son's selfishness—he'd been the recipient of it before, as all parents were. He could only hope Meredith would find the strength to deal with it.

It disturbed Luke how worried he was about her, how much he wanted to go after her, and hold her, and tell her that Mike would be over this in a few hours, he'd apologize and things would be back to normal. The problem was, she and Mike had no *normal* yet, which made this situation all the harder for her.

After giving Mike a long fifteen minutes to cool off, Luke trudged up the back staircase and down the hall to Mike's room. He knocked, then opened the door.

His son was lying on his back, his arm thrown over his eyes. He still wore his soccer jacket, and his muddy sneakers had already smudged the bedspread. "Want to talk?"

Mike grunted and Luke came into the room. He pulled out the desk chair, sat down and waited.

"I'm sorry, Dad."

"I'm not the one you need to apologize to."

Mike uncovered his eyes, and even in the dim light, Luke could see his lashes were wet. "Think she'll get home okay?"

Glancing at the clock, Luke fought to remain calm. Meredith had been gone twenty minutes. "Yeah. I think she will. Why don't you call her in about half an hour?"

Firmly, Mike shook his head. "I can't. I can't face her right now. Will you call her?"

Luke nodded. "Want to talk about what happened?"

"I was a jerk." Luke waited. "I was mad at myself about the game. I took it out on her."

"Why?"

Mike pulled himself up to a sitting position and leaned back against the oak headboard. "Because things get all jumbled with her, Dad. One minute I feel so good about her. The next I'm ticked off that she hasn't been here all my life. Then I forget the things she said about why she gave me up. And how she was when she was eighteen. I just remember that she didn't keep me. It hurts."

"I think she hurts, too."

"Even more now," Mike said.

"What do you mean?"

Mike sighed and grabbed a throw pillow to his chest. His hands bunched on it as he spoke. "We had a great talk last weekend about...things. I think she thought I understood her views pretty well."

"And you don't?"

"I do in my head."

Luke smiled. "Well, maybe it'll take your heart a little longer to catch up."

Michael smiled weakly and checked the clock. "Call her, Dad."

Luke reached for the phone. Mike told him the number. They both waited through six rings. "This is Meredith Hunter. Leave a message at the tone."

No frills for Meredith. He liked that.

"Meredith, this is Luke. Mike and I are worried about you. Call us when you get home."

When he hung up, he said to his son, "It's really too soon for her to be back yet. If she doesn't call in thirty minutes, we'll call her again."

An hour later, there was still no answer.

HALFWAY BETWEEN Sommerfield and Romulus, Meredith swerved off the expressway onto the side of the road. It was dark and it was dangerous with the traffic whizzing by, but she didn't have a choice. She could no longer see well enough to drive.

Numb for the first twenty-five minutes, Meredith had driven the now-familiar route like a robot. Absolutely refusing to let herself remember Michael's words and the contemptuous look on his face, she'd garnered the self-control necessary to get her home. Or so she'd thought. But then she'd been bombarded by images of the child she'd come to love—the child she'd once thought she could *never* love—and the pain had blindsided her.

She put her head down on the steering wheel and sobbed.

Afterward, feeling only slightly better, she started the car, and was careful to check the traffic before she maneuvered into it. A few miles ahead, she spotted a restaurant in the familiar highway rest area and stopped. Once inside, she ordered coffee, which she sat and stared at until it got cold. The place was almost deserted; she glanced at her watch. Eleven-thirty. What did it matter? No one was at home waiting for her. She lived alone, had lived alone for a long time. That independence had once suited her. She liked being accountable to no one—until now.

But now...she'd appreciated Mike's concern when he'd asked to pick her up for the car show, confessing he didn't want her to drive there by herself. She'd also liked it when Luke had checked the alarm before he left that night, admitting they worried about her alone in the condo.

Oh, God, had she lost that?

No! Of course she hadn't. This was just a fight. Families had fights all the time. But she'd felt so close to her son after their talk last weekend. And despite their differences, she'd felt close to Luke, too. If they'd been a real family, she'd be there to work this out with them. But they weren't a real family; she was an interloper.

Without warning, images of her past assaulted her. Damn it, life wasn't fair. She remembered vividly the pain of giving birth to Michael and the greater pain of never even holding him; all she had asked was if it was a boy or a girl. She'd hadn't even seen him until a month ago.

Would she ever see him again?

Stop it, she told herself. This was just a temporary setback. Tomorrow, she'd call him. She'd smooth things over.

But the images refused to stop coming. Because of that, as she stood and made her way to the car, and drove the rest of the way home, she promised herself she'd call Susan tomorrow. Her therapist would help her cope with this newest disaster.

The phone was ringing when she unlocked the door and stepped into the condo. She ignored it. Exhausted, she padded into the living room and crossed to the staircase. She was just by the phone when the answering machine clicked on.

"Meredith, this is Luke. For God's sake, pick up if you're there." Meredith hesitated. "Please, Meredith, we're frantic...Michael's..."

She picked up the phone. "Hello." Her voice, even to her own ears, was sandpapery.

"Oh, thank God."

"Dad, is that her? Is she home?" Meredith heard from the background.

"Yes, son, she is."

"Oh, God," was all Mike said.

"Meredith. Are you all right?" Luke asked.

She cleared her throat. "Yes. I'm all right."

"Did...did something happen on the way home?"

"Happen?"

"You left here two and a half hours ago."

"I did?"

He waited a minute. "Listen, should I come there?"

"No...no. Two and a half hours? Oh, I stopped. I had coffee."

"Oh."

"Dad, can I talk to her?" Meredith heard Mike's pleading voice some distance from the phone.

"Your son wants to talk to you."

Your son.

"Okay, I'll talk to him." *Please, God, don't let me cry.*

A shuffling on the other end, then, "Meredith, thank God you're home. Oh, man, I'm so sorry. About what I said. It was awful. I didn't mean any of it..." Mike's young voice caught. "Can you forgive me?"

She bit her lip hard, then said, "Oh, honey, I can forgive you anything."

"Look, want me and Dad to drive over there now? You sound so upset."

"No, I don't want you to do that. Tomorrow's a school day. I am upset, but talking to you helps. I'll be fine. I promise. I'll call you tomorrow, okay? I'm exhausted and I'm going to bed now."

"Okay. If you're sure. Dad wants to talk to you again. G-good night."

"Meredith." The low husky concern in Luke's voice drained the little strength she had left. She wanted to curl inside it and let it soothe her all night. Gripping the receiver so hard it pinched her fingers, she held her breath as she listened. "We were so worried," he told her. "Are you sure you don't want us to come over?" He pitched his voice a notch lower. "Or just me. I can come alone."

"No. I'm fine. I'm used to taking care of myself." Did the words sound bitter?

"I know. I don't like that."

"Don't worry. I'm fine. Hug Michael for me... Good night, Luke." Slowly, she put down the phone.

In her living room, she noticed a small lamp she'd left burning in the corner, as she always did whenever she'd be out at night. It was all she had to come home to. She trudged upstairs without turning it off.

AT TEN the next morning, Luke dialed the district attorney of Romulus, New York, from his own federal public defender's office. When the operator answered, he said, "I'd like to speak to Meredith Hunter, please."

"Who's calling?"

"Luke Rayburn."

As he waited, he drummed his pen on the shiny surface of his desk. Then he yawned. He'd slept badly and had given up altogether at about five-thirty. At work, he'd used his considerable willpower not to call Meredith, but lost the battle five minutes ago.

"I'm sorry, sir, Ms. Hunter isn't available."

Aware of office red tape, he said, "Give me her secretary, please."

Soon he heard, "Assistant D.A.'s office."

"I'm calling for Meredith Hunter. I'm told she's unavailable. This is Luke Rayburn from the federal public defender's office. I need to know when I can

get hold of Ms. Hunter today. It's important business.''
Well, that was true, even if he was using his professional clout for personal reasons. Hell, he was just too
damn worried to care.

"Just a moment, sir." The secretary's whole tone
had turned cooperative. In seconds she was back. "Ms.
Hunter called in sick. The district attorney wants to
know if he can help you."

"No, thanks." Luke hung up fast.

She was sick? Yeah, sick at heart. Last night on the
phone, her voice was thick with tears and he knew she
wasn't all right. But he was hoping today he could talk
to her, help her understand Michael's teenage eccen-
tricities, help her deal with all this.

And damn, why did he care? Restless, he rose and
went to the small coffeepot he kept in the corner of his
office. Holding his fifth—or was it his sixth?—cup, he
sipped and stared out the window. What a mess. Mike
had been morose this morning, sensing, like Luke, that
Meredith was not okay. He wouldn't talk, except for
monosyllabic answers when Luke questioned him. But,
frankly, at the moment Luke was more worried about
his son's mother than about his son.

He crossed back to his desk, plopped down, took out
a file and tried to read. Partway through, he glanced at
his calendar. Except for a meeting with a client later
this afternoon, today was relatively clear.

The hell with it. Pete, his co-worker, could deal with
any emergency. Luke tossed the file on the desk,
grabbed his gray suit coat and headed out.

Exactly forty-eight minutes later, he was ringing
Meredith Hunter's doorbell.

No answer. He looked at her car in the parking lot.
He leaned on the bell. Still no answer. Tapping his foot

on the concrete porch, Luke scanned the grounds. The leaves were almost off all the trees, a startling contrast to the lushness that had been here when he'd first contacted Meredith. Had it been only a month ago? My God, how had he come to care about her enough to be checking on her at eleven o'clock on a Thursday morning? He hit the bell again.

Finally, the door eased open.

Luke swallowed hard.

Meredith looked up at him with bruised eyes. Mauve smudges beneath them testified against a good night's sleep. Her hair was a tangled mass around her face, which was drawn tight. She'd obviously been wrestling with her own demons—all night and all morning, from the looks of her.

"What are you doing here?" Her voice was scratchy.

He smiled. "I'm worried about you."

A frown made her look even more tired. "You came all the way from Sommerfield just because you're..." She shook her head as if she didn't understand.

"Can I come in?"

Her eyes widened and a muscle pulsed in her throat. "No, Luke, I don't think that's a good idea."

"Why?"

"I'm ah..." She pulled her robe close around her. "I'm feeling pretty raw today."

"I suspected as much."

"I don't want to come unglued...I'm just trying to—"

"Meredith, I'm not leaving you alone. I don't care if you come unglued." He smiled at her. "I'm not bad when it comes to comfort, remember?"

She glanced at his shoulder, then back up to his eyes.

Hers brimmed with anguish. But she stepped back to allow him in.

All the blinds were closed and there were no lights on. Her purse was on the floor in the foyer, her keys next to it. Her shoes were in his path, one behind the other, as if she'd stepped out of them right there.

Crossing to the table, she picked up a mug. "Want some coffee?" she asked, taking a drink.

"I want to talk."

Dark emotion flared in her eyes. "No, you don't."

"Why?"

"I can't...I don't want...I can never..." She slammed the mug down on the table with a crack. "Luke, I can't talk about Michael today. I can't think about what he said without thinking about..."

When she didn't finish, he said, "Without thinking about what?"

"You don't want to know."

"Why wouldn't I want to know something about my son?"

"Oh, God." She threaded her hair off her face, turned away from him and laughed. It was an ugly sound.

He walked over to her, his heart picking up speed. His courtroom intuition was on red alert. More, much more, was going on here than he knew. He turned her to face him. She was trembling. "Meredith, what's going on? I know you were hurt by Mike's accusation last night. But there's more to it than that, isn't there?"

"I can't stop thinking about what happened," she said, her eyes a little glazed.

"Thinking about what happened with Mike?"

"I said I would never think about it again. Susan, my therapist, said that was a good idea. And I didn't.

I hadn't. But seeing Michael.'' She shook her head and stepped back from him. "No, even seeing him, I kept things under control. But last night…after he said those things…the images kept coming and coming and I can't stop them. And I want to…I have to…it's the only way I can live with things.'' She held up her palms. "But I can't stop…''

Luke moved closer. Gently, because he sensed it was what she needed, he ran his hands up and down her arms. "Then tell me and we'll stop this together.''

Her sad green eyes widened. "Tell *you?* Oh, no, I especially can't tell you.''

"Why?''

"You're his father. And Mike can *never* know.'' She grabbed the lapels of Luke's wool suit. *"He can never know!''*

Gripped by the worst sense of foreboding he'd ever felt in his life, Luke struggled against the panic rising in him. Purposefully, he calmed his breathing and willed his hands not to shake. Somehow, he gentled his voice. "All right, Meredith. He can never know. I promise, I'll never tell him. But *you* tell *me*. Okay?''

At first she shook her head, sending her hair into her eyes and onto her cheeks. Then she turned away from him.

"I'll help you stop the images from coming, I promise, Meredith. Trust me.''

She whirled on him then. "Trust you? That's what he said. 'Trust me.' And I did. But then he wouldn't stop.''

"Who wouldn't stop?''

"Tom.''

Tom. Suddenly Luke remembered a name. Thomas J. Stone.

On Michael's birth certificate.

He felt the fiery gnawing of fear in his stomach. "What wouldn't he stop, Meredith?"

Shaking her head again, she stared at him. But she wasn't seeing Luke. She was seeing someone else—or something else—a long time ago. And Luke didn't want to know what it was.

But he had to.

"Touching me," she said abruptly. "He said he just wanted a kiss, he'd stop anytime I said. But he...didn't. I asked him to. Four times." She frowned. "No, five. I can't remember how many times. His lawyer said I was lying because I didn't know how many times, but I wasn't. I asked him to stop."

"But he didn't." Bile rose in Luke's throat as he put together the pieces of the puzzle. He choked it back but his stomach cramped.

"I didn't scream. I was baby-sitting, and I was afraid he would keep going in front of the two little girls, he was so far gone. So I didn't scream. The lawyer said if I didn't scream, then I didn't want him to stop...that I liked what he was doing...but I didn't...I hated it...he hurt me. I was crying. The girls couldn't hear that. It was all right to cry."

Luke felt the moisture form in his own eyes but he willed it back. He reached for her and pulled her to him. The backs of his legs hit the chair and he sank onto it, pulling her to his lap. Holding on to her, he smoothed her hair and crooned, "Yes, it was all right to cry, honey. It's all right to cry now."

And so she did. He rocked her back and forth, feeling his heart rip open a little more with each of her deep, wrenching sobs.

In his mind's eye, he saw Michael as the three-day-old baby that had been brought to them by his lawyer because the hospital wouldn't let the adoptive parents go there to get him.

His baby.

Her baby.

A baby conceived by rape.

It was unfathomable that this child of his heart could have been brought about by such a violent criminal act. Luke shook with suppressed rage at the thought. But he'd deal with that later. Right now, the woman in his arms needed him.

"It's okay, sweetheart. The images will stop coming now."

After several minutes, she stopped weeping. He reached into his back pocket and took out a handkerchief. She eased her death grip on his jacket, so he inched her back a bit. Carefully, the way she deserved to be treated, he wiped her face. She settled back into his arms and closed her eyes. "I never wanted you to know."

"I can see why."

Her eyes snapped open and her body tensed. "Mike can never know."

Luke closed his own eyes at the sickening thought. His anguish was so acute, he wasn't sure he could stand it. "Of course not."

She relaxed again. He held her silently, tightly, for a long time.

"You knew him?" he finally asked.

"Yes, we'd been dating for a few months. I liked him a lot. He was a big jock at South Virginia State University. We had a lot in common. We were both there on soccer scholarships." She scowled. "Only he drank too much. One night, he came over where I was baby-sitting for my sociology teacher. She gave him permission. But I didn't know he was drunk when I let him in. Then, he started kissing me. He said to relax, he'd stop whenever I said so." She paused. "He didn't."

"I take it you prosecuted."

She shuddered and he tightened his hold on her. "Yes. He was gone by the time my teacher got home. I was pretty close to her. She knew something was wrong—I was...bruised...where he'd held me down. When the truth came out, she took me to the hospital."

"Oh, Meredith, I'm so sorry." His lips brushed her hair.

"That's when the nightmare really began." She drew back and looked him squarely in the eye. "A public defender took the case because Tom's parents were dead and he had no money."

It all made sense now. A ruthless public defender. Seventeen years ago, date rape had been unheard of— or at least untalked about. "Now I understand why you gave him up."

"I couldn't risk his ever finding out what happened. The circumstances of his conception." She shook her head. "And I was afraid I couldn't love him, you know, after how he was conceived." Tears pooled in her eyes. "But I do, Luke. I love him so much."

Luke drew her back against his chest; she clung to him.

After a few minutes, she mumbled against his shirt, "But I would have given him up, anyway, I guess. Even if I hadn't been raped. I couldn't have given him the right things then. It was best for him that you got him."

And you got just the nightmares. This remarkable

woman had had to deal with so much horror, and he'd gotten so much that was good and beautiful. He hugged her closer. She burrowed into him.

"What happened to the bastard who did this to you?"

"He was killed in a drunk-driving accident three months after the trial."

God forgive him, Luke was glad.

"Luke, my bias against public defenders... That's why."

"I understand. If the lawyer were here right now, I'd kill him with my bare hands. I understand, honey."

He did. As he rocked and cuddled her, he *did* understand. And he hurt for her, in deep and slicing ways that only made him wonder how her slender body had ever withstood that kind of pain all these years.

CHAPTER SEVEN

LUKE'S FEET hit the pavement hard; the gulps of ice-cold air stung his lungs. But he kept running because, as with Meredith, hours earlier, the images wouldn't stop coming, and he couldn't stand it anymore.

Four out of five rapes are by someone the woman knows.

He let out a string of obscenities. Statistics were for strangers, not for his son.

And now, not for Meredith.

Rounding the corner of his street, Luke pushed himself even harder. The vigorous exercise helped to release what he'd held in for the last twelve hours.

He'd stayed with Meredith as long as he could, then gone home to Michael. Thinking back, he could barely recall what he'd told the boy: that he'd talked to Meredith during the day, that she seemed better, that she would call him. What he vividly remembered was staring at Michael and trying to assimilate that this gentle, sensitive boy had been the product of a violent act.

Meredith had called after dinner, and assured Michael that she was fine, and that she'd see him tomorrow night.

Picking up speed, he thought back to that morning. After her initial confession, Meredith had slept in his arms.

When she'd awakened and showered, he'd fixed her

soup and a sandwich. They had talked, too. Some things he had to know...

They were seated at her small, glass-and-chrome table in the dinette area. Luke had begged off food but nursed a beer. "Was it...were you...was it your first time, Meredith?" he'd asked.

She shook her head. "No. There was a boy from home. I'd dated him steadily all through high school. We'd...made love my senior year."

Luke nodded, relieved that her first sexual experience, at least, had been positive. She'd continued her story. "Danny went to Yale. We'd decided to date other people at college, but neither of us would be serious about it. You know, we wouldn't...be physical with anyone else."

"I understand."

She'd laughed, a sad, rueful sound. "Well, *he* didn't. He couldn't accept the fact I was pregnant."

"Did he know...about the rape?" The word stuck in his throat, and he had to summon considerable effort to get it out.

"Yes." She sipped her milk, not looking at him. "And he couldn't handle it." Meredith sat up straighter and stared ahead. "He got married before he even graduated from college. He has three kids now." Her voice had cracked on the last comment.

Purposefully slowing his pace, he took the slight hill to the high school a little easier.

How had Meredith survived everything? Pregnant at eighteen. The emotional scars of rape. So much loss...

"My parents were wonderful," she'd told him. "My dad was outraged, of course, but he was able to get past it for my sake." She'd stared at Luke. "Just like you have to, Luke. You'll have to put aside your anger...or whatever else you're feeling, and do what's best for Mike."

Solemnly, in the late-afternoon light that slanted through the blinds of her kitchen, he'd taken her hand in his. "I will, I promise," he'd told her. "I won't let you down, Meredith. I won't let Mike down."

Which was why he was out on this godforsaken night running like the Furies were after him. When he reached the school, he jogged onto the track that surrounded the soccer field...

"I lost my soccer scholarship to South Virginia State because I couldn't play the following season," Meredith had told him.

"Didn't they know about the rape?"

"Of course they did. It became public knowledge when I prosecuted. But I lost the case, so I was simply guilty of sexual activity that resulted in pregnancy. Ann Dwyer, the sociology teacher I told you about, put up a royal battle, but no one would listen."

Luke had wondered how this could get any worse—but it did.

"So you went to Princeton?"

"Yeah, it was close to my parents, who were living just outside New York City at the time. And the school had a pretty active Women's Services department on campus, which I knew I was going to need. I'd gotten therapy right after the rape and throughout my pregnancy, but I knew I'd want more support once I got back to school." Her lips formed a slight smile and some of the color returned to her cheeks. "It's where I met Belle. She was involved in...one of the groups."

Luke suspected her best friend had also been raped, but didn't want to ask. *Every five minutes, a woman is raped...* He wondered if a public defender had also been involved in Belle's situation, and if that increased Meredith's bias.

Unable to bear the sight of the soccer field, Luke veered off and took to the streets again.

The images followed him. Meredith had given birth to Mike in October, then started at Princeton in January. She hadn't gone out for soccer there. "I was...changed," she'd said simply.

After Meredith had managed to eat something, they'd gone back to the living room. He knew he had to leave soon, but there was one more thing to talk about...

"Why didn't you have an abortion, Meredith?"

Her face had paled again and his insides had knotted at the thought of his beloved son never existing, but he had to ask.

She sipped the coffee he'd made, and tucked back the hair that fell in her eyes. "I'm not sure. They didn't give you those pills then, like they do now, after a rape, to prevent conception. I thought about an abortion. People advised me to have one. That way, I wouldn't lose soccer...or my reputation...or Danny." She'd shifted on the couch. "It wasn't meant to be that way. I'm not a very religious person, but I think it was meant for me to have that baby." She'd looked over at him. "So I could give him to you, I guess."

He'd gotten up and crossed to her, taken the cup out of her hand and tugged her onto his lap again. Wrapping her in his arms, he kissed her hair, which smelled like a bouquet of daisies. Gently he soothed her back with slow, languid circles. She curled into him, her head on his chest, her fingers fisted in his shirt. His throat clogged as he said, "Thank you for giving up so much so I could have my son..."

Drained by the memories, Luke started to lag. Rape…the public humiliation…loss of a boyfriend… loss of innocence. The words kept coming and coming and he couldn't stop them. A car sped down the street and Luke had to halt his steps to let it go by the intersection.

A stop sign was to his left.

"Stop… It won't stop…. It won't stop," she'd said.

Suddenly, the rage boiled up and out of him. He turned to the sign, and drew back his left hand. Blindly, he smashed his fist into the sturdy aluminum, once, then again, and a third time. Pain splintered through his hand and up his arm as he leaned his head against the sign and finally let the tears come.

THE GRAND JURY CONVENED at nine-thirty the next morning. By then, Meredith had gotten herself together and felt, amazingly, better. Dressed in her favorite red silk suit, she'd managed to cover the ravages of the day before with subtle makeup and an almost-genuine smile.

It wasn't so amazing that she felt better, her therapist had told her on the phone late last night. Susan believed that the burden of withholding the circumstances of her son's birth from Luke and Mike would become too much for Meredith. Sharing it, having someone else know the awful secret, *should* make her feel better.

Unfortunately, it seemed to have done the opposite for Luke Rayburn. Meredith would never forget the look on his face, the agony in those dark, sensitive eyes when she realized what had happened to her. Oh, he'd been strong—he'd taken care of *her*—but Meredith knew how much he hurt, how hard it was for him, and what he would have to deal with afterward.

"All rise." The bailiff stood aside as Judge Eric J. Bancroft entered the court. The jury had filed in on the right.

Meredith sighed, watching from the back pews as the first case came up for decision. She was third on the docket. Having already interviewed her witnesses and prepared her statements, she concentrated on the courtroom. Oak paneling lined all the walls; the thirty-foot ceiling gave it an open, airy feeling. This was one of her favorite places, a place of justice.

Did Luke ever argue in this courtroom? Meredith wondered as she ran her hand along the smooth, cool wood. It wasn't uncommon for a federal public defender to be up against one of her colleagues. It was pure coincidence that she'd never met him before. He'd only joined the federal department last year, where she'd have more chances to run into him than when he'd worked for the county of Sommerfield.

Luke Rayburn was a good man. If she'd had any doubt about that before, his behavior yesterday erased it. He'd been heartbreakingly gentle as he'd held her. Once he realized what had happened, he'd been sensitive to all the nuances and simply listened and consoled.

She frowned; she was worried about him. He'd suppressed all his own reactions while she'd let hers out. For some time now she'd had the feeling he was used to squelching his own needs.

Meredith wondered if he was like that in bed. Though just having the thought made her uncomfortable, there was no use denying she was attracted to him. Especially after yesterday. But she'd been aroused before then by the lean lines of his body and the calm assurance with which he moved. All along, she'd felt herself gravitate toward him physically, but now...

Now it was different. She yearned for his touch more intensely, more graphically. Probably because a bond had been formed, a connection even greater than the fact that she'd given him his son. He knew her worst and deepest secrets and he'd accepted them. She found herself wondering what his lips would feel like pressed to hers. She wanted to know what his hands would feel like on her bare skin, sliding over her rib cage, caressing her breasts. And, somewhere deep down in her gut, she craved the knowledge of what it would be like to have him driving into her with a passion he *didn't* stifle, *couldn't* control.

She also wondered what she'd be like with him. Would she be able to let go with him, would she finally...

"Meredith, you're next," one of the clerks informed her.

Disconcerted by her fantasies, Meredith rose and entered the courtroom proper. Striding to the large pine table on the left, she set down her briefcase and removed her notes from it.

"Ms. Hunter, are you ready?" Judge Bancroft asked.

"Yes, Your Honor," she said, stepping to the podium.

She liked Eric Bancroft. A newly appointed judge, he was tough but fair. Particularly about keeping criminals, even alleged ones, in custody. One of the biggest fears a D.A. had was that the accused would get out on bail after the indictment and commit another crime.

Did public defenders have that fear, too?

Shaking off the memory of how Luke's eyes sparkled with passion as he talked about the law, Meredith outlined her case for the judge.

Her client, Sandra Santori, had been brutally beaten by the accused. Then, he'd raped her at gunpoint. It was going to be a difficult case to prosecute because Sandy was a convicted prostitute with a history of drug abuse. At least there were other witnesses to back her up, as well as two more victims who Meredith had convinced to come forward.

The accused was a drug dealer. And Meredith wanted to get Eddie DeLuca in the worst way. The slime was responsible for selling drugs to kids at Romulus's inner-city school. That Sandy had agreed to prosecute was a miracle.

Would Luke Rayburn be able to defend someone like DeLuca? Again, she quelled thoughts of him as Sandy was led into the courtroom.

A tall, thin woman, the bruises on her face were yellow now, with a tinge of red by her jaw and on her forehead. She was still missing two teeth. Meredith could see her hands shake, even though the accused was not in the courtroom—one of the blessings of a grand jury hearing.

Forgoing the microphone, Meredith crossed to the witness stand. "Are you all right, Sandy?" she asked.

The young woman—she was just twenty—smiled at her. "As much as I'm gonna be in this place. Gives me the willies."

The judge smiled, as did several members of the jury.

Meredith was on her way.

Within an hour, she had all the testimony she needed. The jury's reaction was promising. More than one woman's eyes were suspiciously moist. The four men sat with tense shoulders and granite jaws. Meredith forced herself to remain expressionless during the account of the rape. She didn't take many rape cases, but she'd asked for this one because she wanted Eddie DeLuca behind bars and away from kids like Michael.

Sandy was dismissed and led out to the right. The heavy wooden door across the courtroom creaked open, and Eddie was brought in. Wearing a suit. Clean-shaven. Head down. Posture slumped.

The last time she'd seen him, he'd reeked of marijuana, was wearing a scrungy black T-shirt and jeans and was smoking a cigarette. "Try it, you bitch," he'd said to her. "She ain't gonna get nowhere. Who's gonna believe a stinking whore, anyway? And who's gonna care?"

An hour later, apparently twelve unbiased jurors cared because they handed down a decision that there was indeed sufficient evidence to bring Eddie DeLuca to trial.

"The state recommends no bail, Your Honor," Meredith said firmly. "Mr. DeLuca has prior records of drug dealing and aggravated assault." She smiled to herself, though she didn't let her glee show. "And, he's jumped bail twice before." She'd found out that little tidbit from a snitch who'd known DeLuca when he was operating in New York City.

Judge Bancroft shuffled through his papers. "Anything to say, Mr. Thompson?"

The public defender gave some weak response.

But Meredith had won. And it gave her inexpressible satisfaction to know that DeLuca would be off the streets—for a while at least.

A distressing thought wound its way into her consciousness: Would someone like Luke Rayburn put him back out there?

CLYDE O'MALLEY WAS SCUM. He even looked the part in a battered black leather jacket, an oily ponytail halfway down his back, and dirty fingernails. But he was entitled to a defense and Luke was going to give him the best.

Gingerly, Luke rested his swollen left hand on the podium and listened to Judge Lasser speak to his client. Luke looked at the bandages wrapped around his palm. His reaction last night had been stupid, and he was suffering for it today. Not to mention how he was going to explain his injury to Mike. They'd gotten up late and had barely seen each other before leaving the house this morning, so his son hadn't noticed.

"Mr. O'Malley, your lawyer has advised me you will dispose of the indictment for a plea on counts one to eleven. Is that correct?"

"Yes, sir, it is."

"I have to ask you several questions. And remember, the government can charge you with perjury since you've take an oath."

"Yes, sir."

"Tell me about yourself—your age, your schooling…"

Luke listened as O'Malley provided the information. A female D.A. stood directly across from them at a matching podium. She wasn't as tall as Meredith, and she didn't have Meredith's athletic grace or proud presence. Luke wondered what Meredith was like in the courtroom, how she moved there, how her voice sounded.

All he could remember now was how raw he'd felt after she'd finished crying her heart out in his arms.

Willing his mind away from yesterday—though it was hard because his hand still throbbed—Luke listened to Judge Lasser ask if O'Malley understood the lengthy plea and then read the eleven counts.

O'Malley was a known drug dealer in the city of Sommerfield. He had two prior arrests. This time the police had found a fairly small amount of cocaine when they busted him—but also guns and dynamite. The only reason the defense was able to bargain out a plea was that the police had been working with one of his customers. The teenage boy had been a client, and when the police picked him up for using, he'd agreed to help catch O'Malley. Over the course of several phone calls, he set up a deal with O'Malley, and the police had moved in. Things got complicated when it was discovered the kid was a runaway, and his parents found him. Though they were from out of state, they were rich and had some clout, and were accusing the D.A. of using their son for entrapment. Everything became so convoluted that the prosecution had offered a plea and Luke had advised his client to accept it.

"Has it been explained to you how sentences are determined, Mr. O'Malley?" the judge said.

"Yes, sir."

"And has Mr. Rayburn explained that you will serve eighty-two months in jail. If I accept this, you're stuck with that. It can't be changed."

"Yes, sir."

Judge Lasser finished his questioning about the accused's knowledge of his rights and what he was giving up. Then Lasser addressed the issue of the presentence report. In the end, he set a date, seventy-five days hence, to determine acceptance of the plea and sentencing.

Luke carefully masked his concern when the D.A. across the room asked for bail to be set.

"We request bail conditions remain the same as they have the last few months," Luke said when it was his turn. "Mr. O'Malley has reported to these proceedings of his own volition, and will do so again. He has a lot to lose if he doesn't."

Judge Lasser snorted. "He has a lot of lose if he does show, too. More than six years of his life."

"Still, he hasn't run," Luke argued. "He won't this time."

Piercing O'Malley with a determined glare, the judge told him exactly what would happen if he did not appear in seventy-five days. "When we apprehend you—and I assure you, we will…"

But Luke knew he had won. O'Malley would be released on his own recognizance. As the next case was called, Luke glanced over at the D.A.

Meredith would not have been happy with the judge's decision on custody. Her green eyes would be snapping with anger and her face would flush with challenge. What's more, she'd be disappointed that he'd pushed for O'Malley's release.

Luke sighed. It didn't matter what she thought. He had to do his job the best he could, and it was irrelevant how it conflicted with Meredith's beliefs. Wincing as he picked up his briefcase with his injured left hand, he transferred it to his right. As he walked out of court, he reminded himself that Meredith Hunter had no place in his professional life.

But, in his private one, she definitely had a place. Now all he had to do was figure out what that was.

MIKE BOLTED off the living-room couch as soon as the doorbell rang. Yanking it open, he waited as Meredith stood there gazing at him. Then, without a word, he reached out and hugged her the way he hugged Julie Anne after they'd had a fight.

Dropping the bag she carried, Meredith held him, too. She felt strong and solid, not fragile the way his mother, Sara, had. Meredith's hands went around his neck and she kissed the side of his face. He thought he felt her shiver. Finally, they both drew back, but she held on to his arms. Looking into her eyes, he said, "Meredith, I—"

She put two fingers to his mouth. "Shh. You already apologized. Once is enough."

She let him off the hook. He knew that's what mothers did, and it made him feel close to her. As he moved back to let her in, he caught sight of the package she'd dropped and picked it up. "What's this?"

She smiled a little self-consciously. "You'll see."

Stepping inside, she stopped when she saw his dad. He'd been in the living room, apparently watching them. He hoped his father wasn't mad that he'd hugged her. Mike knew Luke was worried that Meredith would take his mother's place in his memory—which was stupid as far as Mike was concerned. But he also sensed that his dad was afraid Meredith could take Mike away from *him.* Which was just about the dumbest thing Mike could think of.

"Hi," his father said. His voice was funny—soft and kind of goofy.

"Hi." Hers was, too.

Mike wondered why. At the car show, they'd been really weird with each other, and Wednesday night he'd been so mad that he hadn't noticed what was going on between them. Man, he hoped they could find a way to get along.

"Come on in." Mike took Meredith's coat and motioned her through the foyer.

His dad said, "I made a fire in the family room."

"Dad, you shouldn't do that with your hand."

"What happened to your hand?" Meredith asked, looking down at his father's bandages.

"I...ah...lost my temper...and hit something with it. A little too hard."

Mike said, "Yeah, but he won't tell me the details. Must've been something bad..."

He saw Meredith's eyes focus on Luke; some signal went off between them. Again, Mike wondered about the vibes between these two.

"The fire?" his father reminded them.

"Sounds wonderful." She smiled and his father's shoulders relaxed. "Do you have a VCR in there?"

"Yeah, sure." Mike walked beside her through the house. "Why?"

"I want to show you something."

"What?"

"Remember I told you I played soccer in high school?"

"Sure."

"Well, my father was a professional photographer. He videotaped all my games. I want you to see a couple of things."

Mike's heart sank. "Okay." *Don't blow it, Rayburn. You can't keep getting mad at her. She has a right to make a point here.*

When they reached the family room, he went to the machine and put in the first tape. Out of the corner of his eye, he saw his dad go over to Meredith and say

softly—he guessed he wasn't supposed to hear—
"Have you seen these tapes, since…high school?" She
shook her head and his father asked, "Are you sure
you want to do this?"

*Dad thinks it's a bad idea, too. I will not get mad…
I'll just let her show me how it's done right. It won't
kill me.*

"I want to, Luke. I think it's the best way for him
to see."

Damn.

They settled down, Mike and Meredith on the couch
and his dad by the fireplace. The screen came on with
just the date. "It's my junior year. This is the big game
against Penbrook. They were our rivals."

Despite his annoyance, Mike found himself staring
with interest at the video. A huge, burly man with a
beard and the devil in his eyes came on.

"That's your grandfather, Mike," she said.

Mike's jaw dropped and his heart did little flip-flops
in his chest. "Cool!" He glanced at Meredith. Her eyes
were moist.

"He was a wonderful man," she said. "You would
have loved him."

Mike's throat hurt a little, so he just nodded and
listened to his grandfather tell about the tape.

The game started.

"What number are you?"

"Twelve."

"Hey, there you are. You look *young.*"

"I was almost seventeen. Your age."

He watched her—a slim, energetic girl running out
on the field. "You run like me."

"My mother said the same thing."

She picked up the remote.

"What are you doing?" Mike asked.

"Fast-forwarding to the part I want you to see."

"I'd like to watch it all. Wouldn't you, Dad?" And it was true. Even if she was going to prove a point, watching her play was awesome.

She was awesome. At center forward, she took the kickoff with another player. She was as fast as lightning, quicker than some of the guys on his team and one of the most agile players he'd ever seen turning the ball around. And it was all narrated by his grandfather. At one point his deep voice said, "Here comes Mer the Bear up the middle."

"Mer the Bear?" Mike couldn't help asking. "What does that mean?"

"Watch. This play right here."

She'd gotten a fast break but two of the other players caught up to her. So had one of her teammates—who was in good scoring position. The two defenders closed in on Meredith.

"Pass! She's right across from you," Mike murmured.

"Yes," Meredith said dryly. "She is."

But Meredith didn't pass. Instead, she slid the ball through the right defender's legs, circled around her and booted it—into the goal.

Mike hadn't realized he'd stood up. "Yes!" he said, raising his fist in the air.

"Not quite," Meredith said, again in that same tone. "I should have passed."

Luke shook his head in amazement as he watched Mike look down at Meredith, his young eyes shining with relief—and something else. Gratitude.

"Just like me," his son said.

"Yep. Just like you." She picked up the remote and fast-forwarded the tape. "Now watch."

They all did. Another play where Meredith should have passed and didn't. She got up and switched tapes. Two more games in her junior year where she made the same mistake, sometimes scoring, sometimes not.

On one there was a problem with a call. Her father had zoomed in on her on the field. The camera showed her throw up her hands and yell something at the referee. Another player came over to her and said something, but Meredith shook her off. She yelled again. The ref dug out his yellow card; she was temporarily pulled out of the game—the penalty for a personal foul.

Mike swung around. "You got yellow-carded?"

She nodded, stifling a grin.

"What did you say to him?"

"I *said*, 'What's the matter with your freakin' eyes.' He, ah, thought I said something else."

Mike laughed deep from his belly, and Luke realized the sound of his son's uninhibited laughter had been all too rare these last three years. He was grateful that Meredith had brought it to them, even though he felt a pang of guilt over his disloyalty to Sara.

After she put in the last tape, Meredith returned to the couch and sat next to Mike again; she took his hand before she started it. "Remember I told you you'd grow out of this?" He nodded. "Watch."

She allowed them just one more clip—of a play-off game in her senior year. The score was tied. Fifteen seconds left in the game. Meredith was twenty feet from the goal, in possession of the ball. Without hesitation, she passed it to the left wing, who booted it into the net to win the game.

"I rest my case," she said, chuckling.

In the intimate family room, the fire crackled, but no one spoke. Mike blinked rapidly, then said, "Thanks for showing me this."

Reaching up, she smoothed back his hair. "I wanted you to know two things. I understand how hard it is for you to control this urge to take it alone. I was there. I did exactly what you do sometimes." Her eyes danced. "But I beat it. I won the internal battle, and you can, too. You just have to know your flaws, Mike. In soccer and in life. And do your best to overcome them."

His son sighed, then smiled, then hugged her. Luke had to turn away, so much emotion—conflicting emotion—was in his heart. He was still raw from her confession, but it was seeing her on the field that almost did him in. He crossed to the TV to remove the tape from the VCR, struggling to get his feelings in check.

Apparently, she had pressed pause instead of stop and there was a freeze-frame of her emblazoned on the screen leaping into the air with both arms raised. This was Meredith before the rape—free, risk taking, happy, no haunting memories dulling the green of her eyes. This was the girl who had the world by the tail and was going to take everything she could from it. Mer the Bear.

He wanted her back.

Mike had pulled away from her by the time Luke turned around.

"This help at all? With things between us?" she asked, and Luke admired her directness.

"Yeah, it does." Mike ducked his head and seemed to be embarrassed by what he was about to say. "Can we talk about something else, too?"

"Sure."

Luke stayed by the television.

"I was out of line the other night," Mike told her. "I know I don't have to apologize again, but I was a jerk. After I talked to Julie Anne about it, I realized it...it wasn't just the game. I..."

Mike glanced at him. Luke had no idea what his son was going to say. They hadn't talked about this. "Dad, I hope this won't upset you. I promise it doesn't mean I've forgotten Mom, or anything." He turned back to Meredith. "I don't get to see you enough, Meredith. And I get mad about it sometimes. I think that was part of it all. The same thing happened a couple of weeks ago when you had plans and couldn't come to my game." He looked right at her. "I guess I feel you missed so much of my life, I don't want you to miss any more."

Luke's feelings were mixed as he took in his son's words. Foremost was the buried fear that Mike would come to love Meredith more than he'd loved Sara...or more than he loved Luke. Stupid, childish, but still, it was there.

And, underriding everything was the stunning realization that Luke himself felt the same way as Mike. He didn't get to see Meredith nearly enough, either.

Oh, God, how had this happened? And how was he going to put his son's best interests over his own, when he felt such a powerful, intense need to be with this woman?

Silently thanking God, Meredith drew in a deep breath at Mike's declaration. "Oh, honey, do you know how happy that makes me—that you want to spend more time with me?"

Mike smiled a little-boy grin. "Yeah?"

She mussed his hair. "Yeah." Then she took a calming breath. "Let's see. What can we do about it?"

"Well, first off, you know...my birthday's next week."

Meredith watched her son, consciously quelling the feelings that surfaced for her on October thirty-first every year. "Yes, I know."

"We usually have a family party later that night." He rolled his eyes. "After the trick-or-treaters come. I want you to be there, Meredith. And maybe Lydia, if she can."

Meredith nodded, her heart full.

"And I wanna spend more time together. You know, do things together."

"They're advertising a jazz fest in Romulus next Saturday." She smiled again. "I could get tickets. We could go together. Maybe you could—" She glanced at Luke and stopped. His posture had gone rigid, and although he had his lawyer mask on, his jaw tensed. "Um, we should check with your dad, though."

Mike said, "Dad. Is it okay if I go?"

"Sure." Luke pushed away from the wall and returned to the fireplace. He sat down on the hearth, linking his hands between his knees. "You love jazz."

"You could come, Dad."

Luke shook his head. "No, you two should have some time alone together. I'm always here. It'll be good for you. Both of you."

Meredith stifled the disappointment she felt. Had she read him wrong? Was she the only one feeling the closeness...the *need*, for God's sake, to be with Luke as well as her son?

"Okay," Mike said. He looked back to Meredith. "What time?"

"Well, it's all day. You don't have a game, do you?"

"No. Next week there's a Friday game."

"Good, I'll pick you up early, and bring you back late."

"Maybe I could stay overnight with you."

At the comment, Luke shoved his eyebrows together and threw his shoulders back. But he said, "Sure, whatever you want."

Mike chuckled. "Hey, Dad. You could get a hot date for the night." He wiggled his eyebrows. "The whole night."

Though Mike had meant it as a joke, Meredith didn't think it was at all funny. She had to fight the urge to stiffen up; instead, she pasted a sickly-sweet smile on her face. She looked at Luke's large masculine hands. Images of them sliding down the curves of his *hot date's* body assaulted her. She studied his mouth. Visions of his lips, soft and tender at first, then insistent, deepening the kiss—with someone else—battered the defenses she'd built up over the years. "Well, looks like it will work out for everyone," she said glibly.

When she caught Luke's eye, she knew her own betrayed her dislike of the "hot date" he might have next week.

But...so did his.

CHAPTER EIGHT

THE STATISTIC POPPED into Luke's head the following Sunday morning as he watched Meredith from across the kitchen.

Most Americans don't go in for kinky sex. When asked to rank their favorite sex acts, ninety-six percent placed vaginal sex first. Oral sex ranked a distant third. Second place was something that most people never considered to be a sex act at all: watching their partner undress.

Meredith was standing in front of the laundry room. Slowly, she unwrapped a scarf from around her neck. Finger by finger, she drew off the gloves she'd borrowed from his son. As she bent over and pulled Mike's jumbo socks off her feet, Luke saw that her navy blue pants had stirrup things around her soles. Languidly she stood and tugged one of Michael's sweatshirts over her head. Luke swallowed hard, his body reacting to the sight of her arms raised over her head, the feminine curves of her torso evident in the thin white sweater and the clinging spandex.

All in all, she was the sexiest thing he'd ever seen. The statistic proved true for him, all right.

Turning back to the stove, he asked as casually as he could, "Have fun?"

"It was great." He glanced back when his son responded. Mike appeared behind her, inside the laundry room, removing his own outer clothing and now muddy sneakers. "Meredith scored on me twice."

She looked up at Mike and tousled his hair. Luke yearned for her to do the same to him. "Yeah," she said, "but he won, three to two."

Ashamed of his envious thoughts—of his kid, no less—Luke dragged his eyes away from the intimate sight of mother and son in a playful exchange. Just as he'd tried to avoid watching them when they'd gone outside for a friendly game of one-on-one soccer before brunch was ready. Had Sara ever met Mike on his own level like this? The thought made Luke feel even more guilty. When had he started to compare Meredith and Sara? It was blasphemous to her memory. Damn, if he could only stop thinking about Meredith Hunter.

"Smells great, Dad. French toast?"

"Yep." He kept his tone purposely curt to avoid revealing the thickness in his throat when he remembered just how much he'd thought about Meredith yesterday when Michael had gone to Romulus to stay with her. Luke tried to tell himself Meredith was on his mind because of his fear that she would take Sara's place. Or that she'd steal his son's affections from *him*.

But Luke wasn't a liar.

He'd thought about her sexually—graphically, specifically, and in 3-D. Right down to fantasies of what color bra she wore.

"I'll set the table," Mike said, coming into the kitchen and plucking a piece of melon from the bowl on the counter. Luke batted Mike's hand away, but didn't look at him. His son hesitated, then put an arm around Luke's shoulder.

My mood must show, Luke thought. Mike was affectionate by nature, but this gesture was out of the blue.

"So, did you have that hot date while I was gone?" Mike asked.

In the hall outside the laundry room, Meredith had gathered the clothes she'd borrowed into her arms. She dropped them to the floor. Because of Mike's question? Hmm.

"Real men don't tell," Luke said, a little devil in him wanting to test if he'd read her reaction right.

From across the room, he could see her bend down, pick up the bundle and place it on the back stairs. She came fully into the kitchen, leaned against the counter and listened to his son ribbing him.

"Come on, Dad, fess up. While we were listening to those bands play some mean Kenny G, were you snuggled up with a cute little snow bunny?"

"Snow bunny?" Meredith asked.

Mike turned to her. "Last winter, we were taking a skiing lesson. This cute little instructor was all over Dad. Asked him to demonstrate everything." Mike grinned. "She jammed her phone number into his back pocket before we left." He returned his gaze to Luke, a mischievous glint in it. "So, were you, Dad?"

Meredith's eyes fastened on Luke—they were grass green today—and she angled her chin. "Answer the question, Counselor," she said tightly.

"No way." He went along with the game, holding up his right hand. "I plead the Fifth."

The back door rattled with a knock. "Hi, everybody," Julie Anne said, poking her head in. "I saw the silver bullet in the driveway and knew you were home. I wanted to ask Mike if he needed anything at Runson Library. And to see how the jazz fest went."

"Super," Mike said as he set the table.

Julie Anne sniffed the air. "Is that Mr. Rayburn's legendary French toast I smell?"

"Get another plate, Mike," Luke said, laughing.

Meredith turned to the girl. "Working on your paper today?"

"Yep. The downtown library has a book on adoption practices in the 1800s." Julie Anne flipped her long hair over her shoulder. "I have to go down to get it from there, though. They won't send it out, it's too rare."

"Brunch is ready," Luke said.

Everyone moved to the table, sat down and dug into the French toast. The fragrant smell of cinnamon warmed Luke, as did the sight of all of them around his table.

Stacking his plate with food, Mike said to Julie Anne, "Who you going with?"

"Nobody. Why?"

"Jule, it's way in the city."

"No kidding, Rayburn."

"This is Sunday."

Julie Anne turned to Meredith. "Did that jazz fest dull his wits. I *know* it's Sunday."

Serious now—he'd stopped eating—Mike said, "It's deserted down there. Anyone could jump you. Man, you could be raped or killed."

Meredith's fork clattered to the plate. Both kids turned to her.

"I think Mike has a point, Julie Anne," Luke said, trying to cover Meredith's reaction. "You shouldn't go alone."

Sighing, the girl said, "Mom and Dad went antiquing. I can't wait till they get back."

"Still, you can't go alone," Mike said.

Julie Anne turned to Meredith and rolled her eyes. "Is he being sexist?"

"Just cautious," Meredith answered. Her voice was throaty.

Mike looked at Meredith. "How long you staying?"

"Till about five."

"What if I take this chick to the library? We'll only be gone about an hour." Mike scowled. "Is that all right? After what I said the other night about spending time with you?"

Meredith smiled, and Luke's gut clenched. "I think I can do without you for an hour." She glanced at Luke, her eyes darkening. "I'll, um, find something to do. My briefcase is in the car. I can work." When she spoke the last words, her teasing tone was gone.

Thirty minutes later, the kids piled into Mike's car and Meredith faced Luke in the kitchen. They were alone, dangerously alone, he thought.

"I'll clean up." She stood, lifting a dish.

"I'll help."

"No!" He cocked his head at her peremptory tone. "You guys do all the cooking every time I'm here. I insist I clean up. Alone." She averted her eyes. "Go watch a football game or something."

Luke started to protest, but he thought about all the complications that following his instincts would cause. Frustrated, and uncharacteristically irritated by his parental responsibilities, he left without a word.

The den—his favorite room—was in the back corner of the house, its outside wall butting up against the garage. It was isolated from everyone and very private. He trekked down the long corridor and entered it, intending to do some work and forget about Meredith

Hunter. Inside, he crossed the thick carpet he'd covered the hardwood floors with after Sara died, and bent down to the fireplace in the corner. When they'd built this house, one of the few things he'd asked for was a den with a large fieldstone fireplace.

In minutes, a fire warmed him. Instead of going to his desk, he stood before the blaze, searching. This room, and this fire, had given him solace many times in the past, especially during Sara's last days. Bracing his hands on the stone mantel, he watched the golden flames lick at the logs. They flickered, and the wood spat, popping and snapping. Luke inhaled the earthy, smoky scent. Something about the fire, its naturalness, maybe, always cleared the muddle in his mind, always put things in perspective.

As he stared at it, he admitted he wanted Meredith Hunter.

As a woman.

Just for himself.

For a long time, he contemplated the bald fact, wondering how this had happened, trying to wish it hadn't, but unable to do that, either. Half of him felt truly guilty for having these intense feelings for another woman. But the other half rejoiced in them. It was so good to feel this way about her, so elemental, so right. In the flames, he saw the color of her eyes and the burnished highlights of her hair.

"Luke?"

He gripped the mantel. "Yes?"

"I'm done with the dishes."

"Thank you."

"I guess I'll work at the kitch...Luke, are you all right?"

He shook his head. "Go work, Meredith."

There was a long pause, and he thought she'd left. "Luke? Can I come in?"

"No."

"Why?"

He rounded on her. He tried to relax his ramrod stance and ease the tension radiating from every muscle in his body. But he couldn't. Nor could he keep himself from blurting out, "Don't you *know* why?"

Meredith's eyes widened. "Luke?" she repeated with aching vulnerability, taking a step into the room.

"Meredith," he said in a low husky voice. "Don't cross that threshold unless you're ready."

"Ready?"

He closed his eyes briefly, then turned his back to her and braced his hands on the mantel once again. "Just go out to the kitchen."

He remained there for a long time. Just as he was about to move, he felt a hand on his shoulder. *Oh, God.* He expelled a heavy breath.

Slowly, he pivoted.

When he faced Meredith, she saw a look so intense, so powerful in his eyes that she felt humbled.

"Meredith."

She smiled.

He reached out and placed his hand on her throat. It was an intimate gesture, his fingers sneaking inside the rounded neck of her sweater. He rubbed her collarbone. "This is going to take us places," he said, his voice a raspy whisper.

"Yes, it is."

"Do you want to go there with me?"

"Yes."

He smiled then, so poignantly, so gratefully, that Meredith's eyes stung. He studied her face closely without touching it. "I've wanted, for so long, to have the right to look at you. As much as I wanted. To drink in the sight of you."

She swallowed hard.

"And to do this." With exquisite care, he slid his hand from her throat to her hair then to her neck. He tugged. She went forward fractionally with the pressure, and tilted her chin, silently telling him what she wanted. His lips came down to hers in gentle need. They brushed back and forth, but she could feel the strain it took to keep the touch light. For a few glorious seconds, he repeated the butterfly-soft caress.

Then he increased the pressure of his lips; his hands slid to her shoulders to touch, then to grasp. She sensed he was releasing his need for her in increments, trying hard to control himself.

Meredith didn't want control. So she inched closer, and raised her hands to his chest. All the while his lips moved back and forth on hers. His muscles leaped at the touch of her hands.

As soon as his tongue probed at the seam of her lips, she parted them. Welcoming the gentle invasion, she matched it with her own, and his became more insistent, less controlled.

He widened his stance and pulled her between his legs. The feel of his denim-clad hips meeting hers made her arch her lower body to his. He arched back and moaned.

She loved the sound of it.

Deliberately, he lowered his hands to her waist, letting them settle there, knead there. Then he eased them around to her bottom, where his fingers flexed once again in the softness he found.

Conforming her body to his, she moaned. When she felt his erection, hard and insistent, she whimpered.

Sensation shot through her, causing her breasts to ache, and her legs to weaken with the rush of feminine response.

The kiss went on for a long time.

Finally, he pulled back. When she opened her eyes, he was gazing at her with such fierce intensity it made her pulse thrum.

"Meredith...Meredith." She loved the way he kept repeating her name, as if he couldn't get enough of it. Enough of her. Lifting his hand, he traced the arch of her eyebrow, the slant of her nose, then rubbed the pad of his thumb over her lips.

"Do you know how long I've wanted to do this?" His voice was a husky whisper.

"As long as I have?"

A satisfied male smile claimed his mouth. "You have, huh?"

Unflinchingly, she met his gaze. "Yes, Luke, I have." Then she rolled her eyes. "Though I've fought it."

"*You* fought it. Lady, your battle couldn't be half as tough as mine."

"Don't bet on it." She scowled. "There's good reason for us both to fight it, Luke."

He sighed, tugged her to him and rested his chin on her head. His arms enfolded her. "I know. Mike."

"Is that why you didn't come with us yesterday?"

"That, and because I *do* believe you need time together alone."

She was silent for a minute, then answered, "I...I wanted you there. I missed you."

"I thought about you all day...and all night."

She drew back. "No snow bunny?"

That earned her a swift kiss. "You know there wasn't. How could there be when all I wanted was to touch *you*, kiss *you*."

"Oh, God, I want to hear that."

"It's true." He leaned over and buried his face in her neck. She shivered.

"Luke...what about Mike?"

He drew back again but didn't let her go. "I don't know. There's a lot to consider. Especially if..."

"If this doesn't work out."

He frowned.

"We have to be honest about the possibilities," she said.

"I know. But I keep coming to the same conclusion—it's foolish to pretend there's no attraction between us. I've tried to fight it. Because of Michael. But I haven't been able to beat it for weeks. You're going to be around here a hell of a lot—and I'm just not strong enough to resist this pull toward you." He stared at her. "Right now, I think it's better to get our feelings out in the open and deal with them." He gave her a smile so sexy she sagged against him. "If that's how you feel, anyway."

She bumped his middle with hers. "It's how I feel."

He moaned again, kissed her again and said, "Oh, yeah." His lips in her hair, he asked, "So, you want to pursue this?"

Easing back, she looked up at him. "Of course. If it won't hurt Michael."

"We'll have to deal with Michael...later. But first—" he glanced at the clock that hung over his desk "—I figure we've got about ten more minutes of privacy before the kids get back.'' His eyes turned molten. "You wanna talk, or you wanna neck?''

She stood on tiptoe to reach his mouth once more. "I don't want to talk,'' she whispered against his lips.

THEY ACTED like kids themselves the rest of the week, instead of the adults they were...

Luke wanted to jump her bones as she climbed into the Bronco that was parked in the empty high-school lot. She'd been radiant all night as she attended Mike's open house. And it was heartwarming to be able to share his pride in his son's accomplishments with someone—another thing he'd missed since Sara died. At the end of the evening, they'd stopped to talk to the soccer coach, which had been a thrill for Meredith. By the time they left, most of the other cars were gone.

Opening the driver's-side door, Luke slid into the truck; he didn't start the engine, but raised his arm to the back of the seat and rested his hand near her hair. He took a few strands between his fingers as he spoke. "Have fun?''

"Oh, Luke, it was wonderful.''

"I take these things for granted. It's good for me to be with you, to remember how important these events really are. And it means a lot to me to have someone to share them with again.''

She smiled. "He's a good student, isn't he?''

"Yeah.'' A light from the school reflected the glow on her face—over the invitation from Mike to attend this parent-teacher night. Luke felt a pang of sadness at the thought that she'd never heard his kindergarten teacher praise his artwork, never watched him compete in a spelling bee, never seen him in the fifth-grade play.

"Everyone likes Mike, don't they?''

"Yes."

"*I* like him."

Luke grinned, "I like him, too." He cupped the back of her neck. "And I like *you*."

Smiling, she slid over and surprised him with a quick peck on the cheek; then she tried to slide back.

"Not so fast," he said, grasping her shoulders so she couldn't move away from him. "I want a real kiss."

Innocent eyes widened, and even in the dim light he could see them sparkle with mischief. "In the school parking lot? Why, Mr. Rayburn, whatever would people think?"

He raised his knuckles to her cheek and brushed it gently. "That I've been dying to kiss you again for three days, to taste you again."

Her eyes closed. "Do you do that on purpose?" Her voice was as smooth as silk rustling in the night.

"Do what?"

"Say those things on purpose? To make my body respond?"

"Is that what it's doing?"

She nodded.

"Can I see?"

Again she gave her silent consent.

Slowly he unbuttoned her jacket and drew it apart. Still using his knuckles, he whisked them across her breasts. Her nipples beaded under the green silk that had drawn his eyes all evening. "Mmm..." Even to his own ears the sound smirked satisfaction.

She was watching him when he looked up. He said, "I feel like a kid."

"Why?"

Bending his head, he met her forehead with his.

"I've been...aroused all week just thinking about kissing you last Sunday. I've replayed it a thousand times."

"Me, too. I feel fifteen again." They both sighed. "Kiss me now, Luke. Please."

He drew back and tilted her chin up. He started at her forehead. Lightly he brushed his lips there...over her closed eyes...on the tip of her nose...each corner of her mouth.

"Don't tease."

His mouth closed over hers with a fierceness that surprised him. He angled his head, increased the pressure and savored her. Then he drew back, took tiny bites out of her lower lip and soothed it with his tongue.

He liked the way she clutched at his shoulders. He liked her whole response to him. Truth be told, he'd been worried about what scars she might bear because of the rape. But when they'd kissed, she hadn't even seemed hesitant.

When her tongue slid inside his mouth, he clutched back then banded his arms around her. "Oh, Meredith," he whispered against her lips, thinking nothing had felt this good when he'd been fifteen.

Thirty-six hours later, they were in another clinch. Luke was in Romulus on business and Meredith had agreed to have lunch with him. He strode into her office and purposefully closed the door. She rose from her desk, circled it and leaned on the edge.

His eyes never left hers, and he never said a word. All she saw were powerful shoulders encased in a belted, khaki raincoat coming toward her. Her heart sped up and she felt a delicious anticipation race through her. In three long strides, he reached for her, and gave her a searing kiss. His face was cold where she caressed his cheek and he smelled like fall. Mesmerized by his scent, she craved more. On impulse, she reached up and loosened his tie. She undid the two top buttons of a crisp white shirt that carried a faint hint of starch. Standing on tiptoe, she placed her nose in the hollow of his throat and inhaled.

His whole body went taut and he sucked in his breath. "God, woman, what are you doing to me?"

She laughed, startled by the girlish sound. "Maybe I'll give you a hickey."

He chuckled—she felt it where her chest met his. "Meredith, we aren't fifteen. We're two professionals..." He trailed off as she raised her face to his.

Just before she touched his lips with hers, she said, "Necking at noon behind closed doors? Sounds like fifteen to me..."

The following afternoon, they were still doing it.

Only this time, they were back in his den. He'd lit a fire, then crossed the room and turned the lock on the door. Its snick was loud and meaningful. He leaned against the jamb. "It's a role reversal...like my father's gone to the store and I have an unexpected half hour alone in the house with my best girl."

Meredith matched his tone. "Thank God Joey Lubman doesn't drive and Mike had to take him home. How far is it?"

"Far enough." Luke watched her mouth form an impish grin; then he pushed away from the door and crossed to the desk chair. He sat down and patted his lap. "Come here, babe."

"Babe?"

"Well, I'm really getting into this teenage-rebel thing."

Slowly, she rose from the stone hearth where she'd been sitting, all graceful legs and elegant arms, decked out in a one-piece denim suit that made his mouth water. On the way to him, she pulled the tie out of her braid, ran her hands through her hair and fluffed it up.

He squirmed on the seat. "Meredith."

When she reached him, she straddled his lap.

"Oh, God," he mumbled, vaguely aware that he was reduced to one-syllable words whenever she came near him. He gripped her waist and buried his face in her breasts.

Her arms went around his neck as she held his head there. He could smell the faint traces of a light, fresh bath splash, not a heavy perfume or even a sexy cologne. She was soft and warm and he wanted to lose himself in the feel and scent of her.

He felt her kiss the top of his head. Leaning back, he stared up into her eyes. They were dilated, as he imagined his own were. His gaze fell to the buttons of her jumpsuit—tiny silver ones in the shape of hearts. He raised his hand to them, then looked up at her.

She smiled, both with her eyes and her lips.

As slowly as his raging libido allowed, he unfastened each delicate button. He saw his hand tremble, and he thought he'd never been so clumsy. When he'd released them all the way to her waist, he parted the denim.

What he saw underneath made his breath catch. Her breasts were full, and strained against the delicate lace. Visible through the cups were dark nipples.

That he longed to taste.

Afraid of going too fast—and almost out of time—he leaned forward and placed his lips on the silk of her skin over her breastbone. "Meredith, I want more."

She stiffened, almost imperceptively. If he hadn't been nuzzling her, he'd never have noticed it.

But she said, "So do I."

Though slight, and probably unconscious, her reaction concerned him. He thought about the rape again, and how it might have affected her. "Meredith?"

Her body tensed even more. "It's not a big deal. I, um..."

He heard the unmistakable sound of the garage door going up. She glanced toward the wall, then gave him a tender squeeze. "Looks like we've been caught," she said lightly.

Forced to let his concern go, he drew back and studied her. She looked happy, and a little relieved. "All right. Scoot. And button up. I'd do it myself, but my hands aren't steady enough."

And neither was his pulse.

Or his heart.

CHAPTER NINE

"I DON'T BELIEVE IT." Belle leafed through the photocopied article she was trying to read by the dim light of the passenger side of Meredith's car. The two women were on their way to join in Mike's birthday celebration. "Only seven percent of all women talk to a friend about their sex lives."

"Where did you get that survey?" Meredith asked as she switched on her turn signal to exit the expressway that ran from Romulus to Sommerfield.

"From the women's shelter where I volunteer on Tuesdays. We try to provide all kinds of information for the residents."

"It was nice of you to bring along the survey for Mike." Meredith reached over and squeezed Belle's arm. "And I'm not surprised at the statistic. Not everyone is lucky enough to have a friend like you."

Belle smiled, and Meredith was reminded again of the day she'd met Belle at Princeton's rape survivors' group. From the start, they'd shared a special bond, common to women who've been raped. Belle's attacker had been her soon-to-be ex-husband.

Over the years, Meredith and Belle became close friends and Belle had helped her through every one of Mike's birthdays. Usually it took a little wine, a lot of talk and sometimes a distracting activity. Once, they'd gone to New York City to see a Broadway play; another time, they'd camped out in Belle's backyard, and once they'd taken a vacation to the Bahamas. Every year, Belle had been there.

Which was why Meredith felt guilty about not telling Belle what had happened with Luke in the last week. Belle's quoting the survey statistic increased Meredith's guilt. But Belle harbored an unreasonable disapproval of Luke. Though she'd never prosecuted her own rape, as Meredith had, Belle had always been heatedly angry about the chain of events in Meredith's situation. And she'd focused that anger on Tom's public defender, and thereafter on all public defenders. Which was why she couldn't seem to keep an open mind about Luke.

But there was another reason Meredith wasn't discussing Luke. Her feelings for him were too precious to verbalize to anyone just yet. Apparently Luke felt the same way. When he and Meredith had discussed talking to Mike about what had happened between them, Luke had been against saying anything right now...

He'd slid his hand around her neck into her hair. "What are we going to tell him, Meredith? That we've kissed?" He'd shaken his head and that unruly lock had fallen onto his forehead. This time, she'd brushed it back. "Let's wait a little while, and see where this is taking us. Besides, I'll be better prepared to discuss our relationship once the explosions stop going off in my body every time I see you."

Meredith smiled at the memory, hoping those explosions never stopped.

"Where are all the trick-or-treaters?" Belle asked when they turned onto Luke's street.

"Luke said they come mostly between six and eight.

The Rayburns wait until later to celebrate every year, and leave candy outside for latecomers." Meredith smiled weakly as she zipped into the familiar driveway. Her stomach had been doing somersaults all day, as it did every year on October thirty-first.

Michael's birthday.

Belle studied her in the dim light from the porch. "You up to this, kiddo?"

"Yeah." Meredith sighed. "I'm almost afraid to believe it's real, though. This birthday is so different from all the others."

"I know."

Meredith turned to face her friend. "Yes, you do. Have I thanked you enough for spending the last sixteen Halloweens with me?"

"Once or twice," Belle said dryly. "I hope this is a better one for you."

"It will be, Belle. I know what I'm doing."

"I hope you do. I just don't trust Luke Rayburn."

The image of chocolate brown eyes closing just before he buried his face in her breasts swamped Meredith. She fidgeted on the seat. "Come on, friend," she said, breaking the spell that even thoughts of the man could cast over her. "Let me introduce you to my son."

Meredith opened the car door, climbed out and reached into the back to grab the present she'd bought Mike. It had been such a pleasure buying him a birthday gift, picking out the perfect thing, knowing she had the right to give her son a present this year. Her heart was bursting with joy.

Mike whipped open the door before she had a chance to ring the bell. "Hi! Where've you been?"

Meredith smiled into eyes that not only were the

same shape and color as hers, but tonight reflected the same absolute delight that she felt. This was a landmark for him, too. "Your dad said eight."

"Yeah, but it's..." He checked at his watch. "Oh, it's only five of." He shrugged sheepishly. "I guess I was kinda anxious for you to get here. You know, today."

Meredith felt her throat clog. "Yes, honey, I know." Impulsively, she reached out and hugged him.

"It's getting cold out here," she heard from behind her.

"Oh, Lord, Belle, I'm sorry." Stepping back from Mike, she introduced her son to her best friend for the very first time.

"Hi," Mike said, giving Belle a lopsided grin.

Belle bit her lip and blinked. "Hi, Mike."

Moved by Belle's reaction, Meredith slid her arm around her friend's shoulders and together they walked into the house.

As they reached the entrance to the family room, Meredith spotted Luke. He was bending over the fire, adding another log. The muscles in his back bunched and she was swamped with the memory of how those muscles felt under her hands, just last weekend, in front of another fire in the back of the house.

Then he stood, the long lean lines of his body visible through jeans that were a little too tight and a navy long-sleeved thermal shirt. He spun around when her mother said, "Hello, Meredith. And Belle, how nice to see you."

Meredith's gaze held Luke's for a few brief seconds, then she forced herself to look at her mother. Lydia rose from the couch where she'd been sitting with Peg, Paul and Julie Anne, to hug Belle and then Meredith.

"You all right, sweetheart?" Lydia whispered in Meredith's ear.

Meredith squeezed her mother, thinking how lucky she'd been to have this woman, and Belle, all these years. "I'm great, Mom."

Luke came forward when her mother pulled away. He stood a discreet distance from her, hands in his back pockets, but his eyes devoured her. They seemed to burn right through the velour sweat suit she'd chosen because he'd said he liked her in green. "Hi." The word was husky and heartfelt. Then he turned to Belle and held out his hand. "You must be Belle. Meredith's spoken of you."

Meredith loved her friend dearly. She really did. But Belle was never one to conceal her emotions. Her violet eyes frosted over at the sight of Luke and her petite frame straightened. Luke towered over her by almost a foot, but Belle's whole demeanor would have made Goliath shrink before David.

"Hello," she said, holding out her hand stiffly. "I've heard about you, too."

Luke studied Belle for a minute, and Meredith could imagine his lawyer's mind sizing up the chilly greeting. He smiled politely and shook her hand. Then he turned and introduced Belle to his parents, Julie Anne and to the couple on the love seat at the far side of the room.

Seth Sherman greeted both of them warmly, but his wife's response to both Meredith and her friend made Belle's reaction to Luke look friendly.

Meredith took a deep breath and vowed not to let any of this ruin the gift she'd been given: the privilege of sharing her son's birthday.

After sixteen years of missing it.

Through the evening, as she watched him blow out

the candles on his favorite cake—German chocolate— she kept that vow: she tried not to resent that she'd never seen his cake with two or six or ten candles on it. As Lydia's eyes teared when they sang "Happy Birthday," she tried not to remember that her father never got to see his grandson. As Mike sat amidst a mountain of presents, she tried to forget that she'd never seen him receive his first toy truck, his first two-wheeler, his first shaving kit.

"You *made* this, Lydia?" Mike asked as he removed a beautiful fisherman knit sweater from a box he'd just opened.

"Yes." She looked at Peg. "Remember in law school, how I used to knit my way through a study session?"

Peg grinned. "It drove everyone nuts. They'd think she wasn't paying attention. Of course, she'd ace every exam."

With Lydia's gift, came one sent from Nathan's kids—Mike's cousins. Mike was thrilled with the gloves and scarf, and an invitation to spend some time with them in their hometown about a hundred miles outside of New York City.

Mike tackled Julie Anne's gift next. Four CDs of groups Meredith had never heard of.

Luke gave Mike tickets to a Knicks game. She noticed there were three of them. "You like basketball, Meredith?" Mike asked.

"I love it."

Teddy Sherman rose from the love seat where she'd sat like a cardboard cutout all evening. "Open ours next."

Mike picked up a small package. It was about five-by-seven inches, thin and beautifully wrapped. Meredith tensed as she stared at the silver paper. She was standing to the left of Mike, leaning against the kitchen post, so she could see the gift clearly. She forced a smile, trying to quell the fear that this present would somehow hurt her newfound closeness with her son.

Sure enough, inside was a photograph of the Rayburn family and the Sherman family on vacation.

"It's the last time we went to the Bahamas, Michael." Teddy's voice was sad, and if the gesture hadn't been so obviously intended to brand Meredith as an outsider, she would have felt sorry for the other woman.

"Yes." Mike's voice was low and even, but his shoulders had tensed. "Thanks."

Meredith pushed away from the post and leaned over her son. "Let me see, Mike." The room was still. Taking the photo, she perused it carefully. "It's a beautiful picture, and a nice memento." She looked over to the love seat. "What a meaningful gift, Teddy. I'm sure Mike appreciates it."

Again, the silence. Meredith caught Luke's movement out of the corner of her eye. His gaze went from Teddy to Mike then to her. She read admiration in his look, despite his sadness. *Good.* Meredith had rights here, too, and she wasn't going to let anyone take them away.

"One more left," Lydia said, breaking the rope-thick tension.

Meredith smiled at Mike. "It's mine."

He set the frame facedown on the table and smiled at her. "I know." Lifting the bulky package, he shook it. "It's heavy."

Meredith's heart was so full she wondered what she'd done to deserve this joy.

Mike ripped open the package. The brown cardboard

box gave nothing away. He pried out the heavy metal staples and folded back the flaps. Reaching through the tissue paper, he pulled out her present.

But there was no exclamation of "Wow, it's great," or "Neat present" that she expected when she'd lovingly purchased the creamy-soft leather sports bag.

Instead, the room grew even more silent than it was when Teddy gave him the picture. Only the popping of the fire sounded in the too-quiet gathering.

"I...um...your other one was so battered. And I wanted to give you something to do with soccer," Meredith finally said.

He didn't respond, so she knelt in front of him. "Mike?"

When he raised his head, her heart rammed into her rib cage. Huge, fat tears had gathered in his eyes. As she watched, they overflowed and coursed down his cheeks in a way any teenage boy would battle with his last breath. That he hadn't—or couldn't—terrified her.

Automatically, she looked up at Luke. His posture had gone stiff and his face was etched with pain.

"I...I don't understand," Meredith said.

"Oh, for God's sake." Teddy Sherman shot up off the love seat. "Now she's taking that away, too."

Luke whirled on his neighbor and friend. "Teddy, you're out of line."

Meredith straightened and wrapped her arms around her waist. "I don't understand," she repeated.

"Oh, sure you don't," Teddy went on, ignoring Luke's comment.

"Mom, cool it," Julie Anne said.

Abruptly Mike stood. "Just stop it—everybody." His tears kept coming. "Just stop it." Dropping the bag onto the floor, he sidled around Meredith and out of the room. His heavy footsteps resounded on the stairway.

Julie Anne stood and followed him without a word.

Lydia rose from her seat and went to Meredith, placing a protective arm around her. Meredith wanted to lean into it but she didn't. There was too much at stake here.

"Will someone explain this to me," she said as evenly as she could, considering the fact that her stomach roiled.

Teddy watched her. "I'll tell you."

"Teddy," Luke and Seth said simultaneously.

"No, she should know. It's bad enough she barged her way into his life. I won't let her take away everything that's left of Sara." She turned to Meredith, her eyes shining with unshed tears. "Sara gave Mike the *battered* bag he uses. The Christmas before she died." Teddy put her hand over her mouth as the tears streamed down her cheeks. "It was the last thing…he can't forget her…*we* can't forget her."

Luke straightened. "Teddy, we all know how you feel, but…"

Meredith stepped forward. "No, Luke, this is between me and Teddy." Crossing the room, Meredith stood before the woman who hated her; nonetheless, she reached out and touched her arm. When Teddy flinched, Meredith withdrew her hand. "I didn't know about the bag, Teddy. Believe it or not, I wouldn't have bought him a new one if I'd known. I don't want to take Sara's place." She glanced at Luke. "In any way." Looking back to Teddy, she said, "But I do want my own place in Mike's life. I lost him once, and I won't lose him again. I'm sorry if you can't accept that. Or if it frightens you. But I'm here to stay, so you'll have to work it through somehow." Meredith gestured toward her gift. "I'll bring the bag back. I'm sorry it ruined the party." Taking in a deep breath, she finished, "Now, I'll go see to my son." With as much aplomb as she could muster, she turned and walked out of the room.

MIKE HEARD THE KNOCK on his door.

Julie Anne asked from the bed, "You wanna see anybody?"

From his stance at the window, looking out at the stars, he said, "Only Meredith."

Julie Anne got off the bed and opened the door. "Hi," he heard her say.

"Hi."

Mike's gut clenched at the rawness of Meredith's voice.

"He wants to see you, Meredith..." There was a shuffling behind him, then he heard the door close.

In seconds, he felt a hand on his shoulder, a firm but gentle hand that belonged to his mother.

"You okay?" she asked.

He nodded, his throat full of too many emotions to handle.

"I'm sorry about the bag, Mike. I didn't know."

Still facing away from her—he was afraid to look at her, afraid he'd lose it again—he said, "I know you didn't. It's okay."

"I'll bring the bag back."

Propelled by the crazy things he was feeling, he whirled. "No! I don't want you to bring it back! Don't...just don't...it will mean...I want the bag...I want...I want you in my life, Meredith. Don't take it back."

He stared at her for a minute, then threw himself into her arms. She caught him solidly to her, cradling his head against her.

"Don't take it back. Please. And don't go away."

She gripped him tighter. "Oh, Mike. I won't go away. Ever."

He burrowed into her, feeling like a fool, but unable to stop the flood. "Promise?"

"I promise."

She held him and let him cry, soothing him with a hand through his hair, one down his back. It felt so good to have a mother touch him like that again. He'd missed it so much, and he hadn't even known it.

When he was a little more composed, he pulled back. He ran both hands over his eyes, and shook his head. "I'm sorry I lost it."

"Oh, sweetie, never be sorry to show how you feel. Especially with me." She smiled. "Especially with your mother."

It was the first time she'd called herself that. He'd noticed how carefully she always avoided using the word before. He never thought he'd hear her say it— never thought he'd *want* to hear her say it.

But he did. He wanted to hear her say it really bad.

LUKE WAS IMMOBILIZED by the events of the evening. Standing by the floor-to-ceiling windows of the family room, he tried to think of something he could have done to avert what had happened earlier.

He'd had such high expectations for tonight, primarily because both Mike and Meredith had. His son had bubbled around all day at the prospect of having Meredith at his birthday party. And Luke had talked to her several times on the phone since last week and felt the same anticipation coming from her.

And then disaster struck.

"Dad?"

Luke turned at the sound of Mike's voice. Before him was an image he knew he'd never forget in a lifetime: his son stood, red-eyed but relaxed, with his arm around Meredith's shoulders. She had her arm encircling his waist—but it was the look of utter peace on their faces that intrigued him. Both were smiling.

Something had happened upstairs—something good.

"Hi, buddy. You okay?"

Squeezing Meredith's shoulder, Mike said, "Yeah. Sorry I ran out on you." He looked around. "Where is everyone?"

Meredith scanned the empty room, too. "What happened to Belle and my mother?"

"Lydia took Belle home. Your mother said she'd meet you back at your place."

"Grandma and Grandpa?" Mike asked.

"They left, too. Right after Julie Anne and her parents."

Letting go of Meredith, and crossing into the room, Mike stood steadily before him. Luke hadn't realized his son was as tall and broad-shouldered as he himself was. "Dad, I want to keep the bag."

He knew what Mike was telling him. Luke was aware of a dull ache in his chest reminding him that Sara was gone, but it was not the searing pain he usually experienced. Though Sara would never be forgotten—he would see to that—he knew in his heart that both he and Mike had to heal.

"Do you?" Luke said as he jammed his hands into his pockets.

"It's okay, isn't it?"

Shakily, Luke reached out and hugged Mike. "It's more than okay."

From over Mike's shoulder, Luke saw Meredith smile. No tears. No upset. Just a calm, confident smile.

She'd claimed her son tonight. Somewhere in the dark recesses of his mind, the idea still scared him. But mostly, it felt right.

Michael drew back. "What time is it?"

"Almost eleven."

"I'm beat. I'm gonna turn in." He glanced at Meredith, then back to his father, frowning. "Dad, she shouldn't drive home alone tonight. It's too late."

Meredith said to Mike, "I've done it before. I'll be fine. Don't worry."

"I have a right to worry, Meredith," Mike said. "Why don't you stay here tonight? In the guest room."

Despite their agreement to be discreet, Meredith's eyes sought Luke's. Messages were telegraphed.

He saw his son watching them, so Luke broke the contact. "It's fine with me. But Meredith makes her own choices."

"Stay. Please," Mike said.

Meredith hesitated.

"Please."

She nodded. "Oh, all right. I have to call my mother."

Both men laughed at her childlike response. Luke was reminded of their kisses last week and how their playfulness had made them both feel like kids. His body tightened instantaneously.

Twenty minutes later, Mike dumped a pair of his flannel pajamas, a toothbrush and towels on the bed in the guest room while Luke watched from the doorway.

Truthfully, Luke liked having Meredith under his roof, although he would have chosen a different bed. His.

Mike hugged Meredith and Luke good-night, then trekked to the other end of the hall to his own room, where he disappeared. Lounging against the door frame, Luke studied the guest suite with its high ceiling, sitting area, big four-poster and attached bathroom. He remembered designing this wing with the privacy of his guests in mind, and wished now he hadn't been so considerate.

"What's the scowl for?" Meredith asked. She sat down on the handmade quilt, scooted to the wall and leaned against the pine headboard.

Once again, he was hit by a blast of desire so potent it made him grasp the doorjamb. "I was thinking how this suite is too private."

"*Too* private?"

"I can't tell you how tempting you look snuggled up on my guest-room bed. Did you wear that color on purpose?"

She gave him a smile. "Maybe."

"We're going to have to tell Mike soon."

"Why?"

"Because when I first saw you tonight, especially in that soft thing you're wearing, I wanted to throw you over my shoulder and stalk out of the room with you, and forget the party."

Her eyes widened. "Pretty caveman reaction for a liberal guy like yourself."

He crossed his arms over his chest. "Not half as cavemannish as I feel right at this minute. I wouldn't tease if I were you, Ms. Hunter."

She shook her head. "No more teasing." Looking

out the door, she said, "Tonight was tough for him. It's like we made a breakthrough."

"I could tell."

"I'm not sure we should deal him another emotional blow soon...about us, I mean. Certainly not tonight."

Luke sighed, knowing she was right. "Tomorrow?"

"We both have to be in court. I'll be tied up until late. I wasn't planning to come over until Saturday morning." She batted her eyes at him. "Can you wait till then?"

God, it was good to have her flirt with him.

"I'll manage," Luke said dryly. "Somehow. Sleep well." Backing out of the room, he shut the door and swore to himself.

Ten minutes later, he lay naked in his bed, arms linked behind his neck, staring up at the skylight while the moon cast crisscross patterns on his chest. He thought about how Sara had slipped away from him physically and now emotionally, and he felt sad.

Then he thought about how, for a long time, his life had centered around Mike—how he would do anything to make his kid happy.

But tonight—for the first time—he openly admitted the loneliness of being a widower. And for the first time in years, he felt completely alive. Alive...and looking forward to the future.

MIKE WAS SULKING and Meredith couldn't figure out why. If anyone had a right to be on edge, it was her and Luke. Meredith didn't think they could keep their feelings for each other to themselves much longer.

When she'd first arrived, Mike was still asleep, and Luke cornered her in the laundry room as soon as she walked in the door. "I haven't slept well since Mike's birthday two nights ago," he'd said as he unbuttoned her coat and slid his hands inside. He kissed her thoroughly, whispered how good she felt and swore when they heard Mike stirring.

Now, as they cleaned up the lawn and the backyard for winter, things were tense. Meredith and Luke had been excruciatingly careful around each other. Mike had been looking at them strangely as he raked, bagged debris and took the patio cushions into the basement for winter. Meredith had stuck close to him and helped; right now, Luke was on the other side of the yard. The only saving grace was that it was unseasonably warm for the first week in November, and it was pleasant to be outside.

As Mike struggled with a heavy planter he was emptying, Meredith's gaze strayed to Luke. He had on indecently tight-fitting blue jeans, a ragged Stanford sweatshirt and a baseball cap. She sighed and thought about last night's phone call; he couldn't sleep, he'd said. She'd been wide-awake, too...

"What are you wearing?" he'd asked in a silky voice.

"You don't want to know."

"Oh, God."

"I have this weakness...for sleepwear."

"Tell me."

"It's dark green."

"Damn."

"Lots of lace."

"I want my hands on it."

"So do I."

"Inside it."

She froze for a moment, then said, "I want that, too."

"Meredith...I—"

"Go to sleep, Luke," she'd said...

"Mike, I asked for some help here," Luke snapped, drawing her attention from the phone call to the other side of the yard.

"Hold on." Mike yanked the remains of a geranium plant out of the flower box surrounding the stone patio.

His father dropped the rake he'd been using to anchor a load of dirt and wet leaves. The action sent pieces of sticks and wafts of dirt splattering into his face. He stalked to Mike and Meredith. "Could you for once not use that delay tactic when I ask you to do something?"

Mike straightened. "Sor—*ry*," he said sarcastically. "What's with you today? You've been on me since I got up."

"At eleven? Oh, excuse me."

Meredith's jaw dropped. Not only had she rarely seen Luke speak crossly to his son, she'd *never* heard his sarcasm. She recalled a statistic she'd read in one of Mike's surveys. *Sexual frustration plagues sixty-five percent of all men...* Uh-oh.

She said quickly, "I'll help."

"No, you won't," Luke barked at her. "Why don't you go in the house and read or something." He turned to go back to the scattered pile.

Mike's spine stiffened. Meredith knew what was coming before he said it. "Don't talk to her like that, Dad."

Luke halted abruptly and swung around. "Pardon me, young man?"

Mike threw down the small shovel he'd been using, and it clattered against the stones of the patio. "Listen, I don't know why you two have been so stupid around each other since the car show. But she's in my life to stay, Dad, so you'd better get used to it."

This time, Luke's jaw dropped.

Mike turned to Meredith. "You, too, Meredith. You might not like Dad very much but you're going to have to accept him because he's my father. You could at least *try* to talk to him."

Speechless, Meredith sank to the wooden bench behind her.

Mike yanked on the New York Giants cap he wore. "Look, if it's so hard for you two to spend time together, I'll have to divide *my* time between you. I can't take this…standoff much longer."

Luke closed his eyes. All his muscles relaxed. He took in a deep breath before he said in an endearingly soft voice, "Mike, this, um, standoff? You've misinterpreted it."

"No, Dad, don't lie to protect me. You two have been pussyfooting around each other since the car show."

"Yes, son, we have. But not for the reasons you think."

Meredith rose and stood close to her son, too. She touched his arm gently. "Mike, your Dad and I have something to tell you."

"What?"

"Well, Meredith and I have discovered…feelings for each other that don't have anything to do with you."

"No kidding. You act like you can't stand the sight of each other."

Luke threw back his head and raised his eyes to the sky. "Oh, Lord, how did this happen?"

"Mike," Meredith said softly. "It's just the opposite. The feelings we have for each other are...positive. We're..." She looked at the wide shoulders and solid chest of the man behind her son. "We're attracted to each other."

Luke put a hand on Mike's arm. "And we're getting to know each other better—as people, as adults." He took in a deep breath. "As a man and a woman."

A myriad of emotions passed over Mike's face as he looked from his father to her. "No shit?"

"Ah, Mike..."

"Oh, sorry, but hey...you mean, you guys...you *like* each other? *That* way?"

"Yes." Luke gave her an amused look.

"So how come you've been treating each other like one of you has the plague?"

Meredith laughed.

Luke chuckled and said, "We weren't sure you were ready for this. And we were waiting for a good time to tell you."

"Man, I thought you two hated each other's guts so much you couldn't even talk. How long have you...you know, felt this way?"

Luke grinned at him. "It became obvious to us both a few weeks ago."

Mike sat on the bench. "Wow. This is something."

Meredith slid closer to him. "Honey, it won't affect my relationship with you at all, I promise. No matter what happens."

Cocking his head in a gesture so reminiscent of Luke it startled her, he said, "You mean, if it doesn't...work out...between you two."

"Right."

"We both promise you that, Mike," Luke added.

Mike shrugged. "Okay." Then a mischievous light

came into his eyes. "But, man, if it does work
out...you two getting along...then we could be a real
family."

A real family.

The words brought Meredith a sense of joy and
peace she'd never known before.

CHAPTER TEN

WATER RAN DOWN Luke's body as he stepped out of
the shower and crossed to the bathroom door to let out
some of the steam. He winced as he knocked his elbow
on the edge of the vanity. He had to get a grip, pay
attention to what he was doing.

But all he could think about was Meredith. Visions
of her under the hot spray with him, soaping his entire
body with slick hands while the water sluiced over her
naked breasts, drove him to turn the faucet to cold for
a few minutes before he could get out.

From his bedroom, he heard the blare of the television. Knotting a towel around his waist and grabbing
another, he walked out and found his son sprawled on
the king-size bed, a notebook in front of him, staring
at the screen.

"What are—"

"Shh…I'll tell you at the commercial."

A female reporter with blunt-edged hair, a tailored
black suit and starched blouse said, "Twenty-eight percent of men and forty percent of women say that they
don't express their sexuality due to lack of desire."

Aw, damn it. He didn't need this tonight. He had a
date with Meredith in two hours and was desperately
trying to keep his mind off sex.

"Dad, you're dripping," Mike said as he glanced at
his father, then back to the screen.

"Huh?" Luke looked down. "Oh." Using the towel that dangled from his hand, he rubbed his chest, back and arms as he watched the screen.

"Eighty-six percent of all Americans believe that having a close relationship is very important."

Well, I agree with that, Luke thought ruefully. He looked at the king-size bed he'd bought when he refurnished this room two years ago. He missed having someone to link hands with and talk to in the darkness.

Running the towel over his head, he heard, "And coming up next, what do partners find exciting? In a minute, the top ten most appealing sexual acts."

"What *are* you watching?" Luke asked as the screen transformed into bikini-clad nymphs selling a popular soft drink.

"A special broadcast of 'Focus on America.' I'm taping it for my project. Ms. Jansen said we have to use several kinds of sources. Next week, I'm interviewing a psychiatrist in the city who specializes in sexual dysfunction."

"Oh, terrific." Luke was in for a litany of all the problems a man could experience sexually. Not what he needed right now. "Why are you watching it in here?"

"The VCR in the family room didn't work."

"Oh. I'll look at it later."

"If you'd let me have a TV in my own room, I wouldn't be bugging you."

"You're not bugging me. I like to know what you're doing." *It's the subject that's bugging me. Hounding me. Plaguing me.*

"Can I ask you something, Dad?"

"Sure."

"Was it your idea, or Mom's, that I couldn't have a TV in my room?"

Luke coughed, stalling for time. "Your mother's."

"Did you agree?"

Damn, he didn't want to get into this. The truth was, he and Sara had disagreed on a lot about raising Mike. He looked at his almost-grown son and tried to lie, but couldn't, though it didn't set well to be criticizing Sara's views. "No, I didn't agree with that."

Mike sat up straighter and leaned back against the pillows. "Don't take offense, Dad, but why do we still do the things Mom wanted when neither of us agrees with them?"

Luke sighed and sat down on the edge of the bed. "Habit, maybe. Guilt, I guess."

The wisdom in Mike's eyes belied his seventeen years. "Oh."

"Maybe it's time to let go of some of them," Luke said, watching his son carefully. Somehow, he knew they were no longer talking about televisions. "Look, you sure you're okay with this tonight? We haven't talked much about it since Meredith and I told you yesterday."

Mike's grin was so real, it eased the last of Luke's discomfort over his date with Meredith. "Yeah. I'm more than okay with it," Mike said.

"You know, Mike, my dating Meredith, and your feelings for her don't take away from what we felt for your mother. From Sara."

"I know. It's just that sometimes I feel guilty for being happy again."

"She would have wanted that for you."

"For you, too, Dad." Giving him a lopsided grin, Mike slid back down on the bed when the TV show came on, and picked up the remote. "Besides, Julie Anne says you're a hunk, and she thinks Meredith's got major sex appeal. Sounds like a perfect match to me."

Playfully, Luke socked his son in the arm and strode to the large built-in dressers and closets that filled one wall of his bedroom. Reaching into a drawer for underwear and socks, he heard from the TV, "The third most popular sex act is oral sex."

Luke made a beeline for the bathroom.

AN HOUR AND A HALF LATER, when Meredith opened the door to her condo, more than one of Mike's statistics popped into Luke's head. She stood before him in a forest green dress; it was corduroy, with tiny ribs that ran down her body. It had brass buttons, and she'd matched them with earrings the size of nickels. A delicate gold chain draped her throat and there were bangles at her wrists. But it was her hair that made his heart stutter. It was curled and wild all around her face.

"Luke? Are you all right?"

His grin was sheepish. "Yeah, sure. What did you do to your hair?"

She led him into the living room, and faced him again. "I used hot rollers." Touching it self-consciously, she asked, "Do you like it?"

"Like it?" He reached out and snagged a curl, winding it around his fingers. The texture was soft and springy. "It's sexy as hell. Sorry, sweetheart, I was trying to control myself, but you make that impossible." Gently he grasped her shoulders.

She sailed into his arms and clasped him tightly around the neck. "Oh, God, you feel so good," she whispered, her breath on his ear causing him to shudder. "It's been a whole week since you've kissed me."

"An eternity." He crisscrossed his arms on her back. A fierce hunger gnawed at him, and he tried not to hold her too tightly. "Never that long again." He buried his face in the hair that he could envision, all too plainly, spread across his belly for some of the third most appealing sex act. After a moment, he drew back, then lowered his mouth. Though he tried to be gentle, his lips were insistent. They took hers possessively. He was dimly aware that she was just as needy, so he let himself go, probing her mouth until she opened to him. His tongue met hers, and he moaned. She stood on tiptoe, so her body aligned with his. Of their own accord, only partly against his will, his hands left her back and traveled to her bottom. When they closed over her, *she* moaned. His body jerked toward her, and he felt very close to lunacy.

He pulled back because he couldn't remember, in his whole life, being so near complete loss of control. "Meredith. Do you know what you do to me?"

Her eyes were glazed and her cheeks were flushed. Her breathing was erratic. Then she gave him a siren's smile. "We do it to each other, Luke."

"Yeah." He hugged her close, trying hard to still the rampage of his body. "If you want some dinner, we'd better go now."

He could feel her laughing. "I know what you mean."

Twenty minutes later, they were seated in a cozy restaurant in downtown Romulus. It had soft candlelight and even softer music. His body was still humming, and he was having trouble keeping his hands off her, so when the maître d' left, he joked, "You're part of a vast majority, Ms. Hunter."

"Pardon me?"

"Ninety-six percent of all people surveyed said music and candlelight-type romance was important to them."

She groaned. "Oh, God, when is that damned paper due, anyway?"

Luke laughed. "Not soon enough. You ought to be *living* with the new Alfred Kinsey. He's driving me nuts." Briefly Luke filled her in on how Mike had infiltrated his bedroom earlier with the sex show. "And it was the *last* thing I needed."

"Oh, really? Why?" she asked, taking a sip of water. Over the rim of the glass, her eyes sparkled with mischief.

A waiter precluded his answer. They ordered wine. When the man left, Luke took her hand in his. He turned it over and ran his thumb across her wrist. He felt her pulse leap at his touch and smiled. "Seems you *know* why I didn't need that TV show."

Instead of retreating, as he half expected, she covered his hand with her other one. "Yes, Luke, I do."

Again, he wondered about making love to her. From the moment he'd stopped looking at her as Michael's biological mother and begun to see her as a woman instead, he'd noticed that she seemed comfortable with her body. From the moment he'd kissed her, she'd basked in his touch, encouraged it, returned it. A niggling thought came to him—how she'd tensed that day in his den—but there hadn't been a repeat of that intimacy so he didn't know if the action meant anything. He knew that rape victims often had difficulty with intimacy, but Meredith seemed fine. She'd told him she'd gotten therapy, so maybe that was it.

The thought hit him again two hours later when they crossed the entryway into her condo. They'd forgone their original plan to see a movie, ordered two pieces of Chocolate Sin Cake to go and had agreed to return to her place for dessert and coffee.

And what else? Luke was once again so aroused he hurt. Where on earth would he get the willpower to control himself?

"Still hungry?" Meredith asked as he followed her into the kitchen, carrying the dessert.

He set it down on the counter and pulled her back against him. "Yes," he said, nuzzling her hair.

She giggled. "Oh, good. Let's have some dessert."

His mouth closed over her neck and he took a tiny bite. "You taste better than chocolate."

"So do you." Her reply was breathless. "Let's skip the cake."

He eased her around to face him. "You're sure?"

"Yes, Luke, I'm sure."

Slowly he took her hand and led her to the living room. Sinking onto the couch, he tugged her down beside him, sliding his arm around her back. He closed his other hand over her throat and kissed her. It was a deep, searing kiss that set off Fourth-of-July rockets in his body. When he pulled back, he said, "I want more, Meredith."

"I do, too."

He lowered his hand to her dress and didn't even try to stop the trembling. He watched each button slide open, revealing silky skin...and a dark beige lacy garment with a row of cloth-covered buttons. He drew in a deep breath. "What's this called?" he asked hoarsely.

"A teddy."

"I love it."

"I'm glad. I...just bought it today."

"For me?" The knowledge made his blood pump double time through his veins.

Blushing, she said, "Yes, for you."

With his knuckles, he outlined the lace that scalloped her breasts. With his fingers, he undid the minuscule buttons. With his nose, he nudged the silk aside. His mouth tracked tiny kisses around each breast, causing Meredith to squirm. He could feel her breath coming faster and reveled in the knowledge that she was as far gone as he—and they hadn't really done anything yet.

Eagerly, his mouth closed over one pouting nipple. There was a slight jerk of her body—so quick he almost missed it. Then she arched into him, and grasped his head tighter as if to keep him there, as if she was afraid he'd stop.

He suckled her for long, exquisite seconds. When he raised his head, her eyes were unfocused. He started to ease her down, when her hands came to his chest. For a brief second, he feared she might push him away. She didn't. Instead, she unbuttoned his shirt—thank God he hadn't worn a sweater—and eased it aside. Carefully, like a blind person studying braille, she ran her hands over his breastbone, his pecs and down to palm his stomach.

He groaned deep from inside and eased her lower onto the couch. Covering her with his body felt like the most natural thing in the world. She stiffened at first as he pinned her down, but when his bare chest met hers, she sighed and hugged him hard. He kissed her again, trying to consume her. After a few glorious seconds, she broke off the kiss and pulled his face down to her neck. He felt her take a deep breath, then slide her hands down to cup his buttocks. He arched into her with the first real intimacy of her touch.

He didn't realize he'd raised his head until he opened his eyes and saw her staring at him.

The green eyes studying him were cool and clear. Had he looked in a mirror, he knew his would be dazed.

She was calm, rational. He was on the brink of insanity.

Raising her hands to his hair, she lifted her head and kissed him. But it was different. Still passionate, it was...more practiced, deliberate.

She seemed intent on the kiss, as if she was concentrating. It hit him with the force of a steamroller. She was concentrating on her response.

Unfortunately, he recognized the tactic. Perhaps if he hadn't, he could have ignored it. But there was no way it was going to be like this...not from Meredith.

He rolled to his side and sat up next to her on the couch.

"Luke? What's wrong?"

"W-we need to talk." The words stammered out.

"Why?"

Facing her, he noted that her skin was still flushed with desire. "Honey, something just happened here."

"Yes, you pulled away."

As gently as he could, given how his body rebelled at the deprivation of hers, he said, "So did you."

Her jaw tensed and her shoulders went taut; he expected denial. Instead, he saw the glimmer of affirmation in her eyes.

"You want to talk about it?" he asked.

"Maybe." She sat up and drew together the open flaps of her dress, holding them there with her hands.

He reached over and did up the buttons. Then he said, "You shut down, didn't you?"

"No! I didn't shut down."

"Okay, poor choice of words. You withdrew."

"A little bit."

"Too much for me."

She started at the vehemence of his tone. "Luke, it's how I am."

"Meaning?"

"It's just the way I react." She stuck out her chin. "It won't hurt how I respond. Physically."

"Explain it to me, Meredith. I want to understand."

She sighed heavily, then clasped her hands in her lap. "It's the only residue from the rape. At least that's what the therapists think. Some victims can't stand to be touched. Some completely freeze up. It seems I keep a little corner of myself...protected...during sex. It's not so bad."

"Just during sex?"

"Well, with men in general. I need to keep a piece of myself invulnerable."

An important piece, Luke thought, but digested the information without speaking.

"I'm able to have a pretty normal sexual response, though. The few relationships I've had have been pleasurable...satisfying."

"I know."

"It won't interfere with... Wait a minute, you *know?*"

"Yes, Meredith. I know all about controlling yourself but still having a satisfying sex life."

"How?"

"Let's just say, I've had experience with this phenomenon."

"Tell me."

Luke stood abruptly and walked over to her unlit fireplace. He wished it was blazing out some heat; it might take the edge off the cold that had seeped into his bones. "I'm not sure I can. I've never talked about this with anyone."

Unsteadily Meredith rose from the couch and crossed the room. At his back, she circled his waist with her arms; he flinched but she didn't remove them. Instead, she laid her face against him. "Tell me, Luke. Let me give you back some of the comfort and understanding that you've given me."

He stood stiffly for a few seconds, then swiveled around to her. His eyes were so sad it broke her heart.

"Did another woman have this problem?" It was hard to ask, but she said, "Sara?"

He closed his eyes and shook his head.

Meredith was surprised at the denial; she knew he'd loved Sara deeply. She'd stake her life on the fact that he'd never been unfaithful. And she'd thought he hadn't had a serious relationship in the three years since his wife died, but apparently she'd been wrong. That he had cared so much about another woman in the recent past hurt. A lot. But she said, anyway, "Luke, tell me."

His eyes were moist as he stared down at her. He jammed his hands into his pockets and shrugged. "Sara was sick from the day I met her when we were nineteen. She had a severe case of endometriosis, which made her ill every time she got her period, and a lot of the weeks outside of that. Eventually, it's why she couldn't have children. Right from the beginning, things were strained physically."

"I understand."

"So did I. I never pressured her for sex. It was uncomfortable most of the time for her, anyway."

"It doesn't surprise me that you were so considerate."

"She dropped out of college our junior year to have a few operations. That helped."

"Good."

"But she was always so fragile. And I was always very…careful with her."

"And she didn't respond fully?"

He laughed but it was a sad sound. "No, Sara responded just fine. She was very satisfied with our sex life."

"I don't understand."

Luke looked up at the ceiling, where a circular fan whirred softly. "God, I feel guilty even saying it."

"Tell me."

"*I* wasn't satisfied, Meredith. I learned early on to…control my urges, to stifle my more basic sexual nature. I learned how to make tender, gentle love, withholding a part of myself every single time. The passionate, inner part, the part that's uncontrolled." He looked at her bleakly. "The part you withhold."

Stunned, Meredith hugged her waist with her arms. "I…don't know what to say."

He leaned forward and caressed her cheek. "The ironic thing is, I knew right away I couldn't withhold like that with you. What's between us is too electric for me. But I was worried that because of the rape, you might be put off by my…passion."

"Oh, no, I'm not. I want it."

"I know. I've sensed that in the few encounters we've had."

"I'm glad."

"But, you see, I know exactly how you feel, what you do. And I don't want that to define our sexual relationship. I can't bear the thought of you feeling like I felt, doing what I did—walling off that piece of yourself."

He couldn't have found a stronger argument. "I never expected this, Luke. I don't know what to say," she repeated.

"Don't say anything. We'll take this slow."

"What do you mean?"

He brushed her face with his knuckles. "We won't make love right away." His smile was sad. "We'll work up to it, ease into it."

She frowned. "I'm not sure about this—that this is the right way to go about it."

"I am, Meredith." His voice was implacable. "I've been here before. I don't want just a part of you. I won't accept that."

"What if nothing changes?"

"I don't believe that will happen. I *won't* believe it."

"Luke—"

"Please, Meredith, trust me."

She knew she paled, but she couldn't help it. She hadn't trusted a man in seventeen years.

"That's what this is all about, isn't it?" he asked.

"I guess. Partially."

He wrapped her in his arms. "Meredith, I want all of you." He was so determined, she was tempted to believe anything he said. "I want Mer the Bear in my bed."

She smiled at the nickname. Then her heart constricted. "What if she's gone forever?"

"She isn't. We'll find her together." He kissed the top of her head. "Say you'll try."

With more courage than she ever thought she had, Meredith stared into glimmering brown eyes and said, "I'll try."

THINGS WERE LOOKING UP, Meredith thought as she rammed the ball into the low right-hand corner of the court for a shot that was impossible to return. Mer the Bear was back, if not in the bedroom, at least on the racquetball court.

As if to validate her thoughts, she heard Mike call out from the loft above them, "Hey, Meredith, take it easy on the old man."

She peered up at Mike then over to the *old man*. Her mouth watered. He looked like some college kid in his gray fleece shorts and a navy T-shirt. Raking damp hair off his forehead, he gripped his racket and threw his son a disgusted look. "What are you doing here?" he yelled up to Mike.

"Julie Anne and I got a ride here with Brad. I want to borrow your car tonight. We're on our way to the school play and..." Mike hesitated, but finished, "We don't want to depend on the guys to get us home on time on a school night. Besides, we want to pick up Joey, and Brad doesn't want him along." Meredith knew Mike's car was in the shop for a tune-up. "Man, I'll bet you're sorry we came, Dad."

"What's that supposed to mean?"

"Looks to me like she's whipping your butt."

"Way to go, Meredith," Julie Anne called.

"I thought you were teaching her how to play?" Mike said teasingly.

"She's a fast learner. The keys are in my locker in the men's locker room. Get out of here."

"Sure, Dad. Thanks. And, ah, good luck."

When Mike left, Luke faced her. "You gonna stand there smiling, Meredith, or you gonna serve?"

"I'll serve," she said, making her way to the red lines. "Grump."

"What was that?"

"Nothing," she said, hoisting the ball and slamming it for yet another ace.

She beat him fifteen to thirteen.

Luke trotted over to her after the last point, shaking his head. "You sure you haven't played this game before?"

"Nope. This is only the third time." She shrugged. "You beat me twice this week."

"Meredith, I've been playing with Seth for ten years. You shouldn't be able to win so fast."

"Don't underestimate Mer the Bear."

Luke's eyes glowed. She blushed. But it was true. The fast, competitive game sent the adrenaline pumping through her just as it had on the soccer field all those years ago. Winning had given her a high she felt only after an athletic competition—and once in a while after a difficult trial.

And she suspected that was exactly why Luke had wanted to teach her the game. It had been a little more than a week since they hadn't made love in her living room. In the intervening days, he'd kissed her senseless twice; both times, when she'd withdrawn, he hadn't taken it any further. Instead, he'd smiled and told her it would come. She wasn't so sure, but she was determined to trust him.

Luke slid his arm around her shoulders. "Want to get a drink here?"

"No, I need to get going. I have a trial tomorrow." Though his shirt was wet and his hair damp around his forehead, she leaned into him.

"Okay." He hugged her close.

In the parking lot, at her car, she tossed him the keys on impulse. "Here, buddy. Maybe this will help you feel better. I'll let you drive the 'Vette to your house."

His grin was little-boyish. "Hey, I'll lose more often if this is my consolation prize."

Luke went four miles out of their way before he pulled into his driveway. He was flushed with pleasure, chatting about how well the car handled, asking questions about the engine. He switched off the lights but left the car running and glanced at the dashboard clock. "Sure you can't come in for a while?"

"No, I can't. I won't be home until nine, as it is, and I have some reading to do before I go to sleep."

"But you didn't eat. You met me right after work. I'll cook us something. Do you have the material in your briefcase for the trial?"

She nodded.

"You can read here."

Meredith sighed. "Luke, if I come in, you probably won't even get to the stove, and I will *not* read that brief. We'll end up…"

He reached out and threaded his fingers through her hair. "Are you afraid, Meredith?"

"No, of course not." She let out a deep breath. "But, it *is* getting frustrating."

"Don't you think it's gotten better each time?"

"Yeah, I do. It's been longer and longer until I pull back."

"See, I was right. We've made lots of progress." He leaned over, tugged her hair until her mouth met his over the console of the stick shift and kissed her thoroughly. "But you're probably right, when it does happen, I want to have a long, long time to…enjoy it."

"Oh, Luke…"

"Trust me, love."

The word caught her unaware. He'd used other endearments—sweetheart, honey—but never *love*. It made her shiver, wishing for… Oh, God, she wanted this man to love her. She wanted to love him.

Hugging him to her, she said, "I do trust you, Luke. More than I've trusted any other man."

He drew back and gave her a killer smile. "Well, now, that's progress. Drive safely, and call me when you get home."

He opened the door, as did she; he kissed her again in front of the car as she made her way to the driver's side. She got in, but instead of taking off, she watched him jog to the front door and open it. As he turned, the light from overhead illuminated his rugged features and unruly hair. Meredith was more than a little tempted to shut off the engine and run into his arms.

She felt an old, and now-unfamiliar, surge of resentment well inside her. Why did everything have to be so hard? She let it surface, as she'd learned to do, then took a deep breath and said out loud, "You can't go back, Meredith. Concentrate on going forward."

She would, she vowed to herself. She'd win this one. She'd get Mer the Bear back for good.

MIKE SCANNED the gym and found Meredith working at the food station for the holiday craft show held for charity at his school. Wending his way through the crowd, he walked toward her, his heart filled with…something…at seeing her working at his school event. "Hi," he said when he reached her.

She looked up, and that special smile she never used for anyone else lit her face. "Hi, kiddo. Just get here?"

"Yeah. I saw your car in the parking lot. I thought Dad picked you up this morning."

"He did. I let him drive it here."

Mike glanced over at his father, who was scooping ice cream into cones about ten feet away. "Lucky guy."

Meredith was isolated from the rest of the food servers, but she pitched her voice lower, anyway. "Mike, would you like to borrow the 'Vette sometime?"

His heart lurched. Just when he started to get uncomfortable with Meredith dating his father, just when he thought maybe she cared more about his dad than about him, she did something like this—offer to loan him her car, for Pete's sake. Or agree to work at a school charity function when they'd asked for parent volunteers. Julie Anne said it was only normal for him to have some of these conflicting feelings. But she'd also read him the riot act about not blowing it, that this could be a good thing between Meredith and his father. Mike might just get his wish to live with them both if he let nature take its course and didn't interfere with some stupid jealousy thing.

He saw Meredith's smile fade as Mrs. Sherman came through the line and up to pay for her food. Mike stepped to the side and went around the table so he was next to Meredith. He knew Mrs. Sherman didn't like Meredith. Mike wasn't about to stand by and let Julie Anne's mother say anything to hurt her.

"Hello, Teddy," Meredith said calmly. "Nice to see you again."

Abruptly, Mrs. Sherman's face went white. She looked as if she wanted to throw up, but she bit her lip and said, "Hello, Meredith. Nice of you to help out this year."

Meredith clutched the roll of pennies she'd been opening. She stared at Mrs. Sherman, then smiled at her before the woman left.

Mike backed up a step and relaxed his shoulders. "Mrs. Sherman seemed a little friendlier today."

Staring at him, Meredith nodded. "I'm okay with this, Mike."

He widened his eyes innocently. "What?"

She gave him a knowing grin. "You guys don't fool me. You and your dad both have that knight-in-shining-armor streak. I appreciate the gesture, but I can take care of myself."

The line had slowed down again so Mike said, "Can I ask you something?"

"Of course."

"Isn't it nice to have someone take care of you once in a while? Sometimes, I like it when Dad does that for me."

At first, she frowned; then it turned into another smile. "Yeah, I guess I do. I'm just not used to it. But it does feel good." She reached out and squeezed his shoulder. "Just so you guys don't go chauvinist on me."

He was about to give her some smart remark, when Kip Freeman came up behind him and Meredith turned to help a customer.

"Hey, Rayburn, going in for older women these days?" Kip asked.

Mike's eyes narrowed on the soccer player who stood before him. He saw Brad Sloan come up behind Kip. Both had glassy eyes, were chewing gum and sniffling. "What you up to, Freeman?" he asked pointedly.

"Not what *you* are...or what you might be...ah, *up* to." He leered at Meredith. "Who's the fox?"

"That fox is Rayburn's old man's chick," Brad said. "She'd make some stepmother, wouldn't she?" Brad punched Kip's arm, causing the other boy to stagger a bit.

"Hey, watch it," Kip said.

"Watch your *mouth,* Sloan," Mike warned.

"Hi, Mike." The squeaky voice from behind distracted all three of them.

"Hi, Joey," Mike said cautiously. He scanned his soccer buddies. Obviously, these guys were high. If they'd start something with *him*...which they usually didn't dare do...he hated to see what they'd lay on poor Joey.

"Hey, if it isn't dorkhead Joey," Sloan said. "How ya doin', Lubman?"

Joey pushed his glasses up. "Great." He looked around. "You guys come to help out for charity?"

"Nope. We came to pick up girls. How about you?"

Joey turned red.

"He wouldn't know what to do with a girl if he had one on top of him," Kip said, and snorted.

Joey backed up a step.

Kip pushed him back another. "Would ya, Lubby?"

Joey swallowed hard.

Mike said, "Hey, you guys, Mr. Creighton's coming over here. I'd cool it, if I were you. If you know what I mean."

Faster than he thought they could move, given their

state, Kip Freeman took off, with Brad Sloan following.

Mike's father came up behind Joey. "What's going on here, Mike?" he asked, placing a hand on Joey's shoulder.

"Um, nothing. Joey, want to get some pizza?"

Joey looked from him to Mike's father and back to Mike again. "Sure."

"See you later, Dad."

Concerned, Luke watched his son hustle off with his friend and shook his head. Something didn't feel right. He'd seen Mike face down his two soccer buddies, then inch his way in between them and Joey.

"Luke?" he heard from behind.

He turned to face Meredith and all thoughts of the teenagers scattered like the first snowflakes of winter. Today, she was dressed in white—the leg things again and a white sweater. The garment was baggy, but when she moved a certain way, it jump-started his pulse. Her hair was straight and shiny and the lights from the gym accented its reddish tints.

"Hi, sweetheart." His throat clogged with desire. She could shift his body into overdrive in seconds. He leaned over the table, bracing his hands on either side of the money box. "Do you know how sexy you look today?"

Red tinged her checks. She lowered her eyelids provocatively, then raised them up again. The green was almost obscured by the black irises and the black line that rimmed them. "How sexy?"

He straightened or he would have kissed her right there in front of Mike's principal and Teddy Sherman. "You drive me to distraction, woman," he said as he stepped back. "Especially when you flirt with me."

"You do the same to me."

Sucking in a deep breath, he asked, "Want something?"

She licked her lips and he swallowed hard. "Ice cream."

The sweets bar was about ten feet away from cashout. It took him every inch of the distance to get his body to function normally. By the time he got there, her flirting gave him an idea. Scooping out pistachio, her favorite, he piled a cone high and returned to the cashier station. Before he gave it to her, he locked his eyes with hers and sunk his teeth into the creamy treat. He licked his lips after he swallowed. Her eyes dropped to his mouth and he saw her squirm. He handed her the cone and left without a word.

The next time he caught her eye, he had a cookie raised to his mouth. Again, hooking her gaze, he bit into the chocolate chip, pulled it apart with his teeth and chewed ever so slowly. Her face got red and she turned away.

The third time, he sidetracked her in the hall coming off a break. She had a small mound of cotton candy with her. "Mmm, looks good," he said, eyeing it.

She smiled. "It is."

"Feed me a piece," he said huskily, lifting his arm to brace himself against the wall and be closer to her. Without a word, and once again ensnaring her eyes, he watched as she pulled off a section of the sugary confection and raised it to his mouth. His lips closed around it, and her fingers. Reaching up, he held her arm in place by her wrist. The candy melted on his tongue, then he slowly licked first one of her fingers, then each in turn and finally the last. When he finished, she was breathing fast.

According to his body's sensors, things were going just fine.

CHAPTER ELEVEN

"I REALLY SHOULD let you drive." Luke grasped Meredith's neck as they headed to her car after their noon-to-five shift at the craft show. The weight of his hand felt good.

"I thought you wanted to handle the 'Vette again." Actually, she didn't care who drove; she wished they could fly back to Romulus.

"I do, and I am," he said, opening the passenger side of the car and assisting her in. When he got in behind the steering wheel, he continued, "But the newest polls show that women who drive a stick shift are the sexiest to men." He kissed her on the nose and whispered, "I agree."

Meredith clung to his bomber jacket. She was too aroused to question him, so she didn't ask about the absurd statistic.

"Mike's research is getting into the finesse stage," he said as he started the car and headed for the expressway to Romulus. The collar of his jacket was standing up straight, reminding her of James Dean.

"Oh, great."

"Something wrong, Meredith?" He smirked, sliding his hand from the wheel to her knee. "I like this outfit, by the way."

"Thanks. It's comfortable."

"The surveys show that women who dress comfortably are found to be the most sexually appealing to men."

"Luke…"

He flicked on his turn signal and checked the rear-view mirror, ignoring her warning. Carefully, he drove up the ramp and passed several cars before he got back into the slower lane and returned his hand to her knee. "Are you ready for dinner?" he asked casually. Too casually.

"Are you kidding? With all the junk I ate?"

"You know, that's another thing. *Glamour* did a poll that shows women who eat heartily are far more likely to be pursued than dressing-on-the-side gals. Wasn't that ice cream good, Meredith? And the cotton candy? Did I see you sneak a piece of pizza?"

She giggled; she couldn't help it. "*You* are some-thing else, Rayburn."

Again, he didn't respond. Instead, he nestled his hand on the inside of her knee. His large masculine hand that looked so strong but she knew could be so gentle. Sliding it up her thigh, kneading her soft flesh, he told her—this time, without words—just how sexy he found her. Except for when he had to shift, he left his hand there the entire trip home.

When they reached her condo, she fumbled so badly with the key, he took it out of her hands. She noticed his own shook a bit as he opened the door, pulled her inside, shut it and turned the lock.

Early-evening November light slanted through the half-closed blinds of the living room. The air was slightly chilled, as she'd turned down the heat before she left that morning. In the middle of the condo, he shucked off his coat, tossed it to a chair and drew her to him. He slid the jacket off her shoulders and let it fall to the floor. His hands rested lightly on her hips. Unashamedly, he asked, "Where to, Meredith?" His brown eyes deepened to dark burgundy and were just as intoxicating.

"Upstairs, first door on the right."

Leaning over, he put his arm around her back and under her knees and lifted her. He didn't ask if she was sure; he just pivoted and strode to the stairs. She wound her arms around his neck and breathed in the aftershave he'd used that morning. His hair was a little too long and brushed his shirt collar. She fingered it lovingly.

Even carrying her, he took the steps two at a time. Nudging the door open with his foot, he headed straight for the bed. When they reached it, he kissed her with exquisite gentleness and laid her down on the fluffy comforter. His eyes flared at her spread out before him. His Adam's apple bobbed erratically. Except when he tugged his sweater over his head, he never let go of her gaze. Even slower, he unbuttoned his shirt, revealing a track of hair that was a shade darker than the hair on his head. Her eyes dropped to his jeans as he unsnapped the button, then kicked off his shoes.

He looked so male and so sexy that her heart thumped wildly in her chest. He put a knee on the bed; bracing his arms on either side of her, his biceps bunched. "You are so lovely, you take my breath away. I want you so much."

Carefully, as if he was controlling himself, his hands went to the hem of her sweater. His knuckles grazed her stomach as he slid the knit fabric up her body. After he eased the garment over her head, he bent down and kissed the cleavage enhanced by her ecru demicup bra. Then he went for her leggings; she felt his fingertips brush the skin at her waist, her hips, her knees and her ankles. He stopped to pull off her socks and shoes, then removed the leggings. When he straightened, his eyes devoured every inch of her before he lay down next to her. He cupped her breast, nuzzling it. "You always smell so good. What is it?"

"Jean Naté. A bath splash."

"Hmm." His hand moved down and traced every rib. "Perfect. Just perfect." His fingers went lower, outlining her navel, then feathering the lace that banded her stomach. When he cupped her, she arched into his palm. "Oh, love, yes," he said, easing a finger underneath the elastic at the apex of her thigh. She felt it slide into her curls, then part her. "I knew it. I knew you'd be wet."

"Are you kidding?" She gripped his neck and uttered hoarsely, "After what you did to me at the craft show and in the car? I—"

He took her mouth, silencing her. Her hands slid down his side, brushing away his shirt, encountering denim. "Too many clothes on," she mumbled against his lips.

"Then take them off me," he mumbled back.

She grappled with the shirt, but she couldn't maneuver his big body. With an equal mixture of frustration and amusement, she pushed at his chest. "Stand up." Her heart hammered against her rib cage as he uncurled from the bed and obeyed. She came upright, slid to sit on the edge of the bed, then spread her legs and pulled him in between them. Circling his waist with her arms, she buried her face in his stomach, inhaling his scent, kissing his skin, tonguing his navel. He must have removed his own shirt because she watched it fall to the floor.

She ran her hands around to his back and eased her fingers inside the band of his jeans. She inched them down his smooth, firm buttocks, squeezing him. Then she slid her hands out and back around, her eyes closed, her face still buried in his stomach.

When she drew back, she shook her hair out of her eyes and stared at the man towering above her. His head was thrown back, his bare chest flexed and powerful, his hands tightly fisted. He looked both big and vulnerable. He looked both strong and weak with desire.

"Luke...I..."

Before she could tell him how much he meant to her, the phone rang. She jumped, but his hands came down on her shoulders to calm her. "Let it go, love."

Gazing up at him, she murmured, "All right." The answering machine was on, anyway. She buried her face in his stomach again and reached for his zipper. Easing it down revealed navy blue stretch briefs. She kissed the top of them.

From the nightstand, she heard, "Meredith, this is Mike. Oh, man, I was sure you guys would be there. I'm...in trouble." Her son's voice on the upstairs machine sobered her like nothing else could have.

She pulled back just as Luke jerked away from her. He lunged for the phone and snatched up the receiver. "Mike, it's Dad. What's wrong?"

Meredith listened to Luke's end of the conversation. "Yes...uh-huh...Was anyone hurt?...Did they put ice on it?...No....We'll be there as soon as we can. Seth? Oh, okay, then we'll meet you at home and talk with the school tomorrow. Mike, listen to me. It's okay. We'll talk more when I get there."

Luke sighed heavily as he hung up. Meredith's heart

was beating double time in her chest. "What happened?"

"Mike got in a fight at the craft show."

"Mike? *Our* Mike?"

His smile was faint. "Yeah. Seems Brad Sloan and Kip Freeman started picking on Joey when he and Mike and Julie Anne were at a booth. I...think those guys were hassling Mike earlier, but I got distracted and didn't pursue it." He ran a hand over his face. "Anyway, Freeman took Joey's glasses and tossed them around. Mike tried to get them back, and Freeman slugged him. *Our* Mike hit him back. The school's furious about the fight and is instituting disciplinary action."

"Was he hurt?"

"A split lip."

"Oh...that's not too bad, is it?"

Luke shook his head, then raked her body with a purely sexual gaze. She'd forgotten she was almost undressed. Standing, she reached for her sweater, but Luke grabbed her around the waist and pulled her to him, her back against his chest. "Your kid is okay, Meredith, though I *am* worried about these soccer guys." He nibbled at her neck and made her shiver. "Because we can't finish this, I think Mike's dad is in more pain right now than Mike is."

She turned in his arms, lowered her hand and cupped him boldly. "I believe it." She reached up on tiptoe and whispered in his ear, "So is Mike's mom."

ON TUESDAY, two nights later, Meredith let herself into her condo, balancing her briefcase, the *Romulus Chronicle* and some Chinese takeout. Exhausted from a day spent in court, and a weekend trying to straighten out the mess with Mike, she plopped everything down on the kitchen table, ducked upstairs and changed into comfortable pink sweats.

The surveys show that women who dress comfortably are found to be the most sexually appealing to men.

She smiled as she thought about Luke's teasing her and where it almost led them. Frustrated because they hadn't been able to finally make love, she distracted herself with thoughts of Mike. After Luke haggled with the principal on Sunday, Mike ended up suspended from school for one day. The other boys got a week, and after-school detention for the month. Luke was furious with the administration because he believed Mike had been justifiably provoked. But Creighton had explained that it was policy for anyone fighting on school grounds to be suspended. Eventually, Luke had relented. Mike had taken it better than his father had, saying sagely, "Life isn't fair."

That had wrung a slight smile out of Luke, and behind Mike's back he'd given Meredith a searing look.

The smell of sweet-and-sour pork wafted out of the take-out cartons as she poured herself some tea and dug in.

You know, that's another thing. Glamour *did a poll that shows women who eat heartily are far more likely to be pursued than dressing-on-the-side gals.*

Damn, she couldn't stop thinking about him. How he'd looked half dressed in her bedroom. How his muscles bunched under her hands. How his skin tasted.

She yanked open the evening paper to distract herself. Her mouth gaped as she saw Luke on the front page in living color, next to another picture of an innocuous-looking man in a business suit. A sixth sense forewarned her this was not good news. The headline read, Sex Offender Strikes Again. Underneath Luke's picture was a caption, Federal Public Defender Criticized for Getting Confessed Offender Off Last Year.

Meredith's hands clenched on the paper, wrinkling it as she consumed the story. Thirteen months ago, while still working for the county P.D.'s office, Lucas Rayburn defended a laid-off junior executive from a small company just outside Romulus who had been accused of sexually abusing a woman in her apartment. The incident had kinky overtones—the perpetrator made the woman strip, cook dinner for him and parade around naked. The ordeal had gone on for six hours. The case had gone to trial; the man had testified that it was all consensual and that the woman was feeling guilty now. He'd convinced the jury, gone free—and repeated the crime just last night with the exact M.O. This time, the victim's boyfriend came home and caught the guy...who later confessed to both crimes.

Meredith studied the picture. His forehead deeply creased, Luke scowled at the microphone a reporter had stuck in his face. He was quoted as saying, "I feel bad for the victim, but the law determined that Martin was innocent the first time. *I* did not. This is the judicial system—sometimes it works, sometimes it doesn't."

In a corner of the paper, boxed in, was a picture of the woman who had first accused Martin. The camera had caught her wiping her eyes. The caption read, Victim Blames Public Defender Lucas Rayburn. In a scathing diatribe, she denounced Luke's tactics at the trial and called him a monster.

Stunned, Meredith clutched the paper and stumbled into the living room, where she reread the entire story. Intellectually, she knew that this was Luke's professional life, and if she was going to be part of it, she had to understand it.

But her heart kept skipping beats. It was a sex crime. The defendant knew the victim. Luke got the guy off. Then, the perpetrator did it again.

Meredith sat immobile in the living room for almost an hour. Juxtaposed to her doubts were images of Luke holding her in his lap as she told him about the rape; facing down Creighton and fighting for her son's rights; gently arousing her to a pitch where she was sure she wouldn't have pulled back had her life depended on it.

He's a good man, Meredith. And he's probably hurting over this. He cares about people, he's kind, he believes in justice.

Even if this case hits close to home.

She looked at the paper again. And again. And again.

Fifty-five minutes later, Meredith rang his doorbell. Though it was ten o'clock at night, the downstairs was brightly lit. Mike whipped open the door. "Oh, God, Meredith. I'm so glad you're here."

Fiercely she hugged her son. "I just found out. Where is he?"

"In the den."

"How's he taking this?"

"Oh, man, you know Dad. He pretends it's okay, that he did what the law said and no more. But he hurts inside, Meredith. I don't know what to do."

"Come on," she said, grabbing Mike's sleeve and trekking through the house to the den.

What she saw when she got there broke her heart. Luke was sitting in front of the fire, arms braced on his knees, his forehead on his fisted hands. Every muscle in his body was stiff.

"Dad?"

He didn't move. "Go to bed, son, I'm all right."

"Luke?"

His head snapped up. His face was drawn. There were circles under the brown eyes she loved so much. "Meredith..."

In front of her son, who had never witnessed any affection between them, she crossed to the man by the fireplace and reached out to him. He stood and fell into her embrace, holding her so tight it hurt. She felt his face at her neck and his hands clasped around her back.

After a minute she pulled away and heard behind her, "Yeah, well, maybe I will go to bed now."

Trudging to them, Mike stood before Luke, who broke away from Meredith. Unselfconsciously, Mike gave his father a bear hug. He also gave Meredith one, whispered, "Thanks" in her ear and left them alone.

Luke sank onto the couch. He couldn't really believe Meredith was here. He'd tried to call her after the reporters had attacked him this morning, but hadn't been able to reach her. He hadn't wanted to leave a message—they needed to discuss the issue face-to-face. He knew the fact that this case was a sex offense would open old wounds. And he also knew their opposing philosophies about the law would jeopardize their tenuous relationship.

That she'd come to him of her own accord, to help him through this, despite her beliefs, meant more to him than he could express. His chest tightened. It was at that moment that he realized he was in love with Meredith Hunter.

"You don't have to pretend with me," she said as she sat next to him and linked her hand with his.

"Pardon me?" He knew he hadn't spoken the words aloud.

"Are you really all right, like you told Mike?"

Luke nodded. She angled her body to face him, but didn't let go of his hand. Instead, she covered the one she held with her other palm.

"Why did you come?" he asked.

Her eyes widened. "That should be obvious."

"I need to hear the obvious tonight."

"I wanted to be here for you, Luke. I knew you'd be suffering. You're a good man, you care about others."

"I do care, Meredith. About other people. About justice. Even though Martin confessed today, I did what I had to do when the first incident occurred."

"I know."

"And you're okay with this? Even though it's a sex crime, and the victim knew the guy?"

"I have to admit I hate that the guy got off. I guess this is why I'd rather be a prosecutor than a defense attorney, but I respect your views on this, Luke, now that I know you."

Luke wanted to believe her. But some doubt, some niggling distrust crouched in the back of his mind. Consciously, he shoved it even further back and reached for her.

SHE WAS TOUCHING him again three nights later, back in her condominium. Luke had dropped Mike and Julie Anne off at a rock concert in the center of Romulus, and when he arrived at Meredith's, they had four whole hours to themselves. Meredith knew just what she wanted to do with them. And it wasn't talking about the law or their views on it.

She'd ordered an Italian meal, which had been delivered, set her dining-room table with crystal and china she rarely used and changed into a long, black knit jumpsuit. In the candlelight, she stroked his hand and sipped a light-bodied Chianti.

"You look lovely, Meredith," Luke said, his gaze dark and sensual. "You keep getting lovelier every time I see you." He traced the jewel neckline of her outfit with his fingertips. "This new?"

She lowered her eyelids and nodded.

"Oh, love, don't be embarrassed by doing things like this for me. I love these gestures—this delicious outfit, the fancy dinner, the romantic setting."

"I'm pretty obvious."

He grasped her hand and pressed it to the front of his khaki slacks. "So am I."

Sighing, she left her hand where it was, glorying in the feel of him full and firm under her palm. Exerting slight pressure, she whispered, "Let's leave the dishes."

"Oh, God." He met her forehead with his.

Meredith stood and led him to the living room in front of the fire. When she started to tug him down, he held her upright. "I...I want to pick up right where we left off last time," he told her as he unzipped her jumpsuit and eased it off her shoulders, stopping to kiss the bare skin revealed. It made her shiver. She stepped out of her shoes when the suit fell to the floor.

"They're the wrong color," she said, shyly watching his hands caress pink satin and lace tonight.

"I'll make allowances." He traced the edges of the fuller-cut bra and string-bikini panties.

"I think you had your shirt off." She undid the buttons, ran her hands through his chest hair and kissed each nipple. His heart hammered in his chest, under her mouth.

When his shirt was gone, he walked her backward to the couch, which she'd moved closer to the fireplace for the winter. The blaze crackled and emanated warmth. Gentle pressure on her shoulders made her sit; gentler knees parted her thighs; he stood between them. With increasing haste, he whipped off his belt and unsnapped his pants. "There," he said thickly, pressing her mouth to his stomach. "This is right where we left off."

"Mmm." She buried her face in his skin.

For a few moments, she massaged his hips, then inched her hands around to his butt. Firm and smooth, it contracted when she caressed it. She ran her tongue around his navel and felt him start.

He grasped her shoulders hard; it surprised her.

She drew in a deep breath and concentrated on his scent and what he tasted like.

When his fingers dug into her shoulders with more firm pressure, she stiffened slightly.

And when she raised her eyes to his, hers were clear and focused.

"WHERE'S MEREDITH been this week?"

Luke looked up from his desk and removed the glasses he wore when his eyes got tired. And they were tired tonight. His whole body was wearier than it had ever been. "What do you mean, Mike? You saw her Tuesday night."

"Yeah, but you didn't."

"I had court the next day and stayed late at the office. You know how demanding trials are."

Mike's green eyes flared, so much like Meredith's it

caused a sharp pain to arrow through Luke. "Hell, Dad, I'm not a kid."

"I know," Luke said gruffly. He dropped his eyes to his notes.

"I have a stake in this, too, Dad."

Luke's head snapped up. "What do you mean?"

More like a little boy than a young adult, Mike stuck his hands into his pockets and shifted into the room. "I was…I thought if you two…" He glanced up to the ceiling, searching for the words. "If you two ended up together, then we'd be…" He trailed off.

Removing his glasses, Luke summoned the parental side of himself. It was a safe side, just like the lawyer side. It was the man in him he was suppressing—viciously. "Is that what you've been thinking, son?"

Mike shrugged, but angled his chin. The way she did when she made a point. "Well, yeah. Didn't you?"

"I'm not sure what I thought." *Or if I was thinking at all.*

"Did you two have a fight?"

A vision of Meredith assaulted him…

She sat on her couch, bundled in an afghan, tears coursing down her cheeks, while he prowled the living room like a man possessed.

"I'm sorry," she'd said. "I guess maybe that assault case of yours is more on my mind than I'd thought."

Luke had tried hard to rein in his feelings. He knew he was overreacting. But his job, the case, all of it, was too important…always had been, even with Sara.

"Luke, I'm sorry," she'd repeated.

"No, don't apologize. Don't ever apologize for this." He'd looked around wildly. "I've got to go."

Standing abruptly, she blocked his way. "No, please, don't go. Not like this."

He yanked on his shirt and fastened it haphazardly. Searching for his shoes, he didn't look at her, didn't answer. So she grabbed his arm.

"Please, Luke, don't go."

His insides were knotted as he shook her off. Even then, his hands trembled with desire. "I've got to go. I don't know what I'll say or do if I stay here."

"You don't have to control yourself like this around me."

He'd stiffened. "Obviously I do."

For a lifetime, he'd never forget the look on her face when he'd said that...

"Dad? Where'd you go?"

"Nowhere. We didn't have a fight, really. There's...a lot to work out between Meredith and me. It's not always easy."

Mike's face crumpled. Luke was reminded of the horrible night he'd told his son that Sara wasn't going to make it. He tried to tell himself that this wasn't that serious, that Meredith had *not* become that important to them. He wouldn't let her be. But it was too late for that, and he wasn't into self-delusion.

To ease his son's pain, he said, "Mike, this won't affect your relationship with her at all, I promise. You're still going to her place tomorrow, then to your uncle Nathan's for the weekend while I go to the cabin with Seth, aren't you?"

"Yeah, I'm driving over to Meredith's after school on Thursday. Nathan is picking me up there on Saturday morning. I was going to call her tonight to firm things up."

"See, it will all work out."

Mike crossed his arms over his chest. "Are you taking her to the bar association thing Saturday night?"

"Ah, I'm not sure. Seth and I will be back late that day. You're sure you want to visit your cousins this weekend? I could always cancel my plans."

Mike nodded. "I'm sure. I want to get to know them. Can I use your phone to call Meredith?"

Luke looked at his son. He was so transparent. "All right."

He watched Mike dial. Meredith must have answered on the first ring. Waiting for Luke to call? *Don't call me, Meredith. I need some time.*

He'd had the time, he thought as he listened to Mike chitchat with his mother. But it hadn't helped. The wrenching pain that he'd felt when she pulled back, the clawing rejection that he'd experienced hurt then—and now—more than he could bear. Though he knew he was blowing the event out of proportion, he was unable to stop. He was only able to function by stifling it. From experience, he knew that wasn't healthy, but he had no choice.

"Dad, she wants to talk to you." Mike handed him the phone.

Luke covered the mouthpiece. "All right." He ruffled Mike's hair, its texture reminding him of Meredith's silky strands. "We'll discuss this more later."

Mike left and closed the door. Luke put the receiver to his ear to talk to the woman who'd haunted his midnights. "Hello."

"Hi. I didn't call. Mike called me."

"I know," Luke said. "He called from my den. He's worried."

"About you?"

"About us."

"Well, he has good reason, doesn't he?"

"I'm afraid we got his hopes up."

Fear closed in on her at the resignation in his voice. She summoned her discussion with Susan. *All right, Meredith, you had a setback. Now you have to decide if you're going to lie down and take it, or stand up and fight for him.*

"I talked to Susan this week."

Luke cleared his throat. "Meredith, I don't want to get into this on the phone."

"Fine, let's talk when I pick Mike up Thursday."

"He's driving to your place."

"Oh, that's right."

"Besides, I'm going to the cabin with Seth Thursday night." *Maybe I won't go with Seth this year,* he'd said as he cuddled her by the fire. *I'd rather spend the long weekend with you. We could go to the bar association's holiday bash together.*

"Oh, I see." She bit her lip, fighting the hurt his words caused. "Are we going to the bar association bash together?"

"I...ah, I'm not sure I'm going at all. If I do, I won't be back until late Saturday and I won't be able to pick you up. It's in Sommerfield this year, anyway, so maybe it's best if you drive up here by yourself."

I hate the thought of you driving by yourself from Romulus to Sommerfield.

Damn you, Rayburn. Determined, Meredith wound the phone cord around her hand and kept her voice intentionally casual. "That won't be necessary. Lots of people are going from the office." She waited a few seconds, then she pointedly added, "They're having cocktails at Ken's beforehand, then they're driving over to Sommerfield together."

"Well, you wouldn't want to miss that."

"No, I wouldn't. Not the bash, either. Especially

since I have a new dress. I hope you get to see it. I had you in mind when I bought it.''

Susan had said, *Fight for him, Meredith, if that's what you want. The rest will come.*

"Don't count on my being there.''

"No?'' Her bravado was flagging. How could she stop him from freezing her out? What would Mer the Bear do? "Somehow I never pegged you as a coward, Luke.''

"What the hell does that mean?''

"Only this. I backtracked Saturday night. I'm sorry that upset you. And maybe it *was* because of the case. I don't know why it happened, exactly. This isn't a conscious thing. But if you're not willing to experience some setbacks and work through them, then maybe you're not the man I thought you were.''

"Damn it, Meredith. I was hurt.''

"So was I. That's part of life.'' She drew in a breath. "It looks like I'm not the only one that shuts down. You're doing the same thing with me—right now. This whole week.'' She waited before she added, "Think about that when you're up in the cabin with your good friend Seth.''

And she hung up.

And it felt good.

CHAPTER TWELVE

LUKE RAN a finger around the collar of his tux as he listened to Judge Lasser and kept an eye on the door to the hotel's ballroom. Damn her, where was she? Better yet, what the hell was *he* doing here? Nodding once or twice to the judge, who had an audience of four, Luke squelched his anger. Just as he'd been squelching everything else.

In an emotional conflict, men are far more likely to be stonewallers than women. They are more likely to protect themselves by withdrawing. Damn Mike's magazines. When the freakin' paper was finished, Luke was going to burn every piece of research the kid had accumulated.

Meredith had been right about his shutting her out. And it ticked Luke off. To make matters worse, Seth had supported her, if inadvertently.

"You're in a foul mood, Luke," his friend had said after they arrived at the cabin and had settled in before the fire. "Is it the holidays coming up—missing Sara?"

Luke had been shocked to realize he hadn't dreaded Thanksgiving, had even been looking forward to Christmas for the first time in three years.

"No, it's not Sara," Luke had answered.

"Is it Meredith Hunter?"

"Yeah."

"Want to talk about it?"

"It's complicated."

"I got all weekend."

Eventually, Luke had confessed his newfound feelings for Meredith, and told Seth about her accusations that he was shutting her out. But he kept private everything else.

"Well, I agree with her."

From where he stood by the fireplace, Luke had whirled to face his friend.

"You can't be surprised, Luke. I told you this before. You're a master at suppressing your feelings and your real needs…"

So, after stewing about her for two days, he'd come to the bar association reception. He still felt ripped up inside when he recalled the sting of her rejection, how she'd frozen up on him again. But he'd come, anyway. At least it would prove he was *not* a coward.

Restless, he took another sip of his bourbon and water and looked toward the door, then around the room. Vaguely, he wondered if Meredith had ever attended this yearly event in the past; had the mother of his child been in the same room with him and he hadn't even known it? With more than two hundred people present, it was certainly possible.

A group sauntered through the door, chuckling and murmuring to each other as they entered the spacious ballroom. There were six women and four men. Two of the women chatted quietly as they made their way to one of the service bars set up around the room—the one directly adjacent to him. Four men came next then two couples, engaged in intimate conversation.

One of the last was Meredith.

He thought he might swallow his tongue when he caught his first glimpse of her. She was right out of his most vivid fantasy. Literally. He recalled the blinding image he'd had of her that night she said she was committed to a black-tie event and couldn't go to Mike's game. *A flash of a short, sophisticated dress...her long legs encased in misty black stockings...they might be attached to a garter belt and...*

And he'd told her about it, confessed it to her once in an intimate moment. Signaling the bartender, he ordered another bourbon and water. How dare she seduce him with his own fantasy?

When he looked over at the group again, he saw one of the men fetch her a drink. He could guess who the guy was. Mr. A.D.A. Dobson, no doubt, the one on his way to a political career. Surreptitiously, he watched them, denying the notion that he was acting like a kid at a high-school dance, mooning over the prom queen and her date. Dobson was taller than Luke, but not as muscular. His tux was classic, but he'd chosen a red cummerbund, giving him a flare Luke found ostentatious. And he was a little *too* classically handsome.

"You all right, my boy?" Judge Lasser asked. "Look a little green to me."

Luke tore his eyes away from Meredith and her colleagues. "No, sir, I'm just fine."

Lasser followed his gaze to the group. "Ah—there's Dobson." Catching the young A.D.A.'s eye, the older man waved the Romulus contingent over.

Aw, hell, Luke thought. An audience. He had to have an audience the first time he saw her after...

"Dobson, nice to see you again," the judge said.

"Thank you, sir. You know everyone in our office, I think."

"Yes, yes." The judge greeted each of them by

name. Then he said, "Do you all know Lucas Rayburn?"

Luke gripped his glass as they were introduced. He tried to avoid looking at Meredith, but he was drawn to her, pulled by something deep inside him. Up close, his fantasy was even more disturbing. The dress he'd thought was black was a rich green and was covered with hundreds of tiny sequins. It dipped down in the front, had cap sleeves and skimmed her knees. It was a little snug around the fanny—wonderfully snug around the fanny.

Dobson raised his arm and draped it loosely over her shoulders. "Have you met Rayburn, Meredith?"

Luke willed his pulse to calm and jammed his fisted free hand into his pocket. He stared pointedly at Dobson's arm around her, wondering if this was how she was going to get him back, by making him jealous. It hurt.

Meredith smiled a million-watt grin, took a step away from the other man and touched Luke's arm. "Hi." She stood on tiptoe, though the high heels made her a lot taller, and kissed him on the cheek. Right in front of everyone. He got a whiff of her fresh scent before she stepped back. She faced Dobson. "Luke and I are old friends."

Luke had to consciously force himself not to reach for her.

When he didn't respond, her smile faltered. "I'm glad you made it, Luke."

Finally finding his voice, he said, "Yeah, so am I." He scanned her outfit. "I wouldn't have wanted to miss this." Damn, why was he succumbing so easily? He was mad, wasn't he? He had a right to be, didn't he? And hurt. Would one little grin and a peck on the cheek—even if they *were* meant to warn off the competition—make him forget how she'd rejected him last weekend?

A little voice inside him nagged, *That wasn't her fault, Rayburn. Everything she did was unconscious. You're overreacting again... You've been overreacting to this whole thing.*

The rest of the group was joking with him, he realized.

"Yeah, I know him..."

"Met him across the courtroom a few times..."

"Tough break in the Martin case..."

"How long have you been the chief federal P.D.?"

After a few minutes of polite talk, Dobson took possession of Meredith's elbow. "We'd better find a table, Meredith. It'll be hard to get one that seats ten."

Meredith's eyes sought Luke's. Was she expecting him to ask her to sit with him? Was he supposed to say that they'd planned to meet here? When he didn't, her warm, loving eyes became green ice. Very fast.

Uh-oh. Bad move, Rayburn.

She turned to Ken, robbing Luke of her attention and bestowing it on the other man. An intense surge of jealousy flooded Luke. He had it bad, and the knowledge shook him. It kept him from claiming her. Instead, he watched her graceful stride—in three-inch heels and misty black stockings—as she accompanied her colleagues to a table for ten.

If Luke was miserable throughout dinner—trying to catch a glimpse of her, seeing her lean forward to talk to her friends—he was downright wretched when the dancing started. Her crowd took over the floor; they seemed young and vivacious.

Luke felt very old.

God, he'd blown everything. He couldn't seem to get back on track. As he watched Meredith dance, he cursed his decision to come to this damn dinner.

He sulked for about twenty minutes, wondering what she was going to do after the party was over. As he watched her disentangle herself from one partner and glide to another, he realized how attractive and desirable her colleagues found her. Three songs later, when Dobson cut in, Luke stood abruptly. He threw back his chair and stalked out of the room.

Ten minutes later, he returned; the deejay announced a medley of the Righteous Brothers. Luke reached Meredith just as Dobson started to take her into his arms. Clasping his hand over her shoulder, Luke said, "I think it's my turn. You don't mind, do you, Dobson?"

"It's up to Meredith," the younger man said. His eyes told Luke that Meredith may not have seen her relationship with Dobson as serious, but Dobson sure as hell did.

"Meredith?" Luke said softly.

Pivoting to face him, she tossed back her hair. "I guess so. One dance."

Obviously she was still ticked about the seating for dinner. Why wouldn't she be? He'd reneged on his invitation to take her to this thing; then, when he had the chance to make up for it by sitting with her, he didn't. She had a right to be angry at him.

Dobson blended into a crowd that turned invisible once Luke had Meredith in his arms. A little taller in her heels, she still fit him perfectly, her body conforming to his. Her hair brushed his cheek, the aroma of a lemony shampoo tickling his nostrils. Her left hand found a home at the base of his neck, the brush of her fingertips giving him goose bumps. He gripped her right hand and pulled it to his chest, secure next to his heart. They moved slowly to the mood of the music. At a loss for words, he said nothing. Instead, he cradled her in his arms, holding her closer than was socially proper. But he couldn't help himself. He let his body absorb hers, let himself inhale her scent.

Meredith was mad. She held herself stiffly in his arms.

What did she care if he looked like a million bucks in his black tie and tux? Its raven color accented his dark good looks, reminding her of Heathcliff. The comparison was doubly fitting because tonight he was brooding and unapproachable, just like the Victorian hero.

What did she care if his arms felt like heaven around her? She tried not to nestle her head in his shoulder, tried not to inhale his unique scent.

"Relax, sweetheart. Just let me hold you."

It should have made her angrier—his patronizing tone, the endearment. But she hugged his neck tighter as he molded his body to hers. Dimly she was aware that their clinch on the dance floor was inappropriate.

No more than kissing him on the cheek in front of Judge Lasser, though. She'd meant to show him and Ken and everyone that Luke was more than an acquaintance. But he'd rebuffed her. And it hurt.

But God, he felt good. She closed her eyes and fantasized about being alone with him.

All too soon, the song ended. By then, she was dazed with longing. He drew away from her, looked deep into her eyes and pressed something cold and sharp into her left hand. He closed her fingers over it and kissed them gently. With an unmistakable air of possessiveness, he led her off the dance floor, back to her table. Giving her one last meaningful look, he turned and walked away from her—right out of the ballroom.

She didn't open her hand until she sat down. Inside was a key—the older kind, with number 315 on it.

A room key.

To a room in this hotel.

Her heart skidded to an abrupt halt. He wanted her to go to room 315.

Because she knew she should be incensed by his presumptuousness, that she should not simply fall helplessly into his arms, she warred with herself—for all of ten seconds.

Go, you want to go.

No, he shut me out. I'm angry and hurt.

Then why did you stash those condoms in your purse?

Oh, damn, who was she kidding? While her colleagues were engaged in conversation, she rose discreetly and grasped her bag to her chest. She bent down and whispered to her friend, "Deb, I have a ride home. Don't wait for me."

And Meredith left the ballroom, too.

The elevator was so slow, she lost her temper and jabbed at the buttons, trying to hurry it along. Decision made, she couldn't wait to get to him. By the time she reached 315, her cheeks were flaming and her hands shook.

She slipped the key in the lock and pushed open the door.

Luke was standing by the window in the semidarkness. His tie was off, his jacket discarded and the top buttons on his shirt were open. He held a wineglass in his hand and she saw a bottle on the table. At the sound of the door, he looked up.

"I..." He cleared his throat. "I didn't think you'd come."

She closed the door behind her and leaned against it for support. "Why is that?"

"I've been a jerk."

"Why, Luke?"

"Didn't you know that ninety-seven percent of all men are jerks?" He smiled self-effacingly.

She smiled back.

Then he frowned. "I was scared."

"Of me?"

"Of my feelings for you."

Puzzled, she waited.

"I love you, Meredith."

It was as if someone had healed the wounds of her heart. All the years of pain and loss—and loneliness that she didn't even know she felt—melted with his declaration. She was rocked by its power, rendered speechless.

"Look, you don't have to say it back or anything," he told her. "I just wanted to tell you what's got me so churned up."

She stared at him, her eyes filling.

"Meredith?"

Still, she was unable to respond, afraid to believe this was real.

Setting down his wineglass, he crossed to her. When he got close enough to see her face, he lifted his hand and trapped a renegade droplet between his fingers. "Why the tears, love?"

Through watery eyes, she said, "Because I love you, too."

His hand froze. He blinked rapidly and swallowed hard. "Thank God." Cradling her face with his palms, he studied her, as if absorbing her words. Then he said, "I want to make love to you, Meredith. With no expectations. No stipulations. No requirements. We'll work through whatever happens, but right now I want you. I *need* you."

She threw herself at him. "I need you, too, Luke."

His arms went around her, enfolding her in a deep and desperate embrace. Hands tight at her back, he held on to her like a man to a life raft, afraid of losing it. His mouth sought the tender skin at her neck; he sucked there and it sent wild swirls of desire through her. Restless, she arched against his lower body. From deep within his chest, he groaned. "Meredith, you make me crazy. I can't stop these feelings."

"Don't try to stop them."

"I want to devour you," he said, moving his mouth to hers. He nibbled at her lips in an effort to appease a hunger that would not be restrained.

"I want that, too. Do it."

He took her lips possessively. After having his fill, he gentled his mouth on her with a series of shivery kisses.

"I can't believe this is happening," she said, her hands raking his back.

Urgently they slid around to his chest. She tugged on his shirt; when the progress was too slow, she yanked it out of his pants and tore at the buttons. A couple flew to the floor. She met the unyielding contours of his chest with her lips, kissing his breastbone. He grasped her bottom convulsively when she tongued his nipples. His hands inched their way up, fumbled with the zipper at her back. The dress fell to the floor. She stepped out of it and her shoes simultaneously. His arms encircled her naked waist and held her to him;

then he drew back and looked down at her. His eyes sparked with reckless desire. "You are a witch to wear this." Slowly, he lowered his hand and fingered the lace of the black garter belt she wore. He traced each clasp, at first with exquisite gentleness, but as he worked his way to each fastener, his touch grew firmer, less controlled, almost rough.

"The panties unsnap without taking the belt and stockings off. If you're interested."

"Oh, yes, am I interested."

Kneeling, he found the tiny snaps inside and undid them, then tugged off a scrap of black lace. For a moment, he buried his face in her stomach, then stood again. Deftly, he unhooked the matching black bra and let it fall with the dress.

"You are so lovely," he said with aching sincerity as he stepped back. "You make me have to think about breathing."

She smiled. "I want to see you, too. All of you." She chuckled as she pulled off his shirt. "We've never gotten any further than this."

Her hands went to his belt. Without haste, she unbuckled it and pulled it through the loops. Her fingers fluttered against his abdomen as she undid the button of his pants. His body jerked. When she ran her hands down the front of him, cupping him through his trousers, he grabbed her upper arms with a savage intensity she'd never seen from him. "Honey, no, I'm not going to make it if you do that."

"That's all right, you'll make it the second time."

"No, no, Meredith...the first time, I have to be inside you the first time...I..." He stiffened. "Oh, damn. I don't have anything...any protection."

She smiled against his skin. "I do."

He drew back, his eyes intent on her. "You *do?*"

"Yes." She faced him squarely. "I was hoping this would happen. I wanted it."

"You're an angel." He drew her back to him and whispered in her ear, "I hope you've got a lot."

"I do." Slowly, she disentangled herself from him and retrieved her purse, which had fallen to the floor.

When she stood back up, Luke bent over and lifted her into his arms. They made their way to the king-size bed where he laid her down with heartfelt tenderness. He took her purse, got out the condoms and placed them on the nightstand. Easing down beside her, he studied her breasts. "You are so perfect," he said, kneading her with a gentle hand. He placed his mouth over a nipple and she practically ricocheted off the bed. "That's my girl. I love how you respond to what I do to you."

Trailing his hand down her ribs, flexing them at her waist, he finally cupped her. "Ah, yes, and here." He parted her and slid a finger inside her, then withdrew it. She shuddered. "Meredith, love, you're so wet."

"You make me wet sometimes when you're across the room and just look at me."

His smile was male and smug. "Good." He leaned over and breathed in her ear, "I'll remember to look at you more often."

"Oh, Luke." She reacted to both his sexy teasing and the circular motion of his palm.

"Feel good?"

"Oh, Luke," she repeated. "Any better and I'd die."

He kept up the gentle torture for long, sensuous seconds. Then he removed his palm, located the center of her response with his finger and stroked the tiny nub.

When she was ready to splinter apart, he covered her body with his, edging his knee in between her legs, intensifying the hot ache there. "Meredith." He thrust his lower body against hers, making her senses spin. Bending his head, he suckled her; she squirmed against him. He lifted his head and recaptured her lips.

"This has to be soon," he said against them. "I'm too close, it's been too long..."

"Now, then."

He eased to his side and reached over to get a condom. Watching her, he ripped it open with his teeth and held it up.

"Want to?"

"Oh, yes."

She took the latex and reached down. With purposeful slowness and just the right amount of pressure, she rolled it down him. His hands tightened on her arms as she completed her task.

Luke pressed her back into the pillows and scissored her legs with his. He sucked in his breath harshly as he entered her—at first slowly, then with one forceful thrust. Meredith felt his hard length fill her and gasped at the joy and sense of belonging it gave her to be part of him. When he began to move, emotion ceased, thought stopped and sensation overtook her. Pleasure radiated from the point of contact to every nerve ending. He moved a little faster. She reached to caress his buttocks, her nails lightly scraped him, and his restraint broke. He grasped her forearms, held on to her and thrust into her. Spirals of ecstasy burst upon her and she closed her eyes with the force of it. It kept coming and coming, in explosive currents, making her struggle for breath. At its peak, she felt Luke tense, moan and grip her even tighter. The world exploded behind her closed lids where touch and sound and feeling all combined.

Luke surfaced from a pool of sensation so deep, so all-encompassing that for a split second he didn't know where he was. Then he saw her face and remembered every single second of it.

"Meredith." He smiled and arched his hips, moving inside her. She closed her eyes and groaned. He did it twice more before he pulled out.

Frowning, she said, "No, Luke, don't go." But when he cupped her, she jerked with the aftershocks he sent through her.

It was a luxury to see her respond to his slightest movement. "You didn't shut down, love," he whispered.

The curled mass of hair on his pillow was a thousand times sexier than he had imagined in his fantasies. Her eyes were a hazy green. "And you didn't hold back."

He threw back his head and laughed. "That's the understatement of the year. I almost lost consciousness."

"I'm so glad." Reaching up, she rubbed his cheek with her palm. "I love you so much, Luke."

"Oh, sweetheart, me, too." He met her forehead with his. "I can't believe this has happened. That it's worked out like this."

She gave him a satisfied smile. "Believe it."

He studied her face, taking in the fine bones of her jaw, the sculpted nose, the full lips. Out of nowhere, he was seized by a panic he'd never known before. His voice was hoarse when he said, "Meredith, I don't think I could bear losing you now." He knew it was too soon for such a declaration, but he was raw and vulnerable and needed some assurance.

"You've lost so much," she said simply.

He molded his hips to hers, his chest grazing her breasts. "I don't want there to be any more loss in either of our lives."

She smiled. "I agree." Threading her fingers through his hair, she drew him down. "We can work everything out between us, if we both want to." She purposefully arched her hips. "We overcame this one, Luke. I know that together we can do anything."

The words were balm to his troubled soul. It allowed his mischievousness to surface. "Well, let's start with some things we *haven't* done together."

"Anything."

"Ever made love in a whirlpool?"

She shook her head.

He got up, walked to the bathroom and turned on the water in the huge two-person tub. Hurrying back to her, he covered her body with his and said, "After the bath, wanna do some of the third most popular sex act with me?"

"What's that?"

He whispered in her ear, embellishing it with details that made her squirm beneath him.

"I'll do anything with you, Luke," she said, and then added, "I'll do anything *for* you."

Luke closed his eyes with the rush of emotion that swept through him. Her vow was exactly what his battered heart needed.

CHAPTER THIRTEEN

WELL, one of Mike's surveys was wrong. Luke was sure of it as he watched Meredith descend the steps with her son, who for the very first time got the chance to wake up his mother on Christmas morning.

Women have a higher need for intimacy than men, Luke had read yesterday.

It just wasn't true. Luke wanted the closest intimacy with the woman standing at the bottom of the staircase, hair disheveled, wrapped in a terry robe, no makeup and holding Mike's hand. He wanted intimacy that came in the form of secret smiles to each other across the room when their son did something cute, as well as touches and caresses that went deeper and were more significant than he'd shared with anyone else.

"Why didn't you wake me earlier?" she asked as the clock on the wall chimed eight times. "You all look like you've been up for a while."

Peg Rayburn smiled wisely. "Some of us. But Mike just got up and he'd left strict instructions last night that no one else go to the guest room and get you up. He wanted to do it."

Luke watched as tears clouded Meredith's eyes. Her first Christmas with her child had brought all her emotions close to the surface.

First there had been Thanksgiving, two weeks after they'd made love. Lydia was in Florida and Peg and

Paul had gone south until Christmas; traditionally, Luke and Mike spent the day with the Shermans. This year, of course, there was no question about celebrating it with Meredith. And given the situation with Teddy, Luke had been in a quandary about what to do. Julie Anne, bless her soul, had saved the day by having a heart-to-heart talk with her mother; they'd both come into the Rayburn kitchen on the Sunday before the holiday and Luke had witnessed the whole emotional exchange...

"Meredith, my mom wants to talk to you," Julie Anne had begun.

Meredith had stiffened, but smiled at Teddy. "All right."

Glancing nervously at Luke, then back to Meredith, Teddy came farther into the kitchen and sat down on the edge of a bar stool. "I've behaved badly, Meredith. I've come to apologize."

In her fair yet sensitive way, Meredith hadn't denied the need for an apology nor had she gloated. "I know this has all been hard for you."

His neighbor's eyes had misted. "I loved Sara like a sister. She and I were so close. I still can't believe she's gone."

"I'm sorry you lost someone you loved," Meredith said.

Julie Anne crossed the room then, and hugged her mother. Teddy closed her eyes briefly, holding on to her daughter's arm. When she opened them, they were clear. "You know Julie Anne's adopted. I'm not sure what I'd do if her biological mother showed up in her life."

"Mom, I—"

"No, Julie Anne, it's okay. I'd deal with it, and I

know you would, too. We'd be all right, I've come to believe that." She smiled weakly at Meredith. "It just took me a while to figure it all out."

Meredith smiled back.

"I'd like you to come to our house for Thanksgiving, Meredith. I realize I'm the last person you want to spend your holiday with. But I'd like to get to know you. Please...give me another chance."

Meredith had stood and gone over to hug Teddy Sherman...

Luke knew he'd never forget that picture. Or this one, he thought now, watching her standing beside their son. His heart was so full, it frightened him.

"How about some coffee, Meredith?" he said, rising.

"I'll get it for her." Mike let go of her hand.

"No," Luke said dryly, crossing to them and taking that hand in his. "You won't. Go wish your grandparents a Merry Christmas."

"I already did that."

"Do it again."

Mike eyed him with male perception. "Oh, I get it."

"Good." Luke practically dragged Meredith with him into the privacy of the kitchen.

Meredith chuckled and shook her head as he led her to the rear of the house, backed her up to the refrigerator and took her mouth with his. An encompassing peace settled over him, closely followed by a slice of desire. "I don't believe I can't have you right this minute."

She was breathing fast. "Me, too."

"I want you more every day."

"Me, too."

After several more kisses, and one quick dip inside

her robe to caress her breasts, Luke pulled away. "Merry Christmas, Meredith. I love you so much."

Her eyes clouded again.

"Uh-oh. Honey, you can't cry all day."

"I know. This is just so overwhelming. I never thought…" She glanced around at the kitchen, smelling the rich aroma of coffee and feeling the heat of the sun through the glass doors. "I have you, your love, and my son. I'm afraid to blink sometimes, afraid it'll be gone if I do."

"Never!" he said. "Let's get some coffee."

Luke crossed to the pot, trying to control his own overflowing emotions. He didn't want to tell her he felt the same anxieties. He didn't want to make her own understandable fears worse.

But in the last few weeks, he'd been shocked to discover just how happy he could be. All the Christmas preparations had been fun this year, not the chore he'd done out of duty or guilt for the past three holidays. With Meredith at his side, they'd picked out presents for their son, trimmed the tree and spent quiet time in front of the fire.

And the lovemaking. Just the thought of it made him adjust his jeans. When they were together, he lost all sense of awareness. It had been the most intense, satisfying experience of his life. And he wanted more. And more frequently.

Which was why they were planning to go away together at the end of Christmas week. Luke had a conference for a couple of days in Miami and Meredith was going to join him.

"We'd better get in there," Luke said, handing her a mug. "Before your son comes looking for you."

Her smile was brighter than the lights on the Christ-

mas tree and gave him such joy, he vowed it would all
work out despite their fears.

Mike watched Meredith and his dad reenter the living room hand in hand. Man, it had been a trip getting
used to their...physicalness...with each other. At first,
he'd been uncomfortable with it...

"A little of the old Oedipus complex showing,
Mikey?" Julie Anne had teased.

He threw a shoe at her; sometimes she could be a
real pain. Then she sobered. "You know I'm kidding.
Listen, most kids grow up watching their parents kiss
and touch. This is new for you. You're entitled to a
little discomfort. You'll get used to it..."

And he had. Meredith had spent so much time at his
house, he'd become used to their touching, and even
used to the long, goofy looks they gave each other from
across the room.

They'd also included him in many of the things they
did together...movies, car shows, just sitting by the
fire. One of his favorite times had been when they went
to work at a food kitchen during the holidays. Meredith
had participated in this event for years and asked Luke
and Mike if they'd like to come along. He'd gotten a
lot of satisfaction from helping out people who had
nothing. Since he had so much.

Meredith and he had spent time alone as not together, too. His dad had been really busy at work the
last two weeks—with a case he hadn't wanted to talk
about—and Meredith had seemed happy to be just with
Mike. Especially plotting what they'd done for today.
There were going to be a lot of surprised people in the
house before Christmas was over.

"I can't believe he's not begging to open presents,"
Paul Rayburn said. "Remember when he was little, he

used to make signs and picket all around us while we drank our coffee and got the camera set up.''

Mike glanced at Meredith. Sometimes when the past was mentioned, she got all teary. Today, though, she laughed and gave him one of those smiles that made him feel nothing could ever go wrong in his life again. She sank onto the floor next to his dad.

Rayburn tradition had it that each person would open one present at a time, starting with the youngest. Mike had checked, and there were a lot of presents for him labeled, To: Mike, From: Meredith and Dad. ''Which one first, Dad?''

His father shared a quick glance with Meredith, and when she nodded, he said, ''The big one.''

Mike smiled. He didn't really care what it was; he had everything he wanted right now. But he joked around, shook the box and popped the ribbon because everybody was watching. When he ripped off the paper, he pulled back, surprised. ''Wow! Dad!''

The box read, ''Nineteen-inch combination TV and VCR.'' The note was in his father's handwriting. ''For your room, buddy.''

Mike's throat clogged. The sadness the gift represented—the loss of Sara—was still there, as it always would be. But it was joined now by the joy he felt for having Meredith in his life. ''Thanks, you guys,'' he said huskily. Without thinking about it, he got up and went over and hugged Meredith. She smelled fresh and clean and familiar. He went to his dad, hugged him, too—a little longer and a little tighter than he usually did—then pulled back.

Clearing his throat, he said, ''Meredith's next in age.'' From under the tree, he picked up a little box wrapped in gold paper. His hand shook when he gave it to her. "I want you to open mine first. Since I'm the only kid here, I get my way on Christmas."

She smiled and tugged him down to the floor next to her. Tearing off the paper, she opened the box and lifted out the necklace.

Mike loved the delicate gold chain and thin charm it held.

"Oh, Mike," she said breathlessly. "A soccer ball. This is lovely."

He could feel his muscles tense. Man, he hoped this wasn't a mistake. "Um, turn it over."

She fingered the tiny grooves in the ball for a second, then flipped it. "Oh!" Meredith gasped and brought her free hand to her mouth. She was stiff for a minute then her chin began to quiver.

Oh, God, please don't let this spoil anything, Mike prayed.

His dad touched her arm. "Meredith?"

Mike held his breath. Everyone was frowning. Then Meredith looked at him, and he started to breathe again. "It's okay, isn't it?" he asked, knowing it was from the way she stared at him, that the tears were ones of joy. But he wanted to hear her say it.

"It's wonderful. It's...it's..." She knelt up and threw herself at him, almost unbalancing him. He closed his eyes and hugged her. When he opened them, he saw his dad watching them carefully, no expression on his face. Mike hadn't told him about the gift. Oh, he knew about the soccer-ball charm. But the real present, the inscription on the back, was Mike's secret.

After a few seconds, Meredith pulled back, wiped her cheeks, and faced everyone. She gave them a watery grin, cleared her throat and said, "It says, 'Merry Christmas, Mom.'"

Her voice cracked on the last word. Mike's eyes filled. He looked at his dad. His were moist. So were his grandparents'. Man, he'd made everybody weepy.

And it felt real good.

Even after things had settled down somewhat, Meredith could barely catch her breath. She tried to act normally as Luke opened a gift from his parents. But her hand kept straying to the necklace she'd slipped on and her eyes kept going to her son. Her son. *Really* her son. He returned her look with glowing green eyes and that half-man, half–little boy smile.

She watched her mother, who was six months younger than Peg, reach out for the present Mike handed her. Meredith had looked forward to this gift for weeks. Lydia's eyebrows were furrowed with suspicion as she read the tag. "From all of you—Mike, Luke, Meredith, Paul and Peg? What could it be?" She turned over the slim glove-size box and shook it. "It's light."

"Oh, for the love of Pete, Lyddie, just open it. You always did drag this out so."

Lydia smiled. "Yes, because it always drove *you* crazy." But her mother tore at the paper, opened the box and read the card and certificate inside. Then she began to cry.

Mike said, "Man, it's regular waterworks around here today."

Everyone laughed.

"I don't know what to say," Lydia finally murmured.

"Just say you'll come with us," Paul answered.

"She doesn't have any choice, darling. The plane and cruise fares are nonrefundable."

Sniffling, Lydia hugged Peg. "I'd never say no to

spending a month with you.'' She dabbed at her tears and then hugged Paul. ''If you're sure you two love-birds want me with you.''

''Of course we do,'' Paul said. His eyes got a mis-chievous glint in them, just like Luke's did sometimes. ''Besides, Peg's got her heart set on you meeting some handsome stranger and having a torrid shipboard affair. You've got the whole month of January.''

Meredith basked in the warmth of the morning, treasuring the smell of fresh pine and the sight of the blinking lights, as the rest of the gifts were opened. It had been fun buying clothes for Luke, imagining what he'd look like in them, what it would be like removing them. God, she loved him. So much. Too much.

No, she told herself. She wasn't going to think that way. Things were going just fine. Everything was just perfect—except for Belle. Her friend had not taken the news about her and Luke's relationship well. Meredith had never seen Belle so stubborn about anything. She hadn't relented at all. In the end, they'd both agreed not to discuss their differing views on the man. But it saddened Meredith that she was unable to discuss something so important with the woman who had al-ways been there for her.

It was late morning by the time all the presents were opened. Paul, Peg and Lydia had gone out for a walk, and Mike had sneaked over to Julie Anne's to see her presents. Meredith was leaning back against the sofa when Luke reached behind the tree for another box. It was a shirt-size package, done up in delicate pinks and reds, with silver bows.

''What's that?'' she asked.

''A last present for you. I wanted to wait till every-one was gone.''

"Why?"

"You'll see." He handed her the box. "Open it, love."

Meredith looked at Luke. His voice was odd—grave, expectant. She tore off the paper and lifted the lid. Inside was a white shirt with soccer balls on it, several of them, raised and fuzzy, in varying shades of green. She fingered one before she pulled the shirt out of the box and read the caption across the top: Soccer... Invented by Men, Perfected by Women.

She laughed aloud. Pinned on it was a note. It read, "For Mer the Bear." Her eyes locked with Luke's.

I want Mer the Bear in my bed. She gave him a knowing smile. "It's wonderful, Luke. Although after the beating you take at racquetball, I'm surprised that you like the nickname."

"It's not the name I like." He pointed to the shirt. "There's something pinned on one of the soccer balls."

Meredith scanned the shirt. Then her hands started to shake and she couldn't see the present very well anymore. Fumbling, she tried to unfasten the pin in the bottom right-hand corner.

Luke reached over. "Here, let me." He undid it and clasped the gift between his thumb and forefinger—an exquisite marquis-cut diamond ring, simple, unadorned and utterly lovely. She raised her eyes to his, as he said, "Marry me, love."

She cried hard. She couldn't help it. He pulled her to him, his flannel shirt absorbing her tears. His hand gently grasped her neck. "Marry me. Give me the best Christmas present I'll ever get."

Overwhelmed, she buried her face deeper in his chest. After a moment, she pulled back and stared at his glowing brown eyes, disheveled hair and sappy grin.

"So?"

She nodded.

"Say it. Say you'll be my wife. You'll be mine."

"Yes... Yes... *Yes.*" She threw herself at him. When they pulled apart, she looked at the tree, the opened presents, the warmth of the whole room.

Could anything ever be more right than this?

AN HOUR LATER, Luke was whistling in the kitchen as he removed the last piece of French toast from the pan. He glanced around. Meredith had gone upstairs to shower and dress. His parents and Lydia were still on their walk, and Mike hadn't returned from the Shermans. Though he'd told Mike about the ring last night—his son had been elated—he was dying to see the look on their parents' faces when he told them about the engagement.

The phone rang. Luke snatched up the receiver. "Merry Christmas!" he said.

"Merry Christmas to you, too, Luke."

"Seth? Have a nice morning?"

"Yes. Listen, do you think you could do me a favor? I want to clear the driveway before we go to my in-laws. But my snowblower broke. Can I use yours?"

"Sure. If I can find it. I've been having the driveway plowed."

"I know. I'm gonna do that, too, after this."

Luke looked down at the French toast. "I'll get it right now."

He wondered why Seth hadn't asked Mike to do the errand. Hurrying, Luke stuck the food in the oven, turned it on low, grabbed his bomber jacket and went to the garage. He was swearing five minutes—and several little nicks on his hands—later when he finally rolled the dusty snowblower out onto his driveway and headed across the front yard.

He stopped short halfway through the Sherman property. The sun bounced off the snow, turning everything crystalline and temporarily startling his vision. But he could see clearly enough to recognize that he'd been had. Eight people stood in the Sherman driveway—next to a 1977 yellow Mach I Mustang.

Luke let go of the snowblower, jammed his hands into his pockets, threw back his head and closed his eyes. Never in his life had he been so surprised. Never had he felt so loved, so appreciated.

He heard his son say, "Aw, man, now *he's* gonna bawl."

He felt pressure on his arm. "Luke?"

Opening his eyes, he saw Meredith bundled in her hooded coat, green eyes alight, smiling at him.

"I don't know what to say."

"Don't say anything till you know the terms. It isn't quite paid for." She tugged on his arm, dragging him over to the car. "Your parents, Mike and I pitched in for a down payment. But you'll have to sink some of your own money into it to keep it."

Luke ran his fingertips over the shiny yellow surface. It was ice-cold. "When did you do this?"

Shyly, Mike stepped forward and tossed him the keys. His cheeks were rosy and his eyes glowed the same color and with the same anticipation as his mother's. "We've been looking ever since Thanksgiving. When we found it, we got everyone else to go in on the down payment with us. It's been in Julie Anne's garage for three days."

Luke stared at the child of his heart. He hugged him tightly. Then he wrapped an arm around Meredith's neck. "I love it."

He walked to the others and hugged his mother, father and Lydia. "Thanks," he repeated. Then he winked at Meredith. "Although this isn't exactly a family car."

"A family car?" his father asked.

"Yes. We're going to need one." Luke held up Meredith's hand. "We're getting married."

Lydia and Peg cried and hugged him. Then they reached for Meredith, who was being hugged by Paul.

"Enough already," Mike's ear-to-ear grin softened his words. "Come on, Dad. Let's take a look at your gift."

Crossing to the car he'd wanted for twenty years, Luke opened the door and ran his hand along the rich, chocolate interior. It was smooth and plush beneath his fingers.

Meredith said, "Wanna take it for a spin?"

"Are you kidding? Of course."

She looked at Mike. "You go with him, Mike."

Mike cocked his head in question. "Just me?"

"Yeah, just you. I think this is the time for a boything, if you know what I mean. Just don't take too long. I'm dying to see it fly, too."

Luke kissed her quick on the mouth, and swung into the low interior.

His son did the same on the other side.

"Ready, Mike?"

"Yeah, Dad. I'm ready for it all."

"So am I," Luke said.

LATE DECEMBER BROUGHT a heat wave to southern Florida, but it was nothing compared to what was going on in room 660 at the Plaza Inn. Huge, the suite consisted of a large sitting area and a bedroom with a Jacuzzi in a glassed-in enclosure that faced a very private balcony. An hour after he met Meredith at the airport and drove her back to their hotel, he led her to the huge bed and made sweet but searing love to her. As he braced himself above her, he couldn't believe he had four full days to do this.

"Did you know that fifty-four percent of men and twenty-nine percent of women think about sex daily?" he asked her as he brushed damp hair from her cheekbone.

"You've made me a minority." She smiled that sensual smile and his heart did back flips in his chest.

Nudging her with his middle, he said, "Meredith, I want more."

"What do you want, Luke? I'll do anything for you."

Could any words possibly be sweeter than those?

"I know, which is the only reason I dare do this." He rolled off her and padded to the dresser that held his briefcase. He came back with a pile of photocopied material.

She looked at the sheaf of papers. "Mike's surveys?"

"And some of his more interesting articles. Ones he probably can't use for his research project. They're a little risqué."

Chuckling, Meredith sat up and settled into the mound of pillows. "Why did you bring them?"

"For fun. For diversion." He leaned over and traced the line where the sheet met her breasts. "For a different kind of closeness."

"I've never felt as close to anyone as I do to you, Luke."

"I know, honey, me too. I love all the small things we share, all the silent intimacies, all the quiet understanding." He smiled at her. "But I want to do something different with you. Something that's fun, but will bond us together even further."

"What do you mean?" she asked.

His face grew serious. "I want us to share every possible kind of intimacy so that nothing can ever come between us."

"Luke, nothing will come between us. I promise."

"I want to believe that, too. But even though we've come to some understanding about my job, things will come up that could threaten our future." He nuzzled her breasts. "Besides, sex researchers have long known that fantasy is a valuable pleasure booster. One study—"

"All right. No more statistics. I agree."

"Wait a second, don't you want to know what ideas I have?"

"Doesn't matter. I trust you completely. I'll do anything you want." She ran her hand over his cheek. "Anyway, I've got a few fantasies of my own, Counselor. Turnabout's fair play."

"Tell me yours and I'll tell you mine."

"We'll need to go shopping for this." She whispered in his ear.

"For mine, too."

Later that day, they made two stops: a trendy clothes boutique for men and women. And a shop simply called Lovecraft.

On New Year's Eve, the hotel bar was dimly lit and filled with the soft undercurrents of muted conversation. Luke kept one eye on the door as he waited for Meredith. He thought back to their fantasy... experiment. He couldn't remember a time when he'd been more aroused. The harem bracelets...the candy-flavored body gel...the scarves made his entire body tense just thinking about them. The physical intimacy had brought them closer. It had solidified an emotional bond that he now believed would last forever.

Aroused again, he tried to distract himself by thinking about the clothes they'd bought. He tugged at the shiny brown T-shirt he was wearing under a raw silk tan jacket. She'd insisted on both items...

"Too young for me," he'd said.

"Luke, you look like a million bucks in it. These go great." She'd handed him a pair of doe-colored linen pants to try on. They'd bought them.

Apparently, she'd been right. As he waited for her to come to the bar, several women had already hit on him. It had done his almost-forty-year-old ego good, even though he couldn't take his eyes off the door, waiting to see what Meredith looked like in *her* new outfit. They'd gotten dressed in separate rooms and had pledged not to peek.

Good thing, he thought as he watched her slink into the room. He never would have let her out of their suite if he'd seen what she looked like in the clothes he'd chosen for her...

"You can't wear a bra with this," she'd told him as he picked out the dress. Its diaphanous material had slithered in his big hands.

"Nope. You aren't gonna wear one all weekend, sweetheart. But you can put these on underneath." He handed her a scrap of cream-colored lace.

"Luke, these panties are almost nonexistent."

"I know."

Now, he glanced at the high-heeled sandals he'd found for her. They made those legs he loved look even longer. She sat three stools down from him, right around the corner of the mahogany bar. There were two middle-aged couples on the other side of her, the women seated, the men standing beside them.

Meredith didn't look at Luke at first, but focused on the young bartender instead. "Can I have a rum-combo?" she asked.

"Honey, you can have anything you want."

Then she glanced at Luke.

He lifted his glass. "The drink's on me," he told the bartender. "Maybe the lady'll tell me her name."

Giving him a Mona Lisa smile, she said, "Maybe."

The bartender fussed over placing her drink in front of her. Luke expected him to start drooling any minute.

Just then, another woman approached him. "You need a refill, handsome," she said in his ear.

"Yeah, I do," Luke said. "But the lady over there, she already asked to…ah, fill my cup."

The bartender swallowed hard and said, "She did?"

Meredith slitted her eyes. "Yeah, I did. I wanna fill his cup all night long."

The drink Luke was holding almost slipped out of his hand. The woman faded into the crowd and the bartender went to serve another customer. But by then, the two men and women next to Meredith had noticed them.

With a sensuality that rivaled Bathsheba's, Meredith swiveled her chair to face Luke and crossed those damn legs. "There's an empty seat here," she said, glancing at the stool to her left.

He held her gaze. "Yeah, there is."

"Want to come sit with me, big guy?"

Chuckles from behind her.

He fingered the gold chain she'd bought for him. "Depends."

"On what?"

"No bruiser's gonna come lookin' for me, is he?"

"Nah. My date for tonight didn't pan out."

Luke came around the bar with his best macho swagger. He sat on the edge of the stool, his legs spread. Meredith placed a foot on the rung between them. The bartender's mouth gaped. She said to the guy, "He needs a refill. He can have anything he wants."

The man behind Luke sputtered his beer all over his sports coat and his wife's hand.

"What happened to your date?" Luke asked, biting back a grin.

"Well, he got...tied up this morning. And tonight...he wasn't quite himself. So I came here alone." She sipped her rum and batted her heavily mascaraed eyes at him. "You with anyone?"

"No. My date wasn't quite herself, either. Seems she had a little too much...ah...candy today. She wasn't quite up to this tonight, either."

The bartender brought Luke's drink and was staring at them openly. So were the two couples behind them. Very slowly, Luke took a piece of the ice from the glass and rubbed it on her wrist. "Do you know what the ancient Peruvian Indians said about the aphrodisiac properties of ice?"

He leaned over and whispered in her ear. All three men watching them swayed toward her. Her sultry laugh echoed through the bar.

"You know," she purred, "I have a refrigerator

back in my room." She licked her lips. "It's full of ice."

Slowly removing the drink from her hand, he leaned over again and whispered, "This is enough, love. We'd better go. I'm about to deck these guys ogling you."

He pushed his stool back and stood. She slid off the seat, pitching her body into his. "That rum must have gone to my head."

Loud enough to be heard by their entire audience, he said, "Don't worry, doll. I'll take care of you."

Sliding an arm intimately around her waist, just below her unfettered breasts, he escorted her out of the bar.

CHAPTER FOURTEEN

LUKE CHUCKLED from the seat beside Meredith on the 747 that transported them back to reality. Looking over, she saw him shake his head at the magazine he held.

"What are you laughing at?" she asked.

He squeezed the hand he held in his. He hadn't stopped touching her in four days. His strong fingers sent shivers through her body. "It's one of Mike's articles."

"Again? You're obsessed with those statistics."

Lifting her hand to his mouth, he kissed it gently. "I'm obsessed with *you*." His eyes burned with barely suppressed sexuality, then he averted them to the page. "That's what this article says. Most people interviewed said they fear that if they really let their sensuality in, it will overtake their lives."

Meredith's heart stuttered when he held her gaze. "It's overtaken me," she told him honestly. "Because of you."

"Me, too."

"Worried?"

"A little. You?"

She was, but Luke needed reassurance. She gave him a sassy smile. "Nope. We can handle anything together."

Shadows crossed his face. With almost visible effort, he banished them. "Let's get married today."

She smiled. They'd been through this before. Both wanted the commitment immediately, but they'd chosen to wait for Lydia and the Rayburns to return from their cruise.

"It's only a few weeks."

"Twenty-seven days."

"You'll make it through that."

Again, shadows crossed his face.

"Luke?"

The ominous expression vanished, replaced by a purposeful leer. "Yeah, well, I'm already feeling deprived."

Smiling, she slid one arm through the crook of his elbow and pressed her breast against his biceps. She kept the tone light for the rest of the flight from Miami to Sommerfield. They'd be early getting in—about eight o'clock instead of eleven—as the airline had called that morning with an unexpected flight change. Meredith was glad she'd get to spend some time with Mike. They hadn't been able to reach him, it was Tuesday and he was in school, but it would be fun to surprise him.

Luke held her hand again two hours later when they trudged through the airport terminal; he let it go when they reached a corner gift stop. "Get me a newspaper, would you, honey? While I pick up the luggage. I want to see what we missed while we were gone."

Meredith kissed him quickly on the mouth and he squeezed her shoulder gently. She entered the store and found a *Sommerfield Sentinel* from that morning. When she reached for it, her hand momentarily froze. Jerking the paper from its stand hard enough to make the tinny holder wobble, she moved to the side of the store and devoured the news on the front page: Federal P.D. Defends Former Wife Abuser, Now Charged With Bank Embezzlement. Again, there was a picture of Luke. He was accompanied by a tall, good-looking man, identified in the caption as Lou Pendelton. Meredith stared at Luke's scowling face, then read the article:

Once again the Sommerfield federal public defender takes on a controversial case. After having been severely criticized late last month for engineering the acquittal of confessed abuser Mark Martin while working for the state, Lucas Rayburn takes the hot seat on another, similar issue. Louis B. Pendelton was arrested three weeks ago on charges of embezzling two hundred thousand dollars from MainLine Bank. After a surprise internal audit, it was discovered that the teller had a shortage of thousands of dollars in his name. Allegedly, Pendelton had been covering his crime by identifying the next audit and transferring large sums of money to another teller during the audit, then reversing the transfer after the firm completed its investigation. After a routine background check by this newspaper, it has come to light that two years ago, in Bennington County, Pendelton was tried and convicted of the harassment and rape of his wife. But an appellate court overturned the conviction when it was discovered that a tape of the accused threatening the victim had been seized illegally. When Judge John Comos suppressed the evidence, District Attorney Mary McPherson did not seek a new trial, and Pendelton was set free. Rayburn was not available for comment on his client's past; however, previous statements made by Rayburn indicate only information relevant to the embezzlement case would be admitted as evidence. See story on page three of Rayburn's last controversial case.

Meredith folded the paper and struggled to catch her breath.

Even though we've come to some understanding about my job, things will come up that could threaten our future, Luke had said right after they'd made love and he told her what else he wanted from her.

He'd known this was coming. He'd known then what kind of man Pendelton was. And he'd known how it might affect her.

I want more. I love all the small things we share, all the silent intimacies, all the quiet understanding. But I want to do something different with you. Something that's fun, but will bond us together even further.

The words took on new meaning. Her heart pounded wildly in her chest as she paid for the paper and made her way, zombie-like, through the airport to the baggage check. Before she reached Luke, she forced her mind to clear and told herself she could handle this situation without getting upset.

"There you are. I thought you'd ditched me for some hunk." Luke stood by their luggage, his smile wry, his hands jammed into jeans that were so tight they ought to have been licensed.

Sidling close to him, she wrapped an arm around his waist and summoned the times she'd kissed that skin, molded those muscles with her fingers. Hugging him tightly, she wanted to crawl inside him and forget this newest problem. "Never." She looked up and held his gaze. "I got a newspaper. Luke, there's bad news in it."

He scowled as she drew back and handed the paper to him. Carefully, he scanned the article, then muttered an expletive. "This news must have broken this morning and no one could reach me because we were traveling." He read further, then his eyes snapped to hers. "You read it?" he asked warily.

"Yes?"

"And?"

"And what?"

"Meredith, I know how you feel about these things. Last time…"

"Last time I didn't love you like I do now. Nothing…nothing will come between us, Luke. I promise."

Luke knew she believed what she said. But all the way home he was haunted by the fact that her reaction to shut down last time was subconscious; would it happen again? Would she reject him again, or had he touched her so deeply that she couldn't possibly let go of him?

He hoped so. *Please, God, let it be so*. He wasn't sure he could survive without her. His words the first night they'd made love were even more true, after this weekend. *Meredith, I don't think I could bear losing you now.*

He drove home, gripping her hand, his mind whirling with the turn of events. Damn the newspaper. Weeks ago the media had suddenly taken an aggressive stance toward the public defender's office. No one had been able to figure out why. In any case, the papers were causing him more grief than he considered fair. Preoccupied, he almost missed the turn onto his street. Lights were on in the family room when he pulled into the driveway.

"I thought Mike was staying with the Shermans." It was the first comment Meredith had made in miles.

"He is. I told him he could come home when he wanted to, for some privacy, but no parties or anything."

"Someone's here."

"Yeah." He'd noticed a car in the driveway.

They got out of the Bronco. By tacit agreement, they left the luggage in the trunk and let themselves into the house. There were raised voices coming from the kitchen. Automatically, both he and Meredith stopped; they didn't call out, just listened.

"They're using you, sucking you in."

"What the hell makes you an expert on this?"

Luke identified the first voice as Julie Anne's, the second as Mike's.

"I *know* the way these guys operate." Julie Anne hesitated. "I've seen them in action before."

"When?"

"Last year. Just when you start breaking away from them, they suck you back in by pretending to be your friends."

"Stay out of this, Jule. It's none of your business."

"Fine," she shouted. "I'll just go tell my parents that you've got your drunken buddies over. You know my father will throw a fit."

Hearing a door slam, Luke headed for the kitchen

with Meredith behind him. Mike was staring at the back door, hands on hips, shoulders stiff.

"Hi," Luke said calmly.

His son turned abruptly. The look on his face would have had a cop slapping handcuffs on him, no questions asked. "Dad?"

"What's going on?" Luke asked.

Meredith appeared at his side. She crossed to Mike and hugged him. "Hi, honey. We missed you."

Mike returned the embrace awkwardly. He stepped back. "I thought your plane was due in at eleven."

"They changed the flights. We couldn't reach you today to tell you," Luke answered. "We overheard you and Julie Anne, son."

Mike's chin tilted and his jaw jutted out. "It's not as bad as it sounded."

"Why don't we sit down?" Meredith's voice was soothing and it gentled Luke's nerves.

At the table, Luke told Mike what he'd heard Julie Anne say. "What I want to know first is if you've been drinking."

"No, I haven't."

"Were you going to?"

Mike looked up to the ceiling, closing his eyes in typical teenage disgust. "Dad, I don't want to discuss this right now."

"Why?"

"Look, you guys, my friends are right in the back of—"

"Hey, Rayburn—" A glassy-eyed Brad Sloan stood in the doorway to the kitchen; when he wavered, he grabbed on to the frame to steady himself. "Oops, thought your old man—look, I'll just get Kip and we'll take off—"

Luke's chair scraped back and he stood. "No, Brad, you won't." He took several steps toward the boy, scanned his rumpled clothes and sniffed. "You smell like a brewery. By law, if you leave my house in this state, I can be held accountable." Luke put out his hand. "Give me your car keys."

"No way, man." Brad backed up a step.

Out of the corner of his eye, Luke saw Meredith stand and slip into the living room.

"I'm okay," Brad continued. "You can't make me..."

In seconds, Meredith returned with a set of keys in her hands. "I saw their jackets when we came in. These were in the pockets of one of them."

Twenty minutes later, after a disgruntled Mr. Sloan fetched his drunken son and cohort, Luke and Meredith sat back down at the table with their own unhappy son.

"Mike, I can't tell you how surprised I am that you'd be a party to this," Luke said frankly.

Mike's gaze was belligerent. "Dad, join the real world. Kids today drink."

"Not all of them. Do you?"

Mike squirmed and wouldn't meet Luke's eyes. "I've had a few beers."

"Mike—"

"Quit cross-examining me! I don't want to talk about this." He stared at Luke implacably.

After a few seconds, Meredith said, "What did Julie Anne mean, they were sucking you in *now?* Why now?"

The stricken look in his son's eyes twisted Luke's gut. "Have you seen the papers?" Mike asked.

Luke drew back. "About my case?"

"Yeah."

"What does that have to do with you?"

"The kids at school have been raggin' on me all day about it. Saying things about you. Bad things."

Instinctively, Luke stretched out his arm and touched his son. "Mike, I'm sorry you have to go through that. We've talked about this. I thought you understood my views on this job."

Mike glanced at Meredith, then back to his father.

"Tell the truth, Mike. Evasion doesn't help." Meredith's voice was firm, belying no contradictory emotions. It made Luke feel better.

"Okay. No, Dad, I don't understand this time. How can you defend the guy after what he did?"

"All right," Luke said, looking at Meredith, praying she could handle this. "Let's go through it again."

ACHY AND EXHAUSTED, Meredith looked up from her desk. Ken Dobson stood in the doorway, his long torso leaning on the jamb. The pose, and his hand-tailored suit, made him look like an ad from *GQ*.

"Welcome back," he said.

She smiled weakly. Her eyes felt gritty from lack of sleep. She'd stayed late last night with Mike and Luke trying to sort things out, then driven back to Romulus. "Thanks."

Uninvited, Ken came into the room. "Enjoy your vacation?"

Remembering the intimacy with Luke, the feel of his

hands on her skin, Meredith had to consciously keep herself from shivering. "It was wonderful."

Ken cleared his throat. "Mind if I close the door? I need to talk to you about something personal."

"Okay."

He shut the door, sat down in front of her desk and stuck his hands in his pockets. "You didn't go alone, did you?"

She shook her head. "No, I didn't."

"It's Rayburn, isn't it?"

Meredith rose and came around the desk to sit in a chair next to him. "Ken, we never made any promises to each other. We had no commitment. But I would have told you right after Christmas if you hadn't been on vacation skiing. Luke and I are engaged."

Keen blue eyes checked her left hand. "I see." He sighed. "I can't say I'm not disappointed. I thought we had something together."

Surprised, Meredith sat back and studied him. Had she misjudged his feelings? "I'm sorry. Apparently, we looked at our relationship differently."

"Have you considered the ramifications of being married to the federal public defender, Meredith?"

"Like?"

"Like conflict of interest."

"Are you questioning my integrity? Or Luke's?"

His eyebrows rose in honest surprise. "No, of course not. I'm only concerned about your happiness. Everyone in the office knows the Knights have a lot of problems." He was referring to the married couple, one a P.D., one a D.A.

"They seem to handle the stress."

"They separated over the holidays."

"Oh, I'm sorry to hear that. I like Jean."

"It's tough, Meredith, not being able to discuss your work with your spouse. It wears on you."

"Thanks for your concern, but it really isn't any of your business."

"It is if I'm in love with you."

Meredith took in a quick breath. "Ken, I didn't know. We've never...I mean...our relationship hasn't gone that far."

"Because you've roadblocked it. I've tried to tell you in a hundred ways..." He stood and paced. "You've always kept a part of yourself from me...from everyone. I thought I could break down your barriers eventually."

Meredith leaned back and clasped her hands in her lap. "I don't know what to say. I love Luke... I'm sorry."

Ken stopped pacing. "How can you love a man who does what he does?"

Meredith sighed. "Ken, don't."

"He defends guilty people every day."

An unbidden and unwelcome vision of the public defender from her rape trial, Mark Rath, assaulted her. She shook it off. "Ken, please...you've always been a little...extreme on this point—"

"And this latest thing," he said, cutting her off. "The sex crimes. It's no secret in the office that those are the hardest cases for you. That they rip you apart. How can you tolerate his freeing men who hurt women?"

Meredith stood abruptly. "That's enough! I won't listen to this about Luke. You're out of line."

Ken stood, too, towering over her. "I'm sorry if I've

upset you. But I won't apologize for what I've said. My feelings for you give me that right, even if you don't return them. Think about it. I know you. I know you could never do what he does. Can you honestly think it isn't going to affect your relationship?''

MEREDITH WAS STILL reeling from Ken's remarks as she dragged herself into her apartment at eight o'clock that night. Her eyes burned and there was a deep ache between her shoulder blades. Nevertheless, when she heard the phone ringing, she raced to it, hoping it was Luke. "Hello."

"Meredith?"

"Belle, is that you? You sound awful."

"I *am* awful. I need to see you. Can I come over?"

"Of course."

"Be there in five minutes."

After Meredith hung up, she paced nervously, waiting for her friend. When the bell rang, she flew to the door and pulled it open. Belle's eyes were red, her cheeks pale. There were mauve smudges underneath her eyes.

"Belle, honey, what's wrong?"

Belle hurried inside, crossed into the living room, dropped her purse and a manila envelope on a table and shucked her coat. "I've...I've got to talk to you."

Alarmed by her pallor, and her obviously disturbed state, Meredith said soothingly, "Sure. Sit down."

Perched on the edge of the couch, Belle stared at her, fidgeting like a nervous witness. She wrung her hands together as she said, "Meredith, this is one of the hardest things I've ever done."

"Belle, you can tell me anything."

"No, you don't understand. It's not about me. It's about you."

"Me?"

"And Luke."

Meredith tensed. "What do you mean?"

"This case in yesterday's newspaper...it just goes to show I've been right about him."

Meredith shook her head. "This case has nothing to do with him as a person."

"Yes, it does. The man he's defending is a monster. Pendelton was convicted of abuse, sentenced to three years in jail and then got off thanks to some other unscrupulous defense attorney."

"I know...I read the whole story." *Twice.*

"He did terrible things to his wife. He beat her up badly, several times, using a belt. He locked her in a closet for hours. He raped her. After months of that treatment, he got so carried away with his fists, he almost killed her. That's when she left him."

Cold seeped through Meredith. Those details hadn't been revealed in the *Sentinel.* "Belle, how do you know this?"

Her friend got up and paced. Her hands fisted at her sides. "The physical abuse wasn't the worst part. Or even the rape. Emotionally, he'd abused her for years before that."

A memory flashed into Meredith's mind. Belle, seventeen years ago, her black ponytail swinging behind her, her eyes vacant, as she paced just like this in the Princeton Women's Center, recounting the abuse she'd suffered from her ex-husband. *Sometimes he used a belt, sometimes his fists... He used to lock me in a closet...*

"Belle, honey, you're confusing this with your own experiences."

Her best friend rounded on her. "No, I'm not. The shelter where I work Tuesdays was all abuzz about this case. Our sister shelter in Sommerfield housed Pendelton's wife when she finally left him." With shaky hands, Belle picked up the envelope from the table. "Here's the evidence. Pictures of Mrs. Pendelton when she came to the shelter."

Meredith stood. "I don't want to look at those. Where did you get them, anyway?"

"I went over to Gentle House today. I talked to their director. They let me take a look at the records." Her eyes glazed, Belle lifted her chin. "I took the pictures when no one was looking."

Belle pulled out the photographs and threw them on the table. Meredith caught a glimpse of a woman's face more black-and-blue than flesh color. A broken nose. Swollen eyes.

Her stomach churned and she turned away from the sight, clutching her waist. "It doesn't have anything to do with Luke."

"Yes, Meredith, it does. Luke's going to get Pendelton off and that monster will do it again. To some other woman who's not as strong as we are." Her voice cracked. "He's getting a lot of these guys off. Guys who do what someone did to me. What someone did to *you*. It changed our whole lives." Belle was weeping openly.

"You're twisting this around, Belle. You have a skewed view of all defense attorneys. Including Luke in the sweep isn't fair."

"My view isn't skewed. It just isn't fair that defense

attorneys get the guilty off. Whether you admit it or
not, Luke is giving other men the freedom to hurt
women just like we were hurt.''

THE DREAM CAME that night. Meredith was in one of
those half-awake, you-know-you're-dreaming-but-you-
can't-stop-it states.

A woman was on a couch. It was Mrs. Pendelton, in
Ann Dwyer's home. The room looked just like it did
eighteen years ago—warm, cozy and utterly safe. Mrs.
Pendelton was struggling. A man, her husband—Meredith knew his face from the picture in the paper—was
on top of her. His meaty hands bit into her bruised arms
and she moaned. ''Shut up or you'll wake the girls.''

''I don't want this, Louis. Please...don't. You're
hurting me...''

Meredith woke herself with a scream. She bolted up
from the mattress, breathing hard, sweat soaking her
nightshirt. She glanced at the clock—4:01. Lying back
onto the pillow, she blinked to stay awake, fearful of
picking up the dream where she'd left off if she fell
back asleep.

But the dream returned the next night. Again, the
scene was Ann Dwyer's house. Again, a man and a
woman were on the couch. Pendelton slapped the
woman hard on the face. Meredith felt the sting on her
cheek as she writhed beneath him. He reeked of alcohol
and his belt buckle dug into her stomach.

''You want it, you stupid bitch,'' he snapped. ''You
know you do.''

''No, please, no, Tom, I don't. You misunderstood...please...stop.''

Fearful of waking the girls, Meredith struggled with her body, twisting, turning, trying to get free.

Viciously, he ripped off her sweatpants and panties...

Meredith found herself sitting up ramrod straight in bed, gulping for air. Tears streamed down her cheeks and she shook her head. It's just a dream...just a dream. It doesn't mean anything. The red lights of the digital clock blinked 4:24. Trembling, she yanked back the covers and flung her feet over the side of the bed. She got up to make coffee, again unwilling to risk falling back into the dream.

The next night it reappeared, like some eerie ghost, walking the night until its sins had been appeased. Meredith had taken a sleeping pill, hoping to sleep so soundly that no dreams would haunt her. Instead, the nightmare took on a surreal quality...

Two people were moving in slow motion. A large, familiar hand gripped her throat, only it scared her this time, when it never had before. She started to scream, and suddenly there was a blindfold over her eyes, which ludicrously prevented her from crying out. Heavy male weight pressed her into the couch, and for a minute, she couldn't breathe. His hands were gentle at first, as always, but when he reached for her sweatpants, like Tom had, she squirmed underneath him. His touch got rough...his fingers dug into her waist as he tore the clothes off her. His elbow jabbed her raised knee hard enough to bruise her. Suddenly the blindfold was on her mouth, gagging her. She thought she was going to throw up, like that night so long ago.

"It's all right, love," he said in whispers that she'd

heard a thousand times. "You want this...I know you do."

Still in the dream, she told herself not to open her eyes...she didn't want to see...but she did, eventually. She opened them wide...and in the semidarkness, Meredith looked into the face of Luke Rayburn.

LUKE WATCHED the fire in the den pop and sputter, thinking about how everything was going wrong in both his personal and professional life.

The office was a zoo, hounded by reporters all week, invaded by official phone calls demanding to know what the hell was going on up there in Sommerfield. He'd had to stay late for several meetings, which didn't help the situation at home. The constant pressure grated on his nerves, depriving him of the patience he needed to deal with his son.

Mike was silent and surly all week. He'd clammed up completely about the drinking. But Luke knew he needed to discuss the issue of alcohol consumption with his son. He'd thought about grounding Mike, but he didn't really believe that would accomplish anything. Instead, he told the boy that he couldn't see Kip or Brad until this was settled. Mike had frozen him out all week, refusing to talk about anything. The other kids taunting Mike about the case had driven him back to Kip and Brad, and Luke couldn't find a way to separate them.

Meredith had arrived at ten this morning. He'd cataloged her pale face, her nervous gestures, and both caused a painful knot in his stomach. Glancing up at the ceiling in the direction of Mike's room, Luke sighed heavily. She and Mike had gone there almost immediately. Obviously, Mike wanted to talk to *her*. Luke's old nemesis, possessiveness of his son, reared its ugly head.

He was appalled at the stupid, insidious fear of losing Mike to Meredith; nevertheless, it clutched at his heart, its talons digging deep. He tried to shake free of the feeling, suppress it or at least ignore it, but he couldn't. Purposefully, he turned his thoughts to his relationship with Meredith; that didn't make him feel any better.

She'd been busy all week at work, too, after being gone from the office for four days. She'd managed dinner with Mike one night, but Luke had been at the office and he hadn't seen her. She'd been in court yesterday and tied up late into the evening, which was why she wasn't able to come to Sommerfield until today, Saturday.

He'd called her late each night, which had become a habit, but it wasn't the same between them. She'd been tense, and there was none of the intimacy that had been present in their previous phone calls—no sharing work stories, no confidences about their son. And none of the sexy teasing, none of the naughty talk, no complaints because they couldn't touch each other right that minute. As before, her distance and discomfort kicked into all his insecurities, making him act irrationally.

Stupid, Rayburn. You're overreacting. Again. We're all just under a lot of stress. It will work out. Two weeks from today they'd be married. They'd live together and deal with these things like a normal family, in normal everyday ways.

Forcibly suppressing the worry, Luke left the den to

fix lunch. When he called Meredith and Mike, only she came down. His breath caught again at the sight of her. She was dressed in a baby-pink sweater and matching jeans. Her hair was pulled off her face with clips. She looked young and innocent, and he wanted to pull her to him and do old and not-so-innocent things to her. But her eyes were wary and the smudges beneath them testified to her anxiety.

"Mike says he's not hungry."

"I want him down here." Luke tried to brush past her.

"Luke," she said softly, grasping his arm. "He needs time."

"He's had all week. Avoiding me won't help." He pounded up the back stairs, tromped down the hall, rapped loudly on Mike's door and swung it open. Mike was staring out the window, hands jammed into his pockets, shoulders hunched.

"Mike, come down for lunch."

"I'm not hungry."

"Come sit with us, anyway."

"No, thanks."

"I want you to."

His son's body stiffened and Luke recognized the eruption of a teenage tirade seconds too late. "Damn it, Dad, why do you always get your way? Can't I have a say in anything? You're smothering me, making all my decisions. Can't you just leave me alone?"

Stung, Luke stepped back. Was he doing that? He ran a weary hand over his face. He was so damned tired—and scared—he wasn't thinking straight.

"Mike, I..."

"Aw, Dad, just drop it. I feel like hell as it is. Look,

there's a wrestling match at the high school this afternoon. I'm gonna walk over and watch it, okay?''

Regaining some of his usual composure, Luke agreed. "All right. Why don't you ask Julie Anne to go with you?''

Mike snorted. "Julie Anne isn't speaking to me.''

"Why?''

"Because she thinks just like you. Maybe Meredith will go with me.''

Obviously, in more ways than one, Meredith *didn't* think "just like him." The jealousy Luke felt sickened him.

When Meredith and Mike left for the match, Luke returned to the den and sat by the fire and thought about how his life was turning to ashes quicker than the logs in front of him. By the time the two returned, he'd practically convinced himself that he was losing Mike. As for Meredith, he'd decided she was making some kind of unconscious statement by spending her afternoon with Mike, when she and Luke really needed to talk. Again, he knew his thinking was off-kilter, but nothing would come into focus for him.

Mike asked Luke for permission to go over to Joey's, and by five, Luke and Meredith were at last alone...in the house...in the den where so much had started for them.

"I wanted you to stay this afternoon," Luke confessed immediately, hoping to diffuse his ridiculous jealousy by bringing it out in the open.

"I know. I wanted to stay, too. I don't like having to choose between you and Mike. But he's hurting, Luke, and we're the adults. I—''

"No, you don't have to explain. It's childish of me

to be jealous of my own son.'' He gave her a lopsided smile and patted his lap. ''But come over here and show me you missed me.''

Meredith's smile was faked—he would have staked his life on it. But she crossed the room to him and sank onto his lap. Her arms went around his neck, and the scent of Jean Naté enveloped him. Was it his imagination that her body was stiff? That her arms went around him mechanically?

He buried his face in her neck and kissed her there. She started at first, then relaxed into him, but again the action seemed forced. Didn't it? Or was he looking for problems? Was he contriving the evidence because he expected her to distance him physically?

He sighed and set her apart from him. ''We have to talk.''

''I know.''

''I'm a wreck, Meredith. I haven't slept all week.'' He lifted his hand and bushed a thumb over the circle under one of her eyes. ''You, neither?''

''Not much. I've had night—'' She broke off as if she'd decided not to continue.

''What, honey?''

''I've had a tough time sleeping, too.''

She'd changed her mind about confiding in him. Why?

''The case is bothering you, isn't it?''

''Yes, Luke, it is.'' She slid off his lap and went to stand in front of the fire, holding out her hands to warm them.

''It's separating you from me.'' He winced at his accusatory tone.

''Partly.''

I'll do anything for you, Luke, she'd promised him just after they'd made love. *I won't let anything come between us.* What had it taken—four days?

"Is this going to happen every time I take a case you don't like?"

She whirled. "That's unfair. You know there's more to this than my 'not liking' it."

He looked up at the ceiling, searching for answers. "I know. I'm sorry. I'm so beat I'm not thinking straight. I'm saying things I don't mean."

Meredith's eyes narrowed on him. "Yes, I realize that. But it's how you really feel, isn't it? That I'm going to object and pressure you to give up cases like Lou Pendelton's."

He stilled and watched her closely, her exact words sinking in. "I never said anything about giving up the case. Is that what you want?"

"What I want is time to sort this out."

"You didn't answer my question, Meredith."

"Oh, all right. If I could make this decision, yes, that's what I'd want. Pendelton deserves to be in jail. I saw what he did to his wife." She studied him carefully with knowing green eyes. "But you'd never give up the case, would you?"

His breath caught in his throat. "I couldn't, Meredith. Not for you, not even for Sar—" The words were out, slipped past a guard battered by stress, fear and just plain fatigue.

Always the D.A., Meredith caught the slip. Her eyes clouded immediately. She pressed a hand over her mouth and circled her waist with one arm. She just stared at him. Luke felt everything slipping from his grasp and he was impotent to stop the landslide.

"Well," she said finally. "That certainly puts me in my place."

"Meredith..."

"If you couldn't give up a case for Sara, you obviously couldn't give it up for me." The hurt in her voice sliced through him.

"That's not what I meant. You misunderstood."

"Did I? Tell me, Luke. How did Sara feel about your job as a public defender?"

"She hated it. She wanted me to be a corporate lawyer. That's why I can't compromise on this issue. It's the only thing I ever kept for myself."

"And that should make it all right for me?" Her voice climbed a notch. "Do you know how sick I am of playing second fiddle to Sara?" She stepped toward him; her eyes blazed green fire and she was trembling. "She had Mike for fourteen years. She saw him take his first step, she watched him go out on his first date...Sara's had everything I've ever wanted, especially—"

"I notice there was nothing about me in that statement." Luke felt his own temper rise.

Meredith's face went blank.

"You only mentioned your son."

"I wasn't finished. I was going to say especially *you*...she had you for fifteen years, too. She shared all *your* firsts, too. She had you in ways I'll never have you...and now, because of her..."

Luke watched the tears choke back her words. She glanced helplessly around the room. "Oh, God, I hate being like this, hearing us say these petty things to each other." She looked up at him. "Luke, what's happening to us?"

He wanted to go to her, hold her, take away her pain. But something kept him back. In an effort to wade through his tangled emotions, he said, "It'll be all right. In two weeks, when we're married..."

She shook her head. "Luke, we can't get married with all this going on."

His jaw slackened. "You don't mean that," he said.

"Of course I do. We'll have to postpone the wedding. I can't marry you with this between us."

"Then don't let it come between us."

"Do you want me to pretend it's not a problem?"

"I want it *not* to be a problem."

"This isn't something I can control."

"I've heard that before."

Meredith stepped back as if he'd slapped her. And in a way, he had. He'd hit her with something in her past that she'd trusted him with. He'd used it to prove his point. But he couldn't stop. Something inside drove him to push her further. "If you postpone the wedding, I'm going to cancel it." Even as he said the words, he told himself to take them back, that it was the wrong way to close the ever-widening breach between them.

She started to cry in earnest. "Why are you doing this to us?"

"Why are *you?*"

Perhaps if he hadn't been so wrung-out, he might have compromised. Perhaps if his son hadn't come to the doorway just then, they could have worked this through.

"Dad, what's going on? I heard you two yelling from the living room."

Luke looked at Mike. "I thought you were going to Joey's."

"He wasn't home."

Turning to Meredith, Mike said, "Are you all right?" He glanced at his father. "Why is she crying? What did you do to her?"

Luke closed his eyes, his son's accusation cutting deep.

"Mike, it's not his fault," Meredith said. "I'm not feeling well, and we had a disagreement. Walk me to my car, will you?" Meredith pleaded through her tears. "I'm going home now."

"Home? Now? It's not even six o'clock."

"I'll explain it to you on the way out." Without sparing a glance for Luke, she took her son by the arm and quietly left the room.

Luke sank to the chair and stared back into the fire. It gave him no solace this time.

You're being unfair, Rayburn, he told himself as he recalled the things he'd said to her. He winced, remembering how his words about Sara had come out all wrong.

He thought about Florida and the intimacy they'd shared.

How could things change so drastically in just a few short weeks?

CHAPTER FIFTEEN

MIKE THREW his pen down on the library table after he recorded the stupid statistic: *Over fifty percent of the respondents in one survey agreed with the statement, "Romance is full of pain and suffering."* No kidding! It described Meredith and his father to a tee. Last week, he'd spent time with each of them, separately, of course, and they were both miserable. Neither would tell him why.

When the bell rang to end the period, he muttered an expletive under his breath, grabbed the magazine and the rest of his books and stormed out of the library. He kicked three lockers on his way to his own. Instead of relieving the stress, the action only sent pain up his leg.

He swore again.

"Watch your language, young man." Mike looked up to see his English teacher frowning at him. "Michael? I didn't know it was you. I'm surprised at your..." She studied him. "Is something wrong? Do you need to talk?"

He shook his head. "Sorry, Ms. Jansen. I wasn't thinking straight." Excusing himself from his teacher—and the disappointment in her eyes—he headed down the hall, mumbling under his breath, "Join the

club, Ms. J. I'm letting everybody down these days.''
His dad…his mother…Julie Anne.

Why the hell should he care if his father and Meredith were fighting? Accidentally, he'd overheard her
comment about Sara. It hurt to hear how bad she felt.
But something more was going on between her and his
dad. She never came back to see him last weekend.
And she'd refused to come into the house when she'd
picked him up for pizza on Monday. Last night, Mike
had gone to her place for dinner. When he'd asked
about the wedding a week from Saturday, she said it
had been postponed.

Aw, screw it. Screw them. And screw Julie Anne,
too, who was walking down the hall. She turned her
head away as she passed him. But not before he saw
that wounded, you've-hurt-me look in her eyes. He was
stupid to think he could have a girl for a best friend,
anyway. So she was mad. He was mad, too.

When he reached his locker, Brad and Kip were
waiting for him. They were entertaining themselves
with Joey Lubman.

"Hey, twit-head. Come'ere," Brad said, scooping
Joey off the floor with one hand. "I want to reacquaint
you with the inside of this empty locker." Brad pushed
the younger boy up to the wall. Joey sagged against it
like a rag doll. When he spotted Mike, he let out a
relieved breath. Damn, Mike wasn't in the mood for
playing superhero today. Just maybe he wouldn't.

"Rayburn, my man," Kip said silkily. "We were
about to teach Joey a lesson here. Wanna help?"

"Better hurry up, Freeman." Brad clenched Joey's
shoulders, making him squeal. "Looks like baby Joey's
gonna pee his pants any second." Brad laughed evilly.

Mike ignored it, and Joey's yelps, as he grabbed his jacket from his own locker and headed toward the door.

Kip and Brad caught up with him before he reached the exit. Their faces were flushed and they hooted at their prank. "Hey, Rayburn, hold up."

Mike stopped.

Kip punched him on the arm. "We're headin' out for the lake tomorrow night."

"Pretty cold weather for swimming," Mike said, buttoning his coat.

"Only swimming we're gonna be doin' is in a bottle of Scotch." Brad chuckled at his cleverness. "Wanna join us?"

"Can't."

Brad's voice turned soft. "Come on, Mikey. It'll do you good. Make you forget all that crap with your father."

Fleetingly, Mike looked down the hall. Right across from his English class was Joey Lubman, bawling like a baby on Ms. Jansen's shoulder. And Julie Anne was there, her hand settled on his arm.

Mike turned to Brad and Kip. "What time?"

MEREDITH SAT in her office, sad and depressed. Everyone in her life was unhappy—Luke, Mike, Belle.

Belle.

Meredith felt as if she'd lost her best friend. How had that happened?

She checked the clock. Noon. Maybe Belle was free for lunch. Maybe they could talk.

As she picked up the phone, there was a knock on the open doorway. Belle was standing there, looking exactly the way Meredith felt. "Hi. Busy?" Belle asked.

Placing the phone in its cradle, Meredith said, "No, I was just trying to call my best friend to see if she was free for lunch." Belle's grateful smile tugged at Meredith's heart. "I miss you."

"I'm miserable, Mer," Belle blurted out.

Rising, Meredith circled her desk, crossed the room and dragged Belle inside, then shut the door for some privacy. When she turned around, Belle watched her for a minute, then hugged her. Meredith returned the embrace enthusiastically. "Oh, Belle."

"You don't look much better than I do."

"I'm not."

"Come on, let's sit." When they were facing each other, Belle said, "I'm sorry, Meredith. I said some terrible things and I put pressure on you I had no right to exert. It's been keeping me up nights." She studied Meredith's face. "You haven't been sleeping either."

"No."

"Because of what's happened between us?"

"No, though this rift has been horrible. But other things are wrong, too."

"And I haven't been here for you."

"It's all right."

"No, it isn't. But maybe I can help now. I've been back to see a therapist."

"Me, too."

They both laughed. Belle sobered first. "Mine said I need to get over this irrational reaction to defense lawyers and stop hovering over you."

Touched, Meredith reached out and squeezed her

friend's arm. "I've enjoyed the hovering. I've needed it."

"But now you have someone else to do it. Two others."

"Does that make you feel bad, Belle?"

"A little."

"You haven't lost my friendship."

"Not unless I make you choose between me and Luke." When Meredith started to respond, Belle stopped her. "No, don't say anything. It's a conclusion I've come to myself. It's stupid to make you choose between us. I want to be able to accept Luke, and go on with our friendship."

Sighing, Meredith relaxed back in her chair. "He's a wonderful man. Good, kind, moral."

"I've been wrong about him."

"Belle, he really believes in the law, and that everyone has a right to a defense. He'd never do anything immoral. I'm certain of it."

"It doesn't matter to you that he defends people who he thinks might be guilty."

"No, it doesn't. In my head, that is."

"I don't understand."

"I know that the question of a person's guilt or innocence can only be decided by a judge or a jury after all the facts have been presented. But in my heart, I'm having some trouble with this new case. In fact, I've been having terrible nightmares."

"I'm sorry. I never meant for that to happen."

"It's not your fault. Susan said it's understandable that this case would upset me." Meredith thought back to what her therapist had told her just yesterday when she'd confided about her dreams. *It isn't unusual for you to juxtapose the Pendeltons with you and Luke in this scenario. So many aspects of your life are colliding—the rape, finding Mike, falling in love with Luke, his job.*

"What are you going to do, Meredith?"

"I told him I wanted to postpone the wedding."

"That sounds fair enough."

"No, it's not fair to him. Not really. I'm afraid I've lost him." She went on to tell her friend about the argument they'd had about Sara.

"Do you think you shouldn't have negative feelings about her?"

Meredith was not surprised at the question. "No, Susan helped me see that it's an honest, and warranted feeling. Sara got years of Luke's life that I wish I'd had. And she had my son."

"So when Luke used her as a rationale for not giving up the case, you were hurt. Understandably so."

"Yes. But in spite of that, I know Luke shouldn't have to give up this case because of me. I should be able to accept his job."

She turned back to the window and stared out again. Images of Luke flashed through her mind like film clips: how he'd held her after she'd told him about the rape; the relief on his face when she'd shown up in the hotel room after the bar's Christmas party; the self-consciousness he felt in Florida when he'd asked for more intimacy.

"What are you thinking?"

Pivoting, she faced Belle again. "I want to be able to unconditionally accept what he does, Belle. I want to do anything for him, like I said I would."

"You can do anything you want, Meredith. I've seen

you in action. If this is really what you want, you can
do it.''

BY THE TIME Meredith left her office at seven o'clock
that evening, it was dark outside. She'd arranged to
meet her colleagues at Markies, a lawyer's hangout, to
celebrate a big case they'd just won. In truth, she
couldn't bear to go back to her empty apartment. She
missed Luke so much, her whole body ached, as well
as her heart. Nothing was right without him. Even the
few times she'd seen Mike, it wasn't with the usual
undiluted joy. Mike had tried, but the tension with his
father wore through his veneer of teenage nonchalance,
and he'd been depressed during both visits. Which was
why she was glad he was spending the night with Joey
Lubman. It would do him good to be with his friend.

When Meredith entered Markies, she spotted the
D.A. crowd at a corner table. Ken motioned her over.

"Hi, doll. Want a drink?"

A quick flash of Luke leading her out of the bar on
New Year's Eve replaced Ken's smiling face. *Don't
worry, doll, I'll take care of you.*

Meredith joined her friends and tried to participate
in the conversation. They were debating the reasons for
being a district attorney instead of going into private
practice. Above their discussion, she heard Luke's
voice when she'd asked why a bright graduate of Stanford chose public defense.

His brown eyes had sparkled and his face had lit
from within. *Just because people are poor doesn't
mean they deserve the poorest lawyers.*

As she sipped her beer, Meredith realized that
Luke's faith in the law was something they had in com-

mon, not a difference. More so, she loved his strong passion for the profession and his unswerving dedication to helping people. It was all part of him. Part of the man she loved.

She glanced down at her ring. Fingering it, she thought of Christmas morning...the Mer the Bear T-shirt...Mer the Bear on the racquetball court...*I want Mer the Bear in my bed... Trust me, we'll find her together.*

Music began behind her. Ken came over. "Want to dance, Meredith?"

She looked up into his perfectly handsome face. *What the hell was she doing here?*

"No, thanks. I've got a phone call to make."

LUKE SAT in the dark, listening to the phone ring. He should answer it, he knew he should. But he figured if it was Mike, he'd leave a message and Luke could pick it up before he hung up. After the beep, it was quiet.

"Not surprised," he said into the dim and lonely house. "Mike would hardly call from Joey's since he hasn't talked to me in days."

Still, it was irresponsible not to pick up. But he was so damn sick of responsibility, of taking care of everyone, of figuring out everything. He wanted, just for one night, not to have to take care of anything...or anyone.

Liar. If Meredith were here, he'd take care of her. He'd do anything for her.

Except give up a case.

He swore. She had no right to ask him to do that.

Unfair, Rayburn. She didn't ask you to do that. She said she was having trouble with it, needed time to work it out. She only wanted to postpone the wedding.

You're the jerk who canceled it. Had he been smart, and a little more patient, in a week she would have been his.

Luke rose to pour himself a drink. What the hell? No reason not to. Mike was out so Luke wasn't being a poor role model. Meredith was...where *was* Meredith tonight? He had no idea. The realization sent a jagged pain through his gut.

The moonlight gleaming through the window reflected off the silver frame on the bar of the wall unit. Luke flicked on a small light. It was the picture Teddy had given Mike for his birthday. Sara smiled up from the photo. Her blond hair was precisely styled, even though they'd been in the Bahamas. Her neat shorts and top matched the shoes she wore. She looked perfect.

But Sara hadn't been perfect, Luke thought, any more than he was. Nor had their life together been perfect. He'd spent most of it giving her everything she wanted, sacrificing everything to her will. So had Mike.

Well. That certainly puts me in my place. If you couldn't give up a case for Sara, you obviously couldn't give it up for me.

The memory shamed him. He hadn't meant the words the way Meredith took them, but she'd been right about one thing. He'd dug in his heels about the case, unwilling to compromise a tenth as much as he'd always done for Sara.

Why? Had he loved Sara more?

Stupid idea, Rayburn. Oh, he'd loved Sara, fully and completely from the time he'd become a man. But *more* than Meredith?

No, not more. Just in a different way.

And now he loved Meredith deeply. He loved her spunk, her courage, her devotion to Mike…and to the law.

Then why wouldn't you give her a break on this one?

"Because I'm a jerk, that's why," he said into the empty house. A house that would forever be empty without Meredith.

Setting aside the frame, Luke knew it was time to set aside his old habits and fears. Time to begin anew with the woman who had fulfilled every one of his fantasies, both in bed and out.

He strode to the phone, calling himself an ass for ever allowing things to go this far awry.

The phone rang just as he reached it.

God, he hoped it was Meredith. "Hello."

"Mr. Rayburn," a voice asked on the other end. "Mr. Lucas Rayburn?"

"Yes."

"This is Sommerfield Hospital calling."

MEREDITH SQUEEZED Mike's hand between both of hers, willing herself not to cry. It was cold and pale, like his face. "In a lot of pain, honey?" She glanced meaningfully at his left arm.

"A little. But mostly it itches underneath the cast."

Luke bent over the bed and brushed the hair out of Mike's eyes. "You're gonna need help getting dressed, buddy. It'll be just like it was when you were little."

Mike gave him a weak smile, his eyes watery. "I'm sorry, Dad. I was so stupid."

Luke cleared his throat, and Meredith's heart went out to him. She'd never forget the stricken look on his face when he met her at the emergency-room door to tell her that Mike had been in a car accident and was in surgery with a broken arm.

"Yeah, kid, it was stupid. And we'll have to talk about this later. But not right now. Now it's important that you know we love you." His voice quavered. "And we're so thankful that you're all right, we're not even mad."

Her son's face relaxed a bit. "Let me just say one thing, okay? I was gonna call you after I had the two beers. Like we agreed I should if I ever got in this kind of trouble. I wasn't gonna drive back. But Kip and Brad were going back to town 'looking for action.'" Mike rolled his eyes, then frowned again. "They were smashed, they'd been drinking Scotch all night. I knew I was okay…I'd just had the two beers, hours earlier. The accident happened because I hit a patch of ice on the lake road."

Meredith smiled at her son. So much like his dad.

"We know you were sober, son. The blood test was below the minimum for DWI." Luke's face turned dark. "Still, it was a dumb thing to do." He glanced meaningfully at Meredith. "But we all do dumb things sometimes." His look said, *Don't we, Meredith?*

Holding his gaze, she said, "Yes, we do." Then she turned to Mike. "We just need to learn from them. Not do them again. Grow as a person from them. You'll be stronger for this whole experience, Mike. Able to handle things better."

He gave her a wobbly grin. "Yeah, if I ever get out of the house again."

Luke's look was mock-stern. "You'll be grounded for maybe two, three years. That oughtta do it."

All three chuckled, a welcome release after the terror of the night. Then Mike scowled.

"What is it?" Meredith asked.

"I've been rotten to Julie Anne and Joey. Think they'll forgive me?"

Meredith looked to Luke. "What do you think?"

He locked his eyes with hers. "I think if you care about someone, you can forgive them anything." He shifted his gaze to Mike. "We'll call them in the morning."

A nurse came in holding a needle. "Mr. Rayburn, it's 1:00 a.m. Mike needs his rest. You should go home and get some sleep. You, too, Mrs. Rayburn. He'll be out in a few minutes, anyway, after I give him this."

Meredith smiled at the mistake the nurse had made with her name.

Luke grinned, too. "All right, we'll go. We'll be back tomorrow, bright and early."

Leaning over, Meredith kissed Mike's cheek. "Good night, honey. I love you."

"I love you, too, Mom."

Tears clouded her eyes, and he must have seen them. "Hey, Dad," he said, trying to break the tension. "Don't let Mer the Bear go home alone tonight, okay?"

Luke bent over the other side of the bed, kissed Mike, too, straightened and said, "No, I won't. I won't let Mer the Bear go again."

THE RED NUMBERS mocked him from his nightstand—2:05 a.m. Luke lay in his bed, naked, arms linked behind his head, a sheet pulled to his waist. He stared up at the moon shining through the skylight. He sighed.

This wasn't exactly how he'd planned things. He'd *planned* for Meredith to be here with him.

Once they'd gotten out of the hospital, she'd been so upset, he'd insisted she leave her car and ride home in his Bronco. She'd wept wrenchingly in the aftermath of Mike's crisis. She'd managed to keep it together and be strong for her son. But after the tension and sleeplessness of the past week, then the shock of Mike's accident, she'd broken down. He'd shed a few tears of his own, thinking about Mike's close call.

Luke had held her for a good ten minutes in the car, soothing her, luxuriating in the feel of her in his arms again.

He never intended to let her go.

But she'd fallen asleep on the thirty-minute ride from the hospital, which was across town from his house, and he hadn't had the heart to wake her. Instead, he'd carried her from the car to the spare room—he didn't trust himself to put her in his own bed—taken off her sneakers and socks but left on her sweat suit...another thing he didn't trust himself to do—remove her clothes.

It was probably better that they talk this through after she'd had some rest, but damn, he wanted her with him now. Even if they didn't make love, he wanted to hold her. Tell her he knew he'd been a jerk. Promise he'd give up the case if that's what it took to bring her back to him.

Closing his eyes, he willed himself to sleep, but his body wouldn't cooperate. It was as if it had its own internal radar system and knew that Meredith was in the vicinity.

Minutes later, his eyes snapped open when he sensed he was no longer alone.

Meredith stood next to the bed, bathed in moonlight. His breath caught in his throat as he took in her tousled hair, her soccer T-shirt—the one he'd given her for Christmas—skimming her thighs, and God knew *what* underneath it. Her legs were gloriously bare.

"Meredith." Reduced once again to mouthing her name, he could only stare at her.

"I thought you weren't going to let Mer the Bear go again." Humor laced her voice and her eyes stayed locked with his.

He reached out a hand. She linked hers with it. "I'm not, ever again," he said, his voice unmistakably husky.

Her smile was thousand-watt, illuminating the dim interior of his bedroom. "That's good, because I wasn't going to let you, anyway."

Slowly, she placed one knee on the bed, edged her behind next to his thigh and braced her arms on either side of his chest. She leaned over, her hair grazing his cheek. Next to his lips, she whispered, "Kiss me, Luke."

His arms banded around her, crushing her against him. He devoured her mouth, not even trying to slow down. His hands went lower, under the hem of her T-shirt. Oh, God, she had nothing else on.

Like his fantasy woman in Florida, she gave herself freely to the passion of his kiss. Her lips were warm and moist as she searched his mouth, explored him with fiery possessiveness. After an eternity, she lifted her head.

"I want to make love, Luke," she said simply.

"Yes." He threaded the hair back from her face, relishing its familiar texture. Levering himself up to lean against the headboard, he said, "I want to make love to you for the rest of my life. I'll do whatever it takes to make that happen."

She placed two fingers on his lips. "Shh...no ultimatums...no strings...no promises." She held his gaze steadily. Even in the moonlight, he could see the clear, determined look in her eyes. "I'll be fine with this case, with any case you take. I'll work on it with Susan, if I have to. But I'm not going to let it come between us." Leaning over, she kissed his chest, a wet sloppy kiss that made his body buck.

When she sat up, he raised his hand to her neck and massaged it. "You won't have to get used to anything. I'd already decided—before Mike's accident—that I'd give up the case. I was on my way to the phone when the hospital called. Nothing is worth losing you, Meredith." His grip tightened on her neck. "Nothing."

Captured by moonbeams, tears shimmered in her eyes. "I tried to call you, too, to tell you. I'd decided, too, before Mike. I don't want you to give it up, Luke. I won't let you. I want to work through this together. I love the man you are."

His heart, already so full, swelled with emotion for this brave, unselfish woman who was offering him everything. "All right, we'll try it your way first. But if it's too painful, I'll give it up."

A siren's smile hinted at her lips. "Good." She maneuvered her legs so she straddled him. "Then we can do *this* your way."

He closed his eyes briefly, thanking God for giving her back to him. "My way, huh?"

"Yes. I'll do anything for you, Luke. Anything."

He rolled over and gently eased her down, pressing her into the mattress, soothing his knuckles over skin he'd never get tired of touching. "Ah, Mer the Bear. Those are the sweetest words I've ever heard."

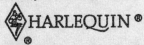

HARLEQUIN SUPERROMANCE®

There's more to the story...

Every now and then comes a book that defies convention, breaks the rules and still offers the reader all the excitement of romance. Harlequin Superromance—the series known for its innovation and variety—is proud to add this book to our already-outstanding lineup.

#733 SOMEWHERE OUT THERE
by
Connie Bennett

Kit Wheeler doesn't believe in UFOs or aliens or government conspiracies. The former astronaut and now respected TV science correspondent wants nothing to do with the crackpots and their tales. Then an air-force jet mysteriously crashes, and Brenna Sullivan, an expert in her own right, has a convincing theory.

Whether you believe or not, you'll enjoy this wonderful story of adventure, romance and the endless possibilities that exist... somewhere out there.

Available in March wherever Harlequin books are sold.

LOVE *or* MONEY?
Why not Love *and* Money!
After all, millionaires
need love, too!

**Suzanne Forster,
Muriel Jensen
and
Judith Arnold**

bring you three original stories
about finding that one-in-a million man!

Harlequin also brings you
a million-dollar sweepstakes—enter
for your chance to win a fortune!

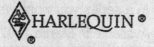

You are cordially invited to a

HOMETOWN REUNION

September 1996—August 1997

Bad boys, cowboys, babies. Feuding families, arson, mistaken identity, a mom on the run... Where can you find romance and adventure? Tyler, Wisconsin, that's where!

So join us in this not-so-sleepy little town and experience the love, the laughter and the tears of those who call it home.

WELCOME TO A
HOMETOWN REUNION

Gabe Atwood has no sooner rescued his wife, Raine, from a burning building when there's more talk of fires. Rumor has it that Clint Stanford suspects Jon Weiss, the new kid at school, of burning down the Ingallses' factory. And that Marina, Jon's mother, has kindled a fire in Clint that may be affecting his judgment. Don't miss Kristine Rolofson's *A Touch of Texas,* the seventh in a series you won't want to end....

Available in March 1997
at your favorite retail store.

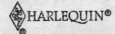

HARLEQUIN®

HTR7

Heartbreak RANCH

Four generations of independent women...
Four heartwarming, romantic stories of the West...
Four incredible authors...

Fern Michaels
Jill Marie Landis
Dorsey Kelley
Chelley Kitzmiller

Saddle up with Heartbreak Ranch, an outstanding
Western collection that will take you on a whirlwind
trip through four generations and the exciting,
romantic adventures of four strong women who
have inherited the ranch from Bella Duprey,
famed Barbary Coast madam.

Available in March,
wherever Harlequin books are sold.

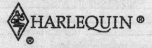

HARLEQUIN ®

®

HARLEQUIN®

Don't miss these Harlequin favorites by some of our most
distinguished authors!
And now, you can receive a discount by ordering two or more titles!

HT#25645	THREE GROOMS AND A WIFE by JoAnn Ross	$3.25 U.S. ☐ / $3.75 CAN. ☐
HT#25647	NOT THIS GUY by Glenda Sanders	$3.25 U.S. ☐ / $3.75 CAN. ☐
HP#11725	THE WRONG KIND OF WIFE by Roberta Leigh	$3.25 U.S. ☐ / $3.75 CAN. ☐
HP#11755	TIGER EYES by Robyn Donald	$3.25 U.S. ☐ / $3.75 CAN. ☐
HR#03416	A WIFE IN WAITING by Jessica Steele	$3.25 U.S. ☐ / $3.75 CAN. ☐
HR#03419	KIT AND THE COWBOY by Rebecca Winters	$3.25 U.S. ☐ / $3.75 CAN. ☐
HS#70622	KIM & THE COWBOY by Margot Dalton	$3.50 U.S. ☐ / $3.99 CAN. ☐
HS#70642	MONDAY'S CHILD by Janice Kaiser	$3.75 U.S. ☐ / $4.25 CAN. ☐
HI#22342	BABY VS. THE BAR by M.J. Rodgers	$3.50 U.S. ☐ / $3.99 CAN. ☐
HI#22382	SEE ME IN YOUR DREAMS by Patricia Rosemoor	$3.75 U.S. ☐ / $4.25 CAN. ☐
HAR#16538	KISSED BY THE SEA by Rebecca Flanders	$3.50 U.S. ☐ / $3.99 CAN. ☐
HAR#16603	MOMMY ON BOARD by Muriel Jensen	$3.50 U.S. ☐ / $3.99 CAN. ☐
HH#28885	DESERT ROGUE by Erine Yorke	$4.50 U.S. ☐ / $4.99 CAN. ☐
HH#28911	THE NORMAN'S HEART by Margaret Moore	$4.50 U.S. ☐ / $4.99 CAN. ☐

(limited quantities available on certain titles)

	AMOUNT	$
DEDUCT:	**10% DISCOUNT FOR 2+ BOOKS**	$
ADD:	**POSTAGE & HANDLING**	$
	($1.00 for one book, 50¢ for each additional)	
	APPLICABLE TAXES*	$_____
	TOTAL PAYABLE	$_____
	(check or money order—please do not send cash)	

To order, complete this form and send it, along with a check or money order for the
total above, payable to Harlequin Books, to: **In the U.S.:** 3010 Walden Avenue,
P.O. Box 9047, Buffalo, NY 14269-9047; **in Canada:** P.O. Box 613, Fort Erie, Ontario,
L2A 5X3.

Name:_____

Address: _____ City: _____

State/Prov.:_____ Zip/Postal Code: _____

*New York residents remit applicable sales taxes.
Canadian residents remit applicable GST and provincial taxes.
Look us up on-line at: http://www.romance.net

HBACK-JM4